Once *in*
Love with
Lily

AUJOERAS PUBLISHING

Once in Love with Lily

CATHRYN K. THOMPSON

For my husband.

Thank you for pushing me to do something new and for believing in me when I didn't believe in myself.

Thanks to Jo Jo, Red, and all the others who remain anonymous inspirations. Thanks to Mrs. Izzard for helping me maintain the integrity of the piece and to Ms. James, Ms. Hall, Mrs. Jones, and Agent Cooper for their words of wisdom. Finally, thanks to Minnie, Frances, and Fritz. This would not have been possible without your incredible advice and support. I love you all!

1
BROADWAY BABY

Lillian strolled into the sunlit kitchen at eight in the morning, barefoot, in yoga pants and a tank top, still glistening from her workout. Charles had apparently been up for a while, despite the fact that he hadn't come home until well after midnight the night before. A to-go cup from The Coffee Bean and Tea Leaf was in front of him on the table just as it had been for the better part of the last ten years. She sighed unintentionally. He was the only man she knew who considered walking from the car to the coffee shop to be part of his morning exercise routine. Come to think of it, it was the only part of his morning exercise routine.

He was flipping through the morning paper and making good headway on a large slab of the cake she'd made the night before. It obviously hadn't occurred to him that she might be saving it for something, in this case, for his assistant's birthday. He was brilliant and incredibly creative, but not one for remembering what he considered to be small, unimportant details. Birthdates, anniversaries, and quite often, letting his wife know that he wouldn't be home for dinner, were not, as he put it, "in his wheelhouse." She'd been left more than once eating her latest culinary creation alone, usually standing at the kitchen counter, debating what to redecorate next or whether or not to change her hair color. Last night she'd decided on a nice Ming yellow for the walls in the kitchen.

"Morning," he said, without looking up.

"Good morning," she grumbled, heading straight for the state-of-the-art one-cup coffee machine on the counter. She hit the button to make her latte. "How's the cake?" she called over the hum of the machine.

"Good. A little sweet. What's in it?"

"Nothing special. Just regular chocolate cake, but the icing is almond covered with a chocolate ganache."

"Fancy," he said, playfully mocking, unaffected by the underlying tone of irritation in her voice.

"Hmm. Yes. I actually made it for Cora's birthday. Too late now, isn't it?"

"Aw, shit. When's her birthday?"

"Yesterday, but I didn't see her. You two were at the studio all day. Is she here yet?"

"Yes."

"I take it you didn't get her a gift, then?"

"You know I'm no good at that kind of stuff. That's what I have her for in the first place."

Lillian shook her head and put on a smile. "Don't worry about it. I'll have flowers delivered later, but you get to tell her that you ate her cake."

"Fine. Thank you," Charles said. He put another bite of cake in his mouth.

She took a plain Greek yogurt from the fridge, added a tablespoon of honey, and began stirring. "I thought maybe you'd taken Cora out for her birthday when you didn't come home last night."

"No. I told you I had a meeting with the producers."

"Long meeting."

"What?"

"You didn't get home until almost two," she said, still stirring.

"Did you miss me terribly?" he asked, trying to imitate her British accent.

2

"No." She smiled again. "I managed. I actually worked out most of the details for the hospital benefit."

"Good."

"I was starting to wonder about you though. I thought it was just dinner with Jones and Gibson."

"It was. But you know how it is. Dinner leads to drinks and drinks leads to… well, you know. Sometimes you have to wine and dine and play the game, right?"

"Which one of them wears the perfume?" she asked, taking a bite of yogurt.

"What?"

"When I picked up your clothes this morning, your shirt still smelled of perfume. It was nice. But it wasn't mine."

"Ah…" he stalled as if trying to come up with an excuse or explanation, but laughed and gave up instead. "Okay. You caught me. Gibson dragged us to Blazing Angels. Are you going to sit down and eat that?"

"I bet he had to twist your arm, didn't he?" she mumbled sarcastically as she took the chair across from him.

"What?"

"Nothing." She shook her head. "So did you work out the deal, then?"

"I think we came to an agreement that will be mutually beneficial."

"And when do you start filming?"

"Two weeks." He went back to his paper.

She cleared her throat. "Danny called last night."

"Your brother? Why? Does he need more money?"

"Louisa quit."

"Who's Louisa?"

"His choreographer."

"Aren't they supposed to start rehearsals soon? Has he found someone else?"

"Not yet. I offered to help him find someone, but he's worried about bringing on someone new on such short notice because it could put them weeks behind schedule."

"Right. Which would mean more money. So, what's he going to do?"

"He has this crazy idea that I should do the show with him."

"Makes sense. When would you need to leave?" he asked, without ever looking up from the entertainment news.

"Monday. But—"

"But what?"

"Well, I'm not sure I want to do it."

That got his attention. "What do you mean you don't want to do it? Doesn't sound like we have much choice, do we. Unless you think we should flush a little more money down the toilet."

"I'm not even sure I *can* do it."

"You have a history in theater and a background in just about every kind of dance there is. Why not?"

"How about because I haven't seen anything but a soundstage in the last ten years? Live theater is just not my thing anymore, is it? A Broadway show with an inexperienced cast and crew—it's a huge undertaking. I'd already be months behind in preparation. I don't know if I have that in me. Even if I don't have to start from scratch."

"What does that mean?"

"Danny said when Louisa stormed off, she left her notes."

"So some of the work is already done?"

"Yes. They want me to interpret her vision and fill in the holes. But—"

"Then it's a no-brainer."

"But taking her work and claiming it as my own? That would be cheating."

"Desperate times call for desperate measures. At least you'd have somewhere to start."

"Charles, either way, I've never choreographed a live show. It's completely different. I'm completely different."

"He knows what he's getting. You just do it your way."

"Then I need Nina. I need her to do my demos. What if she isn't available?"

"She's available. That's what we pay her for. It'll be fine. It may even be good for you."

"How do you mean?"

"It's been seven years since the accident. Don't you think maybe it's time you got over it?"

"It's not that simple."

"Maybe it should be that simple. You're the one who's always saying that God sorts things out. If that's true, then maybe he's giving you a little kick in the ass. You call Nina and Danny. I'll have Cora get started on the arrangements."

She let out aggravated sigh and got up from the table.

He picked up his phone and checked his calendar. He shook his head. "I'll have to be back by the ninth. I have to sit down with the crew and go over a few details before we start," he said, looking slightly put out by the inconvenience.

"You mean you're coming with me?"

"I think I'd better."

"I thought you hated New York."

"Yeah, well, I hate to lose money even more," he said as he stood and picked up his coffee. "I want to set up a meeting with their production team and make sure they know what the hell they're doing. I should have done that a long time ago." He gave her an irritated glance over the top of his cup as he took a sip. "I'll see you later. Cora's waiting for me to go through next week's appointments, which we now need to reschedule." He walked out of the kitchen, still fumbling with his phone. His office door

5

closed a few moments later. She cleared his breakfast items off of the table and sat down at the breakfast bar. She took a deep breath and reluctantly picked up her phone.

* * *

Forty-eight hours later Lillian, Charles, and both of their assistants were aboard the jet headed for the Big Apple. Lillian looked at her watch. They had been in the air for only two hours, but it felt like much longer. She was restless. Anxious. She had good reason to be apprehensive, didn't she? In just a few short hours they would be touching down in New York and the next day she would be on her way to meet with the cast. She hadn't even visited the City on vacation, let alone for professional purposes, in over ten years. A Broadway show was a daunting task and she still wasn't sure she could handle it. And the show, *Love On World Tour*, was something akin to *Love American Style-The Musical.*

"Ridiculous!" She said under her breath.

The plot, if there was one, seemed doomed from the start. Nevertheless, Danny had begged, Charles had insisted, and Lillian had grudgingly consented. What else could she have done?

"Nothing," she blurted out loud.

"Who are you talking to?" Charles asked.

"No one," she sighed. "I'm just trying to remind myself again why this whole thing was a good idea."

"Well, let me see... it's a job, it's exposure, and he's your brother! Besides, it's Broadway, baby! This is exciting stuff! Think of what this'll do for your credibility if it goes well. No pressure."

"I've done Broadway before. It's not all it's cracked up to be." She shook her head and shrugged, looking over at Cora who was watching the interaction from across the aisle. "And stop saying that!"

"You're just nervous. Stop saying what?"

"Broooaaadway, baby! Ugh!" She threw her head back against the seat and closed her eyes. "You sound like some Rat Pack knock-off or something. And don't call me baby! You know I hate that."

"Lillian, think of it this way. Due to unforeseen circumstances, you've been handed an incredible opportunity that some people wait their whole lives for. You've studied ballet, tap, jazz, and ballroom dance with professionals from around the world, worked on stage and screen, and starred in what is probably the most popular teen dance film of all time—and the sequel. Of course the sequel was less popular, as is typical, but I digress. There is no reason you can't handle this. Besides, you said he has her notes. It's not like you have to reinvent the wheel, right?"

She glared at him out of the corner of her eye with pouty lips.

"Come on. Don't look like that. Like it or not, you've got to bite the bullet here. Your kid brother needs you."

"He's not exactly a kid, now is he? He's over thirty!"

"He's still *your* kid brother."

"And then there's the matter of your personal investment."

"There is that. I wasn't going to bring that up again. Look, stop worrying. You'll be fine. And for the record, I was not calling you baby. It's just an expression."

"Fine."

"If you ask me—"

"Fine!" she repeated, throwing her hands up in surrender.

He put his hand on her knee. "Relax! Do you want a drink? Maybe that would help take the edge off."

"That's the best idea you've had all day." She sighed and cracked a smile. "Thanks." She put her hand on his.

He patted her leg and then pulled his hand away to pick up the magazine he'd been reading. "Cora, would you mind? The usual please."

"Of course, sir," she said, springing into action.

Lillian knew she had to pull herself together. She would need to put on a happy face for Danny. If he sensed that she was upset, he would think she was upset with him. It had nothing to do with him really, but he was so sensitive he would most certainly think so. Besides, although she'd had her moments of pessimism and self-pity, she generally considered herself an optimist. As the great Winston Churchill once said, "A pessimist sees the difficulty in every opportunity. An optimist sees opportunity in every difficulty."

"Okay Lillian," she thought, "you can do this. You, the girl from bloody Hackney, are flying from L.A. to New York on your husband's private jet. Seven years ago you were in a wheelchair because some dumb-ass in a Chevy ran a red light. You weren't sure in you'd ever walk again, much less dance. Against all odds, with hard work, determination, and a rich, supportive husband you now have a successful career as a choreographer. So suck it up, buttercup! You can do this." With that, she smiled and took a healthy sip of the Manhattan that had appeared during her little pep talk.

* * *

Two drinks, half a novel, and twelve crossword puzzles later they were touching down at LaGuardia. Danny was waiting there with Steven. They were waving madly as Lillian and Charles stepped off of the plane.

"Jesus. Do they have to wear matching rings?" Charles whispered as they made their way toward them.

"Why shouldn't they? It's legal now and they're happy about it. Just because you don't wear a wedding ring…" Lillian said, surprised that he even noticed the rings.

She hugged and kissed them both. Charles shook their hands gave Danny a half-hearted pat on the back when he was pulled into an embrace against his will. After the pilot had unloaded their bags Charles thanked and dismissed him and they were off to Danny's and Steven's apartment on the Upper East Side.

Charles had tried to convince them that they could rent a car, but Steven insisted on driving them in his new Scion. Even their overnight bags barely fit in the cargo space. Her garment bag was crammed on her lap. Charles was awkwardly holding her makeup case while attempting to answer emails on his phone. It was a good thing neither of them were any taller or they would have had to leave half of their belongings on the street just to have room for their knees in the back seat. The drive seemed almost as eternal as the flight had, especially with the guys chattering away up front. Cora was damn lucky to have escaped that ride to the city. She and Nina had left them at the airport and taken a car filled with the rest of their luggage to the Plaza to oversee the arrangements for the remainder of their stay.

Lillian was thrilled when they arrived at the charming brownstone that Danny and Steven shared on East 78th Street. Steven scored a parking spot in front of the building and was positively elated. Charles must have been happy to arrive too. He had the door open and was prying himself out of the backseat before the vehicle had even come to a complete stop.

"Lil, we are so glad you're here. I can't tell you how much this means." Danny dropped their luggage inside the door.

"Here hon. I'll take that," Steven said, tossing his keys down on breakfast bar. He picked up their bags and took them into the tiny office guestroom.

"I'm glad I could help, Danny," Lillian said.

"Lil, it's Daniel now, remember? I'm thirty-two years old."

"Yes, well, you're still my little brother, Danny," she smiled.

9

"Give it up, Danny!" Steven joked as he came back across the living area to the kitchen.

"Okay, fine. I'll let it go, since you're here to save my ass," he laughed. "Can we get you two anything to eat or drink? A cup of tea?"

"Tea would be lovely, thank you."

"Coming right up," Steven called. "Charles?"

"I'll take a beer if you have it," Charles said, flopping down on the brown, soft leather sofa.

"We have some Blue Moon," Steven said as he put the kettle on the stove and bent down to check the height of the flame.

"Figures," Charles grumbled. He leaned back, kicked off his shoes, and propped his feet up on the coffee table.

Danny sat down at the large, wooden dining table rolling his eyes. Lillian scowled at him. He raised his eyebrows and shrugged with a silent "What?" He gestured toward Charles.

"Charles, would you mind taking your feet down, please?" she asked.

"It's weathered wood and metal. What the hell difference does it make?" Charles said.

She ignored his comment. "Okay, let's take a look at Louisa's notes, shall we?" She sat down across from Danny and pulled out her laptop, a note pad, and a pencil.

"You just got here. You want to work now?" Danny asked.

"Yes, please."

Danny shook his head. He opened his attaché case that was on the chair next him, fished out a bulging manila folder, and slid the folder across the table to Lillian.

"Is this it? Haven't you got a flash drive or anything?"

He shook his head again. "Nope. That's it."

"She is old school, isn't she?" Lillian sighed.

Charles cleared his throat. "If you three are going to talk shop, do you mind if I turn on the TV?"

"No, darling," she answered. "Just keep the volume down, would you, so we can still carry on a conversation?"

Charles didn't answer, but reached for the remote in the caddy on the small metal side table. "Jesus Christ, it's like a God damned Ethan Allan catalog in here."

"Really?" Steven asked, handing him the Blue Moon. "I was going for a New York Brownstone meets London Townhouse kind of thing. Much more Restoration Hardware."

"Oh, sure. Now that you mention it," Charles scoffed, taking a chug from the bottle. He flipped through the channels and settled on the Sundance channel. Then he pulled out his phone to check his messages for the third time since they'd touched down.

Steven brought the tea kettle and three cups to the table. He sat down next to Danny and took his hand. They both stared at Lillian as she began to examine the file. Almost immediately she started to bite her lower lip. Ten minutes later she closed the folder and picked up her tea cup.

"Well?" Danny asked.

"Well…" She repeated, still staring at the folder. She pulled out her ponytail, shook her hair out, and ran her hands through it. She exhaled slowly. "Okay. I'm going to need a copy of the script and the score."

"I'll get them." Steven stood.

"Thanks. Can you show me your costume sketches too? I'd like to get a feel for your vision and see what kind of range of motion I have to work with."

"How bad is it?" Danny asked once Steven was out of the room.

"Let's just say that there's a lot of work to do and I'm glad Louisa's contract was payable upon completion."

"Why?"

"For starters, there are only complete notes on about three numbers here. The rest is a bunch of disconnected chicken scratch if you ask me."

"That good, huh? Can you use any of it?"

She ran her fingers through her hair again. "I don't think so. If I'm going to put my name on it I'd be better off throwing it out and starting fresh." She shook her head, still deep in thought. Steven returned with the script and sketches. Lillian finally made eye contact with Danny.

"I'm sorry for sucking you into this," he said, putting his hand on hers. "I had no idea. I should have realized. If you want out…"

Lillian stood and stretched, trying to pull herself together. She did want out, but this was Danny's dream. She couldn't walk away when he needed her, not that Charles would let her anyway. She couldn't fail either of them. "Suck it up buttercup!" she told herself.

She managed a smile. "I'm here now. Let's do this."

"Thank God!" Danny said.

"Thank Lillian!" Steven corrected.

He and Danny sprang from their chairs and pulled her into a group hug.

"Hallelujah!" Charles muttered from the sofa. "I'm glad that's finally settled."

Lillian, Danny and Steven worked for several hours while she went through two pots of tea. Charles gave up and went to bed around midnight. By one o'clock Danny and Steven were ready for sleep too. Lillian said goodnight and sent them to bed, insisting that she had just a few more notes to make before turning in herself. Two hours later, she finally decided to call it quits.

Charles was snoring away on the sofa bed in the guestroom. Lillian quietly changed into her new pink and white flannel pajamas and slipped into bed next to him. She closed her eyes and focused on her breathing in an attempt to clear her head, hoping to rid herself of the menacing thoughts of failure on the live stage. She couldn't possibly have known that her concerns about the show would soon pale in comparison to the new issue that loomed on the horizon—an issue that would bring with it enough drama to throw her world completely off of its axis.

2
LONG TIME NO SEE

By the time Lillian woke up the next morning, the boys were already awake and seated around the dining table. Danny and Steven were drinking tea. Charles had his usual black tall from The Coffee Bean and Tea Leaf. He managed to scout those places out wherever he went.

"Good morning, Lil," Danny sang out boisterously. "So glad you could join us."

"What time is it?" she asked groggily.

"Half past eight."

"Good Lord. Charles, you're usually up by six. Why didn't you wake me?"

"Well, the guys and I were just shooting the breeze and I thought you might need the sleep."

"Yes, but thank God you're up," Steven called out. "These two have both been in director mode sharing trade secrets and I haven't been able to get a word in edgewise."

"Sorry Steve. I'd have brought you in, but wardrobe really isn't my bag," Charles laughed. "I have people for that. Come to think of it, I have people for just about everything."

All three of them laughed at that. Lillian was pleased to see that Charles seemed to be much more pleasant with Danny and Steven today. A night's rest seemed to have done him good. She hoped his good mood would hold out for a while.

"I don't suppose you brought me a coffee, did you darling?" she asked him.

"No. Sorry. You don't want me to go back, do you?"

"Oh, dear God! Please, Lillian, don't make him go back," Steven said. "He had to walk five blocks."

"Yes! Heaven help us if he has to make that trek again. We'll never hear the end of it," Danny said.

"Do you two always have to be so dramatic?" Charles asked.

Lillian heard the flare of agitation in Charles's voice. "Okay. Never mind the coffee, darling," she said. "Gentlemen, what time do we need to be there?"

"We were due there at nine," Steven said.

"But I've already called and made excuses for you, Sissy," Danny said. "I bought you another hour, so get in there and pretty yourself up so we can get going. I can't have you embarrassing me on your first day, now can I?"

"I think you probably do that well enough on your own, but I shall try to make myself look presentable just the same. Lucky for you, I'm not as high maintenance as I look or we'd never make it. I'll be ready in a few."

* * *

"Well, here we go," Danny said as they arrived at the rehearsal space.

"Yep. This is it!" Steven said. He and Danny smiled widely at each other.

The two of them had been bubbling with talk about the show from the time they got on to the subway at Lexington Station, but Lillian hadn't heard a word they'd said. She was far too busy worrying about how the cast would react to her and her unconventional methods.

Danny held the door open. Steven motioned for Lillian to enter before him, but she hesitated.

"Ah…You two go on in," she said. "I think I need to grab a coffee. We have a few minutes, don't we? I'll be back in five. Do you want anything?"

"No thanks," Danny said. He looked surprised by the sudden burst of words coming out of her mouth.

"Do you know where you're going?" Steven asked.

"No, but I'll manage. I hear you can't walk three blocks anymore without running into a Starbucks in this city."

She headed down 8th Avenue through the throngs of people already crowding the streets. "Ah, New York," she thought. "The honking taxis, the charming street vendors with their poached sunglasses and purses, and the faint smell of homeless that lurks just off of the main drag really give it a certain je ne sais quoi." She crossed the street against the light along with the natives, leaving a gaggle of tourists in the dust. As she suspected, she found a Starbucks in about two minutes. She was pleased to find that the line wasn't too long. There were two registers open so things were moving quickly. She stepped up to the counter and placed her standard order.

"Good morning. I'd like a venti skinny vanilla latte, no foam, with whip."

As she uttered those words she heard something that made the hair on the back of her neck stand up. A lump formed in her throat. At the register next to her a familiar voice placed an identical order. She hadn't heard that voice in over a decade, but she recognized it instantly. She turned to look at him. For a moment she could only stare, her mouth agape.

He looked older, more distinguished, but she would recognize him anywhere. His wavy, sandy brown hair was only slightly graying and a bit longer than before, giving him a more rugged appearance. His cool blue eyes still sparkled with a touch of sexy softness. By the looks of it he was still quite interested in physical fitness and, though she wouldn't dare admit it in public, he was still very handsome.

Tony thought he must be dreaming. It couldn't be her. Surely there were other women in New York who ordered their coffee that way. But that voice... He turned to face her. It *was* her, and she looked as fabulous as ever. The years had been more than kind to her. She still had a dancer's figure. Her long dark hair was a bit shorter than it was the last time he saw her and it was layered to the shoulder, framing her face beautifully. Her large brown eyes, though he remembered them as warm and loving, looked pained or angry. He wasn't sure which. The color had gone out of her face, making her full red lips even more noticeable than usual. He figured it was only a matter of time before she started to bite at her bottom lip.

Time seemed to stand still as they stood staring at one another in the middle of the store. "Excuse me, are you going to pay for that?" one cashier asked.

"Sorry," they both answered. Each of them tossed their cash onto the counter and slipped out of the line of irritable customers behind them. They inched over to the pick-up counter without ever taking their eyes off of one another.

He spoke first. "Lily Josephson. Of all the coffee shops in all the towns, in all the world, you had to walk into mine," he smiled.

The tiniest bit of color returned to her cheeks. She looked away, her lips curled in a tiny nervous smile.

"I wouldn't have come if I'd known that you were here," she said, her voice quivering. "What... ah... What *are* you doing here?"

"I live here, remember? Well, here as in the city, not here at the Starbucks," he went on.

Her heart was racing. Her stomach was doing somersaults. It was all she could do to stay standing. Yet there he stood cracking jokes, calm and collected as always. It was unnerving.

She looked up at him biting her lip, which made him smile again.

"What?" she asked.

"It's just that you… nothing." He shook his head. "What are *you* doing here?"

She tried to give a confident answer. It didn't go as well as she might have hoped. "Work… Working," she stammered. "Danny… ah… my brother—"

"Yes, I know who he is."

"Right. Well, he has a show starting production today."

"Oh. Are you in it?"

"No. Choreography. I'm choreographing it."

"I see." He paused, smiling at her again. "You're looking well. How have you been?"

"Fine," she said, without elaborating. She looked toward the door and then at her phone. The run-through was due to start any minute. "Tony, as exciting as it is to see you," she lied (it was more distressing than exciting), "I have to go. They're expecting me at the studio. So, I really have to go." She picked up her latte, which the barista had set on the counter, and walked out of the shop.

"Aw, bloody hell," he said. "Lily, wait!" He grabbed his cup and took off after her.

She walked quickly, holding her coffee in one hand and her coat closed with the other. The wind was hitting her harder in the face with every step. She knew he was following her, but she refused to look back. By the time she reached the end of the block he had caught up to her. She kept moving without acknowledging his presence for fear that any one of the many emotions she'd been trying to hide might escape.

"Lily, at least let me walk you to wherever it is you're headed. I won't bite, I promise." He grabbed her arm to keep her from getting away again.

She stopped and yanked free of his grip. She took a deep breath, put on her brave face, and turned to face him again. "Too late. We're already here." she said as calmly as she could.

He looked at the name on the door of the rehearsal studio. "You're kidding. This is Danny's show?"

"Yes. So, if you'll excuse me…"

"Aw, bloody hell!" he said again.

"What?"

"It looks like we're stuck with each other, at least for the time being."

"Why is that?"

Just then Danny came bursting out the door and almost ran them over.

"Aw…fuck!" Danny said. A look of panic washed over him as he looked from one to the other.

Steven came rushing out behind him.

"Oh, Lillian, there you are. We were just about to come looking for you. And Tony's here now too. Perfect. Have you two met? Lillian, allow me to introduce you to our set consultant, Tony Ward."

Lillian let out a guffaw. "Steven, darling, allow me to introduce you to Tony Ward, my ex!"

3
THE SHOW MUST GO ON

"Shit, Lil, I'm so sorry," Danny said.

"Shit is right. Did you know about this, Daniel?"

"No."

"How could you not?"

"I swear, Lil, I had no idea."

"He didn't know, Lillian," Steven affirmed. "Tracie invited Tony in on the project and I didn't realize…"

"Who the hell is Tracie?"

"Our set designer, Tracie Roberts. She wanted someone to advise her on the Paris scenes."

"Why him? He's an architect for God's sake!"

"Well, he has an eye for design and he knows Paris. And he came cheap. Free."

"Why?"

"Probably because she's sleeping with him," Steven went on. Danny elbowed him.

"Oh, Christ!" she shouted.

"I am still standing here. You do know that, right?" Tony finally added. He glanced at Lillian. She closed her eyes and shook her head as if she were trying to shake out some terrible image. She inhaled slowly, exhaled loudly, and spoke again.

"All right. Whatever. It's freezing out here and we have a run through to get to. Let's just get on with it."

"Really?" Danny asked.

"Yes, really. We're all professionals, right? Let's get in there."

Tony shook his head and opened the door for Lillian. He followed her inside. Danny and Steven straggled behind.

"What the hell?" Steven whispered. "What's the deal with those two?"

"Long story. I'll explain later," Danny said, heading up the stairs after Lily and Tony. "Let's just get this thing started."

* * *

It was well after one o'clock when they took their lunch break. Lillian was still scribbling notes as the other members of the cast and crew made their way out of the room. Danny snuck up and sat down next to her.

"How's it going?"

"Fine, sweetie," she said, without looking up.

"Nina said she was headed to the Thai place round the corner. Did you want anything?"

"No thanks, love. I'm not hungry."

"You ought to be. You didn't have any breakfast this morning."

"I'll eat later. I'm meeting Charles for dinner."

"Lil?"

"Hmm?" She kept right on working.

He put his hand over hers to stop her from writing. She finally looked up at him.

"Talk to me."

"About what?"

"How are you?"

"I'm fine. I'm just trying to get my thoughts down while it's quiet."

"You're fine? Really? After what happened this morning?"

"Oh. That," she said as if it hadn't crossed her mind until now.

"Yes. That. The guy you were in love with for—how long—forever?"

"Thirteen years."

"Right. So, forever. My God, we all thought the two of you would get—"

"Danny, can we not do this, please?"

"Sorry. I just thought you might want to talk about it. It must have knocked you sideways, didn't it?"

"I suppose so. I never expected to see him again. I never wanted to, really," she said.

"Do you want to talk about it?"

"No."

"But you're going to have to deal with him being around. Don't you think you should clear the air at some point?"

"Why? So he can spell out exactly what I did to drive him away? I don't think so."

"Lil, don't you want to know?"

"No, Danny!" She stood and walked across the room. She was silent for a few moments. Then she turned to look at him again, arms folded. "The past is the past. I'd just as soon leave it buried and keep a comfortable distance. I have too many other things to worry about right now other than whatever did or didn't happen with him."

She picked up her coat and purse and smiled at Danny.

"I think you're right about one thing though. I could use a bite to eat, and a short walk might do me good. Is Fluffy's still open?"

"Yes."

"I haven't had cheesecake like that in ages. Care to join me?"

"No thanks. Too much to do. Steven's bringing me something from Carnegie."

"I'll see you later, then. Be back in a few."

Lillian breathed deeply, allowing the brisk air to fill her lungs, hoping it would help to calm her nerves. She wouldn't burden Danny with it, but seeing Tony again did a lot more than knock her sideways. She'd avoided the subject for most of the morning, keeping busy with work. Now that she'd stopped to think about it again, she felt slightly nauseous. Whether it was from the emotional trauma or the lack of food, she wasn't sure. Either way, drowning her drama in a cup of tea and slice of chocolate marble cheesecake from Fluffy's Bakery sounded like a great idea. It used to be one of her favorite places for a quick bite. She hoped it hadn't changed too much since the last time she was there. It was always a real disappointment when you had something special in mind and the reality didn't live up to the memory.

* * *

Lillian sat down with her tea and cheesecake, took a cleansing breath, and relaxed her shoulders for the first time in several hours. She put the first bite in her mouth and savored the sweet, creamy, chocolaty goodness for a moment with her eyes closed. It was as delicious as she remembered. She was enjoying being alone with her thoughts, but her moment of peace ended all too soon.

"If you eat all that sugar without eating anything else it's going to play havoc with your blood sugar levels. You know you need protein."

She looked up from her cheesecake with an irritated frown on her face. "Belt up, Tony! What in bloody 'ell are you doin' here now? Are you following me? Do you mind if I 'ave twenty damned minutes to myself?"

"Sorry. What are you getting so het up for?"

"I'm not."

"Sure you are. You're accent's slipping like it does when you get angry or ah… you know. Never mind." He chuckled.

She rolled her eyes.

"Anyway," he said, "I wasn't really trying to follow you, but Fluffy's is the place to go around here, especially for cheesecake. Of course, I've always found the name more suggestive of a cat grooming parlor or something, but no matter. Is this seat taken? Mind if I have a seat?"

Without waiting for an answer he started to sit.

"Yes, actually, I do mind. Good God. You've gone and put me right off of the sodding cheesecake now. You enjoy yourself. I'm going back." She stood up, grabbed her coat and purse, and stormed out.

* * *

Fortunately the run-through of the second act moved much more quickly than the first. They were finished by four-thirty. Lillian stood up and stretched. She was relieved to see that her vision for the choreography was starting to come together. Her mind drifted back to food. Having abandoned her cheesecake earlier, she was beginning to feel a bit weak. Annoying though it was, Tony was right about her need for protein. She checked her texts and found one from Charles about dinner.

Danny appeared deeply involved in a conversation with Tracie. Tony was lingering at Tracie's side. Rather than interrupt them and risk forfeiting a clean getaway, she sent Danny a quick text.

- **Call you later. Dinner at Brasserie 8 1/2 if you want to come with.**

She had just reached the bottom of the stairs and was about to exit when she heard Tony come bounding down behind her.

"Lily, can we talk for a minute?"

"Do we have to do this now, Tony? Charles and I have dinner plans."

"I think Chuck can wait, Lily. He's had twelve years. I'm asking for about twelve seconds."

"Don't be disrespectful, Tony. It doesn't suit you. He's Charles and I'm Lillian." She opened the door and stepped outside. He followed her.

"I can't call you Lillian. It sounds like an old grandmother and you're anything but," he said, giving her a once-over.

"It was my grandmother's name. You know that."

"Yes, but I've known you since you were a girl. You'll always be Lily to me. I'm sorry."

"Fine. Was that what you had to say? Can I go now? It's freezing out here."

"No. Look... Lily, I know you were surprised to see me this morning. I was surprised to see you too. But to be honest, after all of this time, I'm also a bit surprised that you're so angry with me, especially considering—"

"What did you expect?" she interrupted. "Did you think I would just fall into your arms? The last time I saw you—God!" She stopped, choking on the thought, and shook her head. She looked away to keep him from seeing that she had begun to tear up.

"I'm not asking for warm and fuzzy, but something a little less than hostile might be nice."

She stood staring at the ground, the wind whipping her hair about her face. "I'm sorry. I didn't expect to be angry, but I am. I thought I'd moved on, but seeing you again— it's like tearing open an old wound."

"Maybe it would help if we sat down and talked about it like rational adults."

"I don't want to talk about it, Tony."

"Some things never change, do they?"

"What's that supposed to mean?" She looked back up at him.

"You still think if you avoid something long enough it will go away."

"It's not that."

"Isn't it?"

There was long pause before she spoke again. For the first time since their meeting that morning, the harshness in her eyes started to soften. When she spoke again, her tone was just a touch kinder. "Look, whether you hurt me, or I hurt you, or we hurt each other—it doesn't really matter anymore, does it? It's over. We're over, and we have been for quite some time. I can't dwell on that now. I have a job, a marriage, a life to think about. And none of those things concern you. Not anymore."

"Well, we are sort of working together here though, aren't we?"

She pursed her lips, irritated again. He was making a valid point.

"If you don't want to deal with things right now, fine. Let's not deal with them. But as far as dealing with each other—well, what I'm asking is—we loved each other very much once. Do you think we could try to be friendly— civil, at least? You know—at least for the sake of the show?"

There was another long pause as Lily seemed to contemplate the offer. By the look on her face he could tell he'd hit a soft spot. Tony shut up and waited patiently.

"Yes," she finally answered. "We can be friendly—or civil, at least. For the show. For Danny."

He reached out his hand to her. She left him hanging for a few seconds and then slowly took his hand as a sign of peace. It was a small step, but Tony seemed satisfied with it. He would have to be. As they stood there, hands still clasped, Charles stepped out of his chauffeured Town Car and came walking toward them.

Tony noticed him first and let go, putting his hands into his coat pockets and shifting his weight a bit.

"Oh, hello, darling," Lily said, clearing her throat. What are you doing here? I thought we were meeting at the restaurant."

"Your brother sent me a text that you were done for the day. My meeting was finished, so I decided pick you up and have Cora move our reservations."

"Oh. Well, that's a surprise."

"Obviously," he smirked.

Lily wondered why Charles was looking at her and Tony so strangely, as if he'd caught them in some sort of delectation. "Ah, you two don't really know each other, do you?" she asked, moving past it.

"Well actually—" Tony started out.

"No. We don't," Charles cut him off.

"Charles, this is Tony Ward. Tony, Charles George."

"Tony Ward? As in your ex-boyfriend?" Charles asked, giving Lily a quizzical look.

"The same," she said. "He's been brought on as a design consultant for the show."

"And that's not going to be a problem?" Charles asked.

"Well, no. We've ah… we've called a truce for the time being," she said.

"For the sake of the show," Tony pointed out.

"Good," Charles said. "You said yourself this is a big job. You already have enough issues to deal with. We don't need any more of the old baggage getting in the way of your work, do we, hon?"

"Of course not," Lily agreed with a weak smile. "Do you mind if we get going please, darling? I'm starving."

"You're not starving," Charles said sharply.

"Ha!" She forced a laugh. "Fine, darling. I'm famished, then. Can we just go, please?"

"Sure. We should go anyway if we're going to make it through traffic. Tony, catch you later," he said.

"Good night," Tony answered. He gave a slight wave as Charles took off toward the car.

Lily paused a moment and gave Tony an almost unnoticeable nod before turning to follow her husband.

The corners of Tony's mouth turned up in a rueful smile as he watched her walk away.

4
JUST ONE WEEKEND

The following week the company moved into the theater space. On Wednesday morning, Lily kissed Charles goodbye and sent him home on the jet. She was actually somewhat relieved to see him go. She would have much more time to concentrate on her work without having to concern herself with his moods or whereabouts.

Of course, there was still the Tony issue to contend with. He had been visiting every day at lunch time to chat with Tracie as she finished plans for the sets. And the last two days he'd stayed after to watch the performers as they practiced. Lily made it a point to exchange pleasantries with him upon arrival or departure, but tried not to do much more to acknowledge his presence.

That afternoon Lily and Nina were working the chorus dancers through a jive number. Lily studied them, scribbling madly on her notepad while Nina led the troupe through the steps. As they started the routine over for the third time, Lily was distracted by the extremely loud marimba ringtone echoing in the empty theater. She turned to see whose phone it was.

"Ugh. Tony," she said, rolling her eyes. She watched him stride up the center aisle chattering away. Just as he disappeared from view, Danny's voice came at her from the back of the house.

"Hey, Lil, can I borrow you for a sec?"

She tossed her notepad down on the edge of the stage and headed down the steps to meet him, sighing as she walked.

"What's the matter?" he asked, as she approached him, frowning.

"It's nothing, love. I just have yet to see this number all the way through. Whatcha need?"

"I was wondering if we could take a look at the action leading up to the Elvis number after dinner. I'd like your opinion on some of the movement there."

"Sure."

They stood there watching the jive for a minute or two. "This one's looking good. I love what you did with Carrie's solo too."

"Yeah, it's not bad," she said.

"Not bad? Are you kidding? The crew was raving about it all morning."

"I just think it needs more."

"More what?"

"I don't know. More flash. More spice. It needs to be bigger. And so does that damn Elvis number for Hank and Natalie."

"Well, keep at it. You'll get it." He put his arm around her shoulders and gave her a gentle shake.

She smiled. "Yes. *We* will," she said, leaning her head on his shoulder with her eyes still on her dancers.

"Are you sure you're all right? You seem—"

"I'm fine, sweetie. I'd better get back up there, though. The left flank looks a bit rough."

"Okay," he nodded. She took off up the aisle.

"Nina," she shouted on her way back up, "let's try it once more from the top, please. Mark, Smith, Michael—watch the timing. You're falling apart," she said sternly. "And Jack, sharpen up those kicks, will you? This is a jive, not a ballet number."

When they finally broke for dinner, Lily headed off to find Danny and, pulling her phone from her pocket, realized she had several missed calls. Three were from Christine, one of her closest friends from school. They still kept in touch, but it had been several weeks since they'd spoken.

She checked the time. It would be ten in the evening in Paris. She decided it wasn't too late to return the call and dialed, hoping nothing was seriously wrong.

"Oui," Christine answered.

"Allo. Bonsoir, Christine. C'est Lily. Tout va bien?"

"Oh, oui Lily. Everything is fine my dear," she said in heavily accented English. "I'm so glad you called me back."

"Of course. I saw that you called three times, but you didn't leave a message."

"Because I needed to talk to you in person. I have a grand favor to ask you."

"Qu'est-ce que c'est?"

"I need you to come to Paris."

"Why? Is something wrong?"

"I know you told me that you could not come to Adrienne's wedding, but now you must."

"I can't. I—"

"No, no, no. You must! Jean-Pierre and I are going to… we are going to get married again too."

"What? Do you mean you're going to renew your vows?"

"Oui. For our anniversary. It has been twenty-five years for us. We are finally going to have the church wedding that we missed the first time."

"I'm so sorry, Christine, but I really don't think I can get away just now. I'd have to see about taking time off. I'm working with my brother and we're really just getting started with this show."

"S'il te plaît, Lily. For me? You must come. You and Tony were with us the first time. You were the ones who believed in us. In our love. You were our good luck charms. You must be there… for luck."

"Have you asked Tony as well?"

"Of course. Jean-Pierre talked to him earlier. He has agreed to come. Now it is up to you."

"I don't know."

"Lily, I understand that the two of you are not the best of friends—"

"Ha! We weren't even *speaking* until last week."

"But you are speaking now, yes?"

"Yes, but—"

"Good. Then can you please—how do you say—bury the hatchet? For just one weekend? So you can be here with me. Please!"

"Why do I have the feeling I'm going to regret this?"

"You won't regret it! Everything will work out. You will see. And you don't have to worry about a thing. I will send your boarding passes by email. Your flight is tomorrow and I have already made your hotel arrangements."

"You don't have to do that. I can take care of that myself. I can afford it, you know?"

"Yes, I know. So can we. Besides, it's done."

"You were quite sure I would agree, weren't you?"

"Oui. I was hoping… that I could appeal to your romantic side! À bientôt, ma chérie."

"Okay. Ciao."

She hung up and set the phone down on the chair next to her. With a groan she dropped her head into her hands.

"Who were you talking to?" Danny asked as he walked up.

"Hey. Oh… ah… that was Christine."

"Your Parisian friend?"

"Yep."

"Everything okay?"

"For her, yes. For me—that remains to be seen."

"What's up?"

"Her daughter is getting married this weekend and I'd already told her that I couldn't make it, but now she and her husband have decided to renew their vows and she's begging me to be there because I stood up for her the first time. She thinks it'll be some kind of bad omen if I'm not there. She even booked the flight and made hotel reservations."

"So what's the problem?"

"Well, obviously it's not good timing with us just getting started on the show, is it?"

"No, but we can probably manage for a few days without you. I don't know about the circles you run in, but in my case, these kinds of things don't come up every day. I think you should go."

"You do? Really?"

"Sure. Besides, Nina will be here with us, right? And maybe Paris will give you a little inspiration for those tough numbers you've been working on."

"Maybe." She groaned again. "Damn it, Daniel. I was really hoping that you would be less accommodating."

"Sorry?"

"Tony is going to stand up for Jean-Pierre."

"Oh."

"Exactly. Last week I didn't even want to be in the same room with him and now I have to spend a weekend in Paris with him?"

"Which scares you more? The idea that you'll spend the whole time fighting with him or that you won't?"

"What are you implying?"

"Well, you have to admit that he is still about as charming and handsome as ever, isn't he?"

"I hadn't noticed."

"Oh, come on!"

"Daniel, I'm married and he's got a girlfriend."

"I didn't realize that slipping a ring on could cause blindness," he snickered.

"You really do find yourself amusing, don't you?"

"Yes. Quite."

"My point is we've both moved on with our lives. The past is… the past."

"If that's true, then it shouldn't be a problem."

"No. I guess not. It's still bloody awkward though, isn't it?" she said, standing and picking up her phone. "I'll see you after dinner, sweetie. I'm gonna go call my husband and see that he's made it home. I guess I'd better get started packing too, though I haven't the slightest idea what to wear to the wedding. I didn't really bring much formal wear with me."

"Oh, say it isn't so!"

"What?"

"You may be forced to shop in Paris!"

"Pity, isn't it?" She laughed. "See you in a bit." She kissed him on the cheek and walked off.

* * *

The following day Lily left rehearsals at three-thirty, picked up her suitcase from the Plaza, and headed for the airport. Ever prepared and punctual, Tony was already seated at the gate reading by the time she got there. Before he had a chance to notice her, she decided to head for the bar. She ordered one drink and then another. After nearly two hours in hiding, she heard the final boarding call come over the loud speaker. She could put it off no longer. She would have to face him. She gathered her things and returned to the gate. She was relieved to find that he was already at the front of the line preparing to board. Her relief didn't last long.

"There you are. I was beginning to think you'd decided not to come after all," Tony said, as Lily came to a stop in the aisle.

Lily rolled her eyes. "Lovely. Christine managed to get us two seats together. How very thoughtful of her." She reached up to shift some items in the overhead compartment to make room for her bag.

"Do you need any help?"

"No. Thank you. I've got it."

She sat down and buckled her seatbelt, assuming there was bound to turbulence of one kind or another. Neither of them spoke again until the flight attendant came by to serve drinks. Lily ordered a Manhattan and Tony asked for scotch on the rocks. She glanced around at the other passengers and fiddled with her glass for several minutes, taking occasional sips. When the silence finally became unbearable she took one more drink and cleared her throat.

"It's too bad your girlfriend couldn't come along."

"Who?"

"Your girlfriend. Tracie. It's too bad she couldn't join you. Paris is a lovely place for lovers."

"I don't think I'd really call her my girlfriend."

"Oh. So what it is then? Just a casual fuck?"

"Jesus!"

"Shit!" She dropped her face into her hands and had a moment before looking up. It had come out faster than she could stop it and she was mortified. "God! I'm sorry. I didn't... I'm sorry. That is *not* how I was intending to start off this conversation. You can sleep with whomever you want anyway. It's obviously none of my damn business," she mumbled. "God! I'm sorry. I... I'd *really* intended to be much more adult about this whole thing."

"So much for small talk, hmm?" he said. "Lily..." He reached over to put his hand on her wrist as she held her glass with both hands. "Why don't you try to relax a bit, okay? You're wound up tighter than the queen's corset on coronation day, for goodness sake. Just... relax."

She eyed his hand, fighting the urge to pull away. "I don't know what's wrong with me. I'm just so..."

He let go of her and picked up his glass.

"Worked up?" he asked, taking a drink.

"Yes."

"Feeling awkward?"

"Yes."

"Nervous and uncertain?"

"Exactly. The funny thing is, I usually pride myself on being able to hide my feelings, you know? But for some reason..." she trailed off, frustrated by the fact that he could throw her off her game so easily.

"Listen, if we're going to get through this weekend, let's get something straight, okay? Going to this wedding together—well, it's rather like being invited to a dinner party and running into an old friend that you haven't seen in years. It's odd at first, but you talk a bit. You reminisce. You have a few drinks. You have a good time and then you go home. That's all it is."

She turned and looked him in the eyes for the first time, her lips parted as if she wanted to say something, but no words came. Instead she just shook her head.

He pressed his lips together and gave her a small painful smile as he nodded. "Before all of that we were friends," he reminded her. "Really good friends. If we can find any part of that again, wouldn't it be nice?"

"Do you really think that's possible?" she asked.

"I'd like to think so. I'm willing to try it—if you are."

She looked pensive for a moment, then nodded slowly. She raised her half empty glass. "Here's to... fresh starts. For old friends."

"I'll drink to that." He raised his glass too and they both took a healthy swallow and settled back in their seats.

Once the inflight meal was finished they both pulled out their laptops and started working. After a while Lily looked over at Tony.

"Do you want to see what I'm doing?"

"Hmm?"

"Well, you keep trying to look over my shoulder so I thought you might want to see what I'm doing."

"Sorry."

"No. It's all right. Have a look." She turned the computer so that he could see the screen. "I'm just programming some step sequences and then I can see what it all looks like."

"That's really incredible."

"Isn't it? When you think about at all of the advances in technology just in the last ten years..." She nodded toward the images on his screen. "Remember the days when architects actually had to draw up their plans? And there was no containing all of your rolls of paper. They were all over our bedroom. Do you remember?" She glanced at him and smiled.

"Yes." He smiled too. "That was much more of a pain in the ass, but every once in a while I get the urge to sketch something just to prove that it can still be done, you know?"

"I know what you mean. But I could never do what I do without it now," she said.

"Do mind if I ask you a question?"

"No. What?"

"Do you ever actually dance with your performers?

"No, not really."

"You don't dance?"

"No."

"Why not?"

"Do you want another drink?" she asked.

She reached up and hit the call button for the flight attendant. Once they had been served, Tony started in again.

"You never answered my question."

"What question?"

"How is it that you can be a sought-after choreographer and yet you say you don't dance?"

"I don't know that I'm that sought-after. I married well, so people in the business tend to take notice. And my brother was desperate." She laughed.

"Is that why you married him?"

"My brother?" she teased.

"Ha! No. Your husband. Is that why you married him? To make it in the business?"

"No. Of course not. That's not what I meant."

"At any rate, you seem to be doing all right for a dancer who doesn't dance."

"Well, I do dance on my own. Just not for other people. I haven't performed in front of anyone—except Nina—since the accident. Did you hear about that?"

"Yes, I read something about it or saw it on the news. That was more than five years ago, wasn't it?" he asked.

"Yes. Seven, actually. But it took a long time to get me up on my feet again."

"Was it really that bad?"

"I don't really remember what happened, but I'm told I—you don't really want hear about it, do you?"

"Go ahead." He was looking at her intently.

"Well, I suffered head trauma and had several rather serious internal injuries. I had a fractured pelvis and multiple spinal fractures, which took three different surgeries to repair, but they wouldn't do those until the swelling went down and some of the other injuries had healed. When I woke up after a week or so in a coma all I knew was that I couldn't move from the waist down. It turned out that none of the injuries to the spine were complete. Thank God. But not being able to repair the damage and start rehab right away took a toll. Once the surgeries were done I had to practically learn to walk again. It was a slow process and a bit of a struggle. There were days when I didn't know if I could do it and even if I did, I didn't know if I would ever really dance again. That was the only thing I ever wanted to do anyway. Some days I just wanted to give up."

Her voice cracked. She stopped and took a drink. After a long pause she went on.

"Charles wouldn't let me quit. He never stopped pushing me. He just kept finding new treatments, experimental and otherwise. We went through hours and hours of physical therapy every week.. Every day for a while. We tried electrical stimulations, acupuncture, chiropractic—the list is endless really. You probably don't need any more boring details. Besides, it's depressing stuff."

"I had no idea it was so serious. And you really don't remember anything?"

She shook her head. "I remember the last few seconds before it happened and then—nothing. But then, I was unconscious for the next eight days. Actually it's funny…" She stopped, wondering if she should share what she was thinking or not.

"What?" he asked quietly.

"It seems that not only did I not remember what happened, but my mind even went so far as to invent some things that hadn't happened."

"Like what?"

"When I woke up, I was absolutely certain that you had been there. I even asked Charles where you were. He thought I was crazy. I was, I guess. We weren't even speaking at the time. It didn't make any sense to think that, but I would have sworn it. Funny, the tricks the mind can play, isn't it?"

"Mmm. Funny," he said. "You don't seem to show any effects now."

"I suppose it couldn't be obvious to the casual observer, but I've lost a lot of control and I have to work a lot harder to do the simplest things. My technique is just not as sharp and my balance isn't what it should be. I can't trust my body the way I used to. I need regular adjustments to keep things in place. When I haven't been realigned in a while, things can get shifted or pinched and they don't work like they should. Sometimes I still wake up with nightmares about losing my footing and falling flat on my face on stage. I feel like I never know if my body's going to give out on me, so I don't give it the chance."

"So then how do you do what you do? You just program it all into your machine and…"

"Well, sort of. I do still have my own studio so I can plan things out on my own. Then I put down notes or plug them into the computer and I bring in Nina and walk through things with her. After I've communicated my vision to her, she's the one who demonstrates it for me.

Instead of her taking notes for me, I take the notes and then tweak where necessary."

"Do you and Nina ever dance together?"

"Well, we…" She looked up and noticed the rather lustful look on his face. "Tony! What's in that drink of yours?"

"Sorry!" he laughed. "Don't you miss dancing? I mean really dancing?"

"Sure. Sometimes. But… Life changes, you know? It is what it is. Listen, enough about me. What about you? How are things with you?"

"Oh, well, business is good. Boring for those who aren't involved in it. The firm's doing well. We have projects in the works on multiple continents. I guess I've done all right for myself professionally."

"And personally?"

"Well, now that Mum and Dad are semi-retired, they're off traveling a lot. So, I've been spending a lot of time managing their affairs while they're away."

"That's not really what I meant. I meant… romantically," she said cautiously.

"That's a whole other story." He gave a small chuckle and shifted in his seat. "Certainly things have not gone as my mother would have hoped. She would have liked to have me married with children by now."

"So why aren't you?"

"You really aren't pulling any punches tonight, are you?"

"Sorry."

"It's getting late."

"I guess we should try to get some sleep, shouldn't we?" she said.

"Probably a good idea," he said, shutting down his computer.

"Just as well. I can't seem to figure out what to do with this damn routine anyway." She powered hers off too and stowed it under the seat in front of her. She arched her back and sighed.

"This show really has you stressed, doesn't it?"

"Yes. It's just such a huge job. I really wasn't prepared, but neither Danny nor Charles left me much choice. Danny and Steven have worked so hard. I couldn't say no. Danny's hoping Paris will inspire me. We shall have to see about that, won't we?" she laughed.

5
WELCOME TO PARIS

Lily and Tony made their way through the underground tunnel to baggage claim, then through the maze of covered tubes in the terminal leading to the taxi lineup. As they stood waiting, Lily sent quick messages to Charles and Danny to let them know she'd arrived safely. She was otherwise quiet, absorbing the dulcet tones of the French language being spoken around her. Before long, the smell of smoke began to fill her nostrils. She turned to see a man a few feet behind her who'd lit up right in front of the no smoking sign.

"Bienvenue à Paris," Lily whispered.

"What?" Tony asked.

"Nothing. Just noticing the smoke."

"We're almost up. We'll be away from it in a minute."

"Oh, it's not bothering me. It's just so… so European," she smiled. "It's nice to be back after so long."

"How long has it been?" he asked.

"Almost eight years, I think. Charles doesn't really like to travel to Europe."

"What? Who doesn't like to travel to Europe?"

"Charles doesn't."

"Why not?"

"It's too antiquated. More people should speak English. The smoke irritates his asthma."

"Lovely," Tony said with a frown.

"What?" Lily asked.

"Ah… It's lovely—to be here." He coughed. "Look! Our turn."

The next taxi pulled up and he opened the door for her to get in. By the time he put the bags in the trunk and got in himself, she'd already told the driver where to go and was busy chatting with him, indulging his flirtatious commentary. She allowed the receptionist at the hotel the same courtesy, happily accepting his offer of extra towels and the promise of complimentary breakfast. The young man bid her farewell and kissed her hand as he gave her the room keys. Tony just laughed as he picked up their bags and followed her to their rooms.

"What a beautiful room! Très chic," she said as she opened the door and looked around. The bed rested on a turquoise accent wall with a white leather headboard and crisp white linens. The accent pillows were covered in a matching shade of blue and brown toile. On the dark wood side table was an arrangement of white calla lilies and the floor-to-ceiling sheer drapes that covered the opposite wall were silk screened with oversized images of the flowers as well.

"Oh, look!" She rushed across the room, pulled the drapes, and threw open the glass doors that led to a tiny balcony. "La Sorbonne! Gah! Tony, is there any place on Earth like this city?" She backed up and sat down on the bed, still admiring the view. She ran her hand over the brown chenille throw covering the foot of the bed. "The bed isn't half bad either," she said.

"Do you think you'll have a rest then?" he asked, putting her bag down next to the bed.

"Are you kidding? We have the whole day before we're supposed to meet them for dinner. I want to experience Paris again. I also need to find a dress for the wedding."

"Oh. Well, I'll leave you to that then. See you later."
He turned to leave.

"What are you going to do?"

"I'll probably get settled and then go for a coffee and a croissant or something," he said.

"Well, did you want to meet for lunch later?"

"Ah, maybe." He sounded surprised. "If you've finished your shopping by then."

"It's a little after ten now. Why don't we meet back here... say around two and we can go from there."

"Sure. Mind—the two of us about Paris together—there might be talk," he joked.

"Ha! As long as that's all there is."

"Enjoy your shopping," he said as he left.

She heaved her suitcase up onto the bed and opened it to unpack. When she was finished, she donned her red wool pea coat, stashed her room key safely in her purse, and headed out.

She wound her way through the crooked streets of the Latin Quarter, trying hard to take it all in. The smell of fresh baked baguettes and croissants still wafted from the boulangerie near the hotel. Café owners just opening up were setting out their sandwich boards with the day's specials on them.

Local women with their shopping bags were already beginning to file into the butcher and other shops. She stopped for a minute outside the fromagerie and admired the many wedges and rounds of camembert, brie and the like in the cases. Then she remembered that she was on a mission to find a suitable dress and moved on, only briefly allowing herself be distracted by the sweets in the chocolatier two doors down or the numerous booksellers in their stalls.

Several hours and boutiques later, she returned to the hotel with her arms full of packages. She hung her new purchases in the closet and consulted her phone. No messages other than a text from Danny telling her to have fun. She still had another hour before she was supposed to meet Tony for lunch, so she decided to go back out for a short walk.

She left the hotel with no real destination in mind, but the power of memory pulled her in the direction of the river. She ended up on the Quai Saint-Michel just downstream from Notre Dame on the left bank, where she'd spent countless hours during her youth. It was no coincidence that Tony had found his way there as well. He was seated on the edge of the wall staring out over the river. She strolled up quietly, hands in her pockets, and stood behind him.

"Fancy meeting you here," she said.

"Oh, hello." He glanced up at her.

"It's still an impressive sight, isn't it?" she said softly.

"Spectacular," he nodded.

She sat down a few feet away from him with her feet dangling over the edge. They watched the people going by and the boats on the river without speaking for what must have been half an hour. After a while she took her hands from her pockets and blew on them.

"Are you cold?"

"A bit."

"We can go if you want to. Get some lunch."

"No. Not yet. I like it here. I just wish I'd thought to bring some gloves."

His eyes lit up. "Wait here a minute. I have an idea."

"Where are you going?" she called after him.

"I'll be right back. Don't go away."

A few minutes later he returned, carrying a large thermos and two small cups. He sat back down next to her again, closer this time. She caught a whiff of his cologne. The familiar scent made her smile.

"I think this just might do the trick," he said as he handed her one of the cups.

"I thought maybe you went to buy some gloves."

"Nope. This is better. It will warm your hands and your insides too."

"What have you got in there?"

"Vin chaud."

"Brilliant! Where did you get the flask?"

"You are not the only one who knows how to get what you want."

"What are you talking about?"

"Oh come now. I watched you work your magic on the receptionist," he laughed. " I had a nice little chat with the young lady in the café round the corner this morning. I used it to my advantage."

"I see."

He poured some of the mulled wine into her cup. She wrapped both hands around it and inhaled the aroma of the cinnamon and cloves.

"We certainly spent a lot of hours here, didn't we?" she said.

Tony nodded. He watched her face as her lips curved into a gentle smile. The November wind whipped through her long dark hair. Seeing her sitting there like that gave him pause, and his thoughts drifted.

* * *

It was April. They were sitting on the quay with a bottle of wine, bread, and cheese. It was dusk, and the glow of the setting sun on the Seine was a sight to behold. The Eiffel Tower stood proudly in the distance over his left shoulder. The grandeur of the Notre Dame loomed in front of him just across the river. Still, Tony was more impressed by the object of beauty to his right. He studied Lily in the waning light as she told a story of something one her classmates had said or done. He couldn't quite follow the story, but not because he wasn't interested in what she had to say. He just happened to be more interested in her face at the moment.

He'd known her since she was twelve. He'd thought she was beautiful even then, but as she'd matured, her features had become even more beautifully defined. When they first met, he thought she was a pretty little girl, but that day he saw before him an exquisite young woman. Her skin was flawless, her large brown eyes soulful, and her lips—full, luscious. They practically begged to be kissed.

They had always been just friends. If fact, they'd been best friends, but he had been hoping for more for quite some time. The trouble was, he wasn't entirely sure how she felt. He knew she cared for him a great deal. She depended on him. She might even say that she loved him. But did she love him the way he loved her? Did she still see him as just a protective older brother? It was hard to tell. She was young. He knew that. But she would be eighteen soon, and she had always been mature beyond her years. She'd had to be. And he was only nineteen anyway. The difference wasn't that big. He had been with other girls his own age, but none of them made him feel the way she did.

She'd finished her story and was looking at him as if she were waiting for him to say something. He only stared back.

"Tony?"

"Hmm? What?"

"I asked you what you thought. You haven't answered."

"I'm sorry. It's just…"

"Just what?"

"You look… so beautiful tonight."

"Tony, please," she said, smiling shyly and lowering her eyes.

The spring breeze blew her hair across her face. He reached over and gently brushed it out of the way with his fingers, tucking it behind her ear and slowly tracing his way down her jaw line with the backs of his fingers. Her gaze met his. For the first time he saw a different look in her eyes. His hand still under her chin, he tilted it ever so slightly upward. Her lips parted invitingly. His moment had finally arrived. He only had one shot at making their first kiss perfect. Depending on her reaction, it might be their only kiss. He leaned in and kissed her gently, slowly, savoring her lips. It was everything he could have imagined and more.

He stopped and smiled at her nervously, waiting to see what she would say. She didn't say anything. To his surprise, she tilted her head, leaned in, and kissed him back.

* * *

"Tony," Lily said, dragging him back into the present.

"Hmm? What?"

"What were you thinking about?"

"Nothing."

"Come on. That's a very pensive face for nothing."

"I was just thinking—you don't want to know."

"Tell me."

He shook his head.

"Come on," she coaxed.

"I never could resist that smile," he said, which only made her smile wider, though she tried to hide it. "I was thinking… that we were… sitting right here. In this very spot. The first time I ever kissed you."

"Hmm. Only we were farther down there, weren't we?" she asked, nodding to the left.

"No. We were sitting there, but then that guy sat on the end, and he was smoking like a chimney and hacking, remember?" he laughed. "So we moved down to get some peace and quiet."

"Oh, you're right."

"I know. Because you were trying to tell me about Brigitte and Claire."

"And you weren't listening anyway."

"I was listening. I was trying to, but I was distracted. You were... so beautiful."

"That was... some kiss," she said as they stared into one another's eyes. Then, suddenly, she broke from his gaze and looked down. "You know, I am quite hungry all of a sudden. Could we go to lunch now?"

"Of course," he said, springing to his feet.

He collected the thermos and cups in his left hand and held out the right to help her up.

"I hear there's a great restaurant round the corner if you're in the mood for oysters," he said.

She spun to put her feet up on the edge and reached for his hand. He pulled her to her feet.

"Oysters?" She sounded skeptical.

"They're supposed to be deliciously fresh."

She hesitated a moment and then said, "Why not? Oysters! Ooh—and onion soup!"

"Shall we?" He put out his arm.

She looped hers through his, and off they went. Even a day ago it would have seemed strange to walk arm in arm with him, but somehow at the moment it felt like the most natural thing in the world. For a change, she wouldn't question it. She would just enjoy the moment.

On the walk back to the hotel after their leisurely lunch, they passed a crepe vendor and Lily's eyes grew wide. "Oh, that's the perfect dessert. Let's stop for a crepe. Do you want to?"

"If you like," Tony said, chuckling at her excessive excitement. He marveled at the owner, an older gentleman in small gray cap, who was managing to smoke a cigarette, make their crepes and flirt with Lily all at the same time. She was watching his every move as he swirled the batter smoothly around on the large circular griddles, forming perfectly round paper-thin pancakes. He flipped them and folded them in half and proceeded to put the toppings on.

Then he doubled them over twice more and slipped them into the wax paper cones. He handed them both to Lily, and when she tried to pay him, he insisted that she need only pay for Tony's, because crepes were free for ladies today. Lily thanked him and turned to Tony, handing him his.

"Here you go. One banana and Nutella crepe. Lucky for you he didn't skimp on the Nutella either," she laughed.

"Yes! I hate that." He laughed. "What did you get?"

"Just butter and sugar. Simple, but really yummy," she said as she bit off a large piece.

"Yummy?" he teased.

"Yes," she answered with her mouth full. "Mmm!"

She licked her lips. "Oh my God! That is fabulous! How's yours?"

"Good. Want a bite?"

"No thank you."

They ate as they walked. Lily cooed happily with every bite. His was gone, and she was nearly finished with hers by the time they reached the hotel.

Outside her door, she fished for her key. Once she'd managed to open the door, Tony handed her the crepe wrapper that he'd been holding. "Oh, thanks." She took it and started to fold it up as if she were going to toss it out.

"Aren't you going to eat the last bite?" he asked.

"I don't think I can. I'm stuffed."

"You're kidding? That's the best part you've got there with all of the butter and sugar melted into a little pool of goodness at the bottom of the cone."

"Oh, well in that case…" she took the last bite out of the wrapper and held it out.

As he opened his mouth to question her, she popped it in, then licked the butter from her fingers. He was obviously surprised, but not displeased.

"See, I was right. Yummy!" he said, smiling as he chewed.

"It's getting late. We'd best freshen up before tonight's festivities, hadn't we?"

He nodded as he swallowed.

"Well, thank you for a lovely lunch," she said quietly.

"My pleasure."

"See you in a bit, darling," she said as she closed the door.

"Darling?" he murmured, tilting his head. He turned and walked toward his room.

6
EXCESSIVE CELEBRATION

After traveling, shopping, and socializing for hours at dinner with the wedding party, Lily was exhausted. She often had trouble sleeping away from home, but that night. she was out the moment her head hit the pillow and she slept until after noon the next day. Fortunately, she and Tony were not expected to attend the civil ceremony, which bought her a bit of extra time. Still, by the time she finished her coffee at the café down the street, she barely had time to shower, primp, and put on her new dress before they had to leave for the church.

Once she was ready she knocked on Tony's door. He greeted her quickly without really looking at her and rushed back into the bathroom.

"Are you about ready?" she called to him.

"Just about. I'm working on my damn tie. I don't know what hell my problem is today."

"Just as well."

"Why?" He came back out, with the tie in his hand, and, from across the room, noticed her in the plum colored pin-tucked jersey dress. He stopped and smiled, examining her.

"Did you find that dress yesterday?"

"Yes. Do you like it?" She twirled around for him to see the rest.

The flared hemline ended an inch above the knee displaying her legs nicely. Sheer mesh insets created a striped pattern on the front and back yokes, which showed just enough skin to be intriguing.

"Very nice. It's a great color for you."

"Thanks."

She stood smiling at him, thinking he looked quite nice in the light gray suit.

"What's that?" he asked, pointing to the small unwrapped box she was holding.

"Oh…" she said, snapping out of it. "I actually bought this for you." She held out the box for him to take. He opened it.

"You bought me a tie?"

"Not just a tie. A silk damask plum shimmer tie with a matching pocket square."

"Ooh. Sounds much more exciting. That's very thoughtful. You didn't have to do that."

"Well, I thought it would go nicely with my dress. I'm glad to see it will work with your suit too."

"Matches the room as well," he chuckled.

"So it does." She smiled, noting the purple accent pillows and modern plum stripe painted all the way around the room.

"Let's see if I can manage this one," he said as he took the tie out of the box.

"Here. Allow me." She slid her coat off her arm and tossed it and her handbag onto the bed.

"Were you always this tall?" he asked as she stepped up and met him eye to eye to slip it around his neck.

"Nope. It's the shoes. They give me an extra four inches." She tied a nice, neat Windsor knot on the first try, grinning as she tightened it.

"There." She stepped back and admired her work.

"Thanks." He pinned it and buttoned his vest. She picked up his suit coat from the chair and held it out for him. He slipped into it and put in the pocket square. "Well?" he asked when he'd finished.

"We do clean up well, if I do say so. Ready?"

He helped her on with her coat and opened the door for her.

* * *

Lily and Tony had prime seats in the front pew at Saint-Germain-des-Prés along with Gigi and Miguel, who were witnesses for Adrienne and Vidal. Lily started to tear up the moment Adrienne appeared at the end of the aisle on Jean-Pierre's arm in her flowing white gown. Christine followed in an elegant, full-length ivory chiffon gown. Lily was thrilled to see that Christine's father was escorting her. Her parents had refused to give her their blessings for their first wedding because they'd wanted her to finish school first and said she'd be throwing her life away. They couldn't have been more wrong.

The ceremony, a traditional Catholic mass with two sets of wedding vows, was long, but Lily didn't even notice. She listened intently to the readings of love and commitment and was impressed by the tradition and pageantry of the mass. She was moved to see the way Vidal looked at Adrienne as he recited his vows with stars in his eyes. The quiver in his voice was enough to disprove any theory claiming all Spaniards were machistas. Jean-Pierre and Christine still looked at each other with the same sparkle she'd seen when they were teenagers, but when they spoke their vows this time, they were not overly emotional. Their words rang out strong and clear as they reaffirmed their commitment to one another. No doubt. They would be together forever.

"Romance is not dead," Lily whispered. Tony smiled and handed her his handkerchief. She dabbed gently at her watery eyes. She could only pray that her waterproof mascara was holding up under the strain.

* * *

Lily and several of the other girls from her class at the conservatoire gathered around Christine at the cocktail reception. Christine exuded pure joy as everyone showered her with love and congratulations. They toasted their friendships and the bride and groom. Christine thanked them all for being there to share the day with her and then skipped off to find her husband.

Margot shared recent pictures of her children, and Brigitte gave a brief history of her love life, which was more like a dissertation. In an attempt to avoid further unwanted details from Brigitte, Lily turned to Emilie.

"You've been very quiet, Emilie. How about you?" she asked. "How are things with you and André?"

"We divorced two years ago."

"The bastard was cheating on her with his secretary," Brigitte said.

"Oh. I'm so sorry. How awful!" Lily grimaced.

"It's not all bad. There are some advantages to being single again," Emilie smirked. She casually took a sip of her drink and turned her attention to someone across the room.

Lily followed Emilie's eyes, trying to ascertain who she was ogling. There, in the direct line of fire, was Tony. Lily rolled her eyes and shook her head.

"Good Lord," she mumbled. She turned away and washed the thought down with another swallow of wine.

Having eaten only a pastry with coffee all day, by the time the cocktail hour ended, Lily was more than ready for the dinner celebration. With most Parisian affairs good food and drink were of the utmost importance, and she knew their menu would not disappoint.

After four delicious courses and several glasses of champagne, Lily had to excuse herself. When she returned from the ladies room, the music had already started.

Adrienne, Vidal, and his family were dancing up a storm. Jean-Pierre and Christine stood to one side of the dance floor watching their daughter and her new in-laws. Lily saw them touch their glasses together in a toast. Christine said something to him and smiled as she lovingly touched his cheek. Jean-Pierre responded with a surprisingly lengthy kiss that made Lily flush just watching it.

Tony found Lily admiring the croquembouche a few minutes later.

"It looks delicious, doesn't it?" he said, coming up behind her.

"Yes. I absolutely love these things."

"What's not to love about a tower of cream puffs bound by caramel? Ooh," he said as he heard the next song start up. "This is nice Latin number. Would you care to dance?"

"Oh, ah… I don't think so."

"Come on. Vidal's parents—what are their names?"

"Antonia and Juan José."

"Well, they look pretty good out there, but I'm pretty sure we could give them a run for their money, you and I."

"Tony—"

"This is a great song," he said again, as if he were trying to challenge her. He began to move his feet and hips to the music.

"That looks a bit like cumbia," she said. "Where did you learn that?"

"A spicy little Dominican by the name of Rebeca De La Cruz," he told her. "The same place I acquired my limited knowledge of Spanish. You know—dos cervezas. ¿Dónde está el baño? Stuff like that."

"Is that all she taught you?"

"No, but the rest of it is probably not appropriate at this stage of our relationship. Are you sure I can't convince you to dance?"

"No. Thank you."

A female voice interrupted, "Well if you are not going to dance with this handsome man, do you mind if I do?"

Lily turned to see who it was. "Oh, hello Brigitte. Be my guest," she snickered.

"Excellent! Shall we?" Brigitte said, snaking an arm around Tony and dragging him out onto the floor as he looked back over his shoulder at Lily.

Lily returned to the table and watched the two of them. Brigitte, anything but shy, was all over him.

"Lascivious cow!" Lily said to herself as she downed another glass of champagne.

* * *

By the time they left the party it was nearly three a.m. As they walked through the streets, Lily clung to Tony's arm like a life raft.

"Hey… Let's not go back to the hotel just yet," she said, speaking slowly with very intentional enunciation. "Let's go for a walk. I want to walk across the Pont des Arts."

"It's a bit late for sightseeing, isn't it?" Tony asked.

"Maybe a little," she giggled. "But it's such a lovely view. And I want to see the padlocks. Are they still there?"

"Yes. The government's tried removing them, but couples still come from all over to leave them there."

"See. True love endures. Let's go," she said, pulling him in the direction she wanted to go.

"Aren't you tired?"

"No. Come on. Please!"

She smiled at him and he caved.

As they ambled across the bridge arm in arm, Lily admired the countless locks of all shapes and sizes attached to the railings.

"Just think—all of these were left here as symbols of undying love. So many of them. Isn't it romantic?" she asked. Then she stopped and looked out over the river.

"Oh Tony, look at that," she sighed, resting her head on his shoulder.

The air was crisp and the sky was clear, allowing them a truly breath-taking view of the Pont Neuf over the Seine and the city beyond that shone with a golden glow by night. After a few minutes they continued on across toward the Institute of France and in the direction of the hotel, enjoying the sights and sounds of a city surprisingly still alive for that time of night.

A few blocks from the hotel, Lily suddenly stumbled and almost fell over. "Bugger!" she grumbled.

"Christ, Lil. Are you all right?"

"Yeah. But my shoe isn't. The bloody heel just broke off."

"That's what you get for wearing stilettos on a walking tour of Paris!"

"No kidding. I'm lucky I didn't break my damn ankle. Ouch!" she said, hobbling along for a few steps. "Hang on a minute." She let go of his arm and took the shoe off, putting it and the heel into her very large purse.

"What are you doing?"

"I'm going to save the damn thing and have it repaired," she said as she took the other shoe off and put it in too. "That's better. Ooh, I turned it pretty good though. Damn! It's colder than I thought. We'll have to walk fast!"

"Are you crazy? You can't go barefoot."

"Well, I can't bloody well walk four inches taller on one side now, can I?"

"Give me your handbag."

"Why?"

"Just give it to me."

She passed it to him, and he put it over his shoulder. Then he bent down, scooped her up. He took a moment to steady himself and started walking.

"OH! Tony! What in bloody 'ell are you doin'? You can't carry me all the way back to the hotel."

"Well, I can't let you walk. God only knows what you might step on. Or in. Can't be too careful with an ankle either."

"Don't be ridiculous," she said, trying to sound angry but giggling in spite of herself.

"Calm down, will you? It's barely two blocks. If you'll kindly stop flailing about you'll make it a lot easier on me. Not to mention draw less attention to yourself."

"You're gonna hurt yourself."

"Please. You don't weigh a thing. I think your handbag weighs more than you do. What the hell is in this thing anyway?" He nodded toward his right shoulder.

She laughed heartily, throwing her head back and then bringing it back to rest on his shoulder as she wrapped her arms around his neck.

"A couple of bottles of champagne."

"A couple of… Christ! You nicked the champagne from the party? Have you no shame?"

"I didn't nick it. Christine gave it to me."

"What are you going to do with two more bottles?"

"Drink it!"

"All of it?"

"I might! We're in Paris, it's the good stuff, and my 'usband isn't 'ere to monitor 'ow much I've 'ad," she said. "And don't you dare start judging me!" she added.

"Judge you? Hell, I'm gonna help you drink it!" he laughed.

When they arrived at the hotel, Vidal's parents were arriving as well. Juan José opened the door and allowed Tony to carry Lily in. They smiled at each other, and Antonia made a comment in Spanish. Lily squealed, "Oh, no! We're not. I just broke my… never mind!" She gave up trying to explain, and laughed again.

"What are you laughing about now?"

"I didn't get it all, but I recognized a few words. I'm fairly certain she said you were taking me to bed."

"Ha! I wish," he said under his breath.

"What?"

"What?" he repeated.

Once outside his room he put her down gently and took his key out of his pocket. She followed him inside because he was still holding her bag.

"Have a seat, why don't you, and let's have a look at that ankle," he suggested.

She sat on the edge of the bed and worked off her coat. "It's fine, really. I only turned it. I'm sure it's fine."

"Well, you don't want to take any chances. Especially not with your ankles. Good Lord, you ought to have them insured. Or do you?" He went to his travel bag and pulled out an instant ice pack. Then he hurried into the bathroom and grabbed a towel. He cracked the icepack to activate it. "Here. Sit back."

She scooted back until she was leaning against the pillows. He put the ice pack on her ankle and wrapped the whole thing in the towel.

"Can I get you anything else?" he asked.

"Yes. You can break out one of those bottles of bubbly, please. When did you become Florence Nightingale, anyway?"

"I had a girlfriend who was a nurse. I guess she got to me," he said as pulled the first bottle out of her bag.

"A nurse? What was her name?" she asked.

"Melissa."

"And your Rebeca? What did she do? For a living, I mean. I have a pretty good idea what she did for you," Lily snickered.

"She was a flight attendant," he answered as he popped the top. He found two plastic cups, poured, and handed one to her.

"Tchin Tchin," she said, holding it up. He did the same. They both took a drink. "Damn, that's good stuff," she said.

"So, why the sudden interest in my ex-girlfriends?"

"Just curious." She took another swallow. After a few minutes she started in again. "So how did you ever end up with Tracie?"

"I don't know. The same way I ended up with a lot of the women I've dated, I suppose." He sat on the bed next to her, leaning against the headboard. "Why?"

"Just making conversation." She smiled and took another drink. "How did you meet her?"

"At an afterparty. We had a mutual friend opening in a show."

"How old is she?"

"Ah, twenty-nine, I think."

"What? You're about to turn forty-five for goodness sake!"

"You're a fine one to talk. Your husband is damn near sixty and you're only forty-three. Besides, she approached me, thank you very much! Women do still find me desirable, you know."

"I can see that. He is *not* sixty."

"Close enough. What do you mean?"

"He's fifty-six. There've been women eyeing you everywhere we go."

"Really? Where?"

"Please. Do you mean you really didn't notice? The restaurant last night. The dinner tonight. And... AND... the girl you chatted up in the café yesterday."

"Which women at the dinner?"

"Well, Brigitte, obviously!"

"You can't count her. She was always a bit of a trollop."

"How about my friend Emilie, remember her? She was asking me about you. And you know she's divorced now."

"Is she? You might have mentioned that sooner."

"Tony!" She swatted at him.

"What? You're the one who brought it up." He laughed.

61

"I know it's none of my business, but what do you see in her?"

"Who? Emilie?"

"Tracie!"

"It isn't your business. But if you must know, she was cute, artistic, and interested."

"In what?"

"If you have to ask…"

"Oh, God!" she rolled her eyes.

"Anyway, she's a nice girl," he said.

"Yeah, nice in the sack!"

"Ha! Well, there is that," he said.

She swatted him again, but couldn't help laughing. As their chuckling died down, Lily fidgeted with her half-empty cup, still smiling, but without making eye contact. Tony watched her out of the corner of his eye, enjoying her smile.

Noticing that her drink was low, he got up to refill it. She watched him walk around the bed, jacket and tie off, vest open and shirt partially unbuttoned. She reached down and took the ice pack off of her ankle and handed it to him. He took it into the bathroom and then returned for the bottle.

"So…" she paused and took the last swallow from her cup.

"Oh boy. Here we go again," he said.

"Have you had many women?"

"Lil…"

"What?"

"That's the champagne talking," he laughed.

"No. Come on. You're an attractive guy and…" She paused as if she wanted to take those words back, but it was too late. They were out there. She continued, "I just wondered if—I mean—we've established that you don't have too much trouble getting women's attention."

He brought the bottle back to the bed and sat down again, emptying the bottle into their cups.

"Well, I have not been celibate, obviously."

"So..."

"So?"

"How many women have you had?"

"Lily, you don't really want to know the answer to that."

"Come on. I can tell you. Two."

"Two women?" he teased.

"No! Two men!"

"Hmm. Okay, well, it's more than two. All right? Twelve years is a long time."

"A lot more?"

"Lily!" he said sternly.

"Why didn't you ever marry any of them?"

"I don't know. I guess I never found one I wanted to marry."

"So that's it. You're not going to tell me?"

"I'm not one to kiss and tell, darling."

With that, he stood up and crossed the room.

"Do you still find me attractive?" she asked.

He dropped the empty bottle into the trash can with a thud, pausing there without turning around. After a moment he walked back toward the bed and stopped at the end of it, slowly removing his vest and laying it gently over the chair.

"You're a beautiful woman, Lily," he answered hesitantly. "I always thought you were beautiful. Even when we were kids and you were dancing around in your little tutu in your aunt's studio. Before your teeth were fixed, when you still wore glasses."

"Oh good Lord, not the tutu!" she laughed. She slunk down onto the bed, replaying the awkward memory.

* * *

Class had ended, and most of the other students had already left. She was sitting on the bench in Aunt Sarah's studio taking off her toe shoes and putting on her tennis shoes before walking to the train station to head home, as she always did. She looked up and saw a young boy standing in the doorway. He looked to be thirteen or fourteen. Not too much older than she. He seemed to be watching her, though she couldn't think why he would want to. She didn't recognize him, but then she couldn't exactly make him out from that far away without her glasses on. She smiled shyly, and he smiled back. She picked up her glasses and put them on. Then she glanced at him again. He was still staring at her, which seemed very odd to her. She wasn't used to boys paying her much attention at all, especially not cute boys like this one. She felt compelled to say something, if for no other reason than to break the awkward silence.

"Hi," she said quietly.

"Hi," he answered, still smiling.

"Was there something you wanted?"

"What?"

"Can I help you with something?"

"Oh, no. I'm just waiting."

"Waiting for what?"

"I'm Anna's brother."

"Anna? Oh, right, the new girl. Do you have a name—Anna's brother?"

"Tony."

"Well, hello. Tony. I think Sarah's... ah... Miss Wells is just giving her a class schedule or something. She should be back in just a minute."

"No rush. Do you know her well? Miss Wells?"

"She's my aunt."

"Oh. My mother says she's quite talented."

"She's a great teacher."

"She must be if you're one of her students. I mean—I saw you dancing a moment ago. You looked good, so she must be a good teacher."

"Ah... Thanks. I think."

"That's a nice tutu." He chuckled a bit and smiled again.

She flushed, realizing for the first time that she was standing there talking to the cutest boy who'd ever paid her any mind in a somewhat raggedy, old, faded purple tutu that probably made her look like a little girl instead of a mature young lady on the verge of adolescence.

"Umm. Yeah. My mum gave it to me a couple of years ago for my birthday, and I haven't had the heart to get rid of it yet."

Just then Sarah and Anna came back in to the room. Anna gathered her things and walked over to Tony.

"Ready to go?" he asked her.

"Yes. Sorry it took me so long."

"No problem. It was nice to meet you... Miss Wells' niece."

"I ah... Lily."

"Lily? Like the pretty white flower?"

"Yeah."

"It suits you. Maybe I'll see you on Thursday? Lily." He hesitated, then walked away with Anna. Lily just stood there smiling awkwardly.

* * *

"What happened to your glasses?" she heard Tony ask. "Are you wearing contacts now?"

She didn't answer. She was still staring blankly, holding on to the distant memory.

"Lily?"

"Hmm? Oh. LASIK," she said in a strangely wistful manner.

"You're awfully quiet all of a sudden," Tony said. "Where did you go?"

"Oh... I was just... thinking," she said, twisting a lock of hair around her index finger.

"About what?"

"It was a beautiful wedding, wasn't it?"

"Yes it was."

"I always wanted a wedding like that. The big white dress and champagne and dancing and all that."

"You did?"

"Sure."

"Your wedding to Charles, it wasn't what you imagined?"

"No. Not at all. It was very small, very private. Just us in the garden. It all happened so quickly, you know?"

"No. I don't know."

"Well, I didn't really even think it was an option. I didn't think he was the marrying type. One day, after he'd been away on business, he came home with a ring and said he'd thought about it and decided we should make it official. That was it."

"Then what?"

"He called his friend, the judge, and then I put on a nice dress, and we got married."

"Just like that?"

"Yep."

"Not much of a romantic, is he?"

"Oh, I don't know. In his way he is. He said he'd never thought about marrying anyone until then and he didn't want to wait another day. Danny was still in town, but he was leaving once school was over. It was actually perfect timing. There was something sort of sweet about it being just us."

Tony looked over at her, wondering what else she was really thinking beneath her small smile. She sighed and reached over to set her cup down on the bedside table.

"They looked so much in love, didn't they?" she asked. "Not just Adrienne and Vidal, but Christine and Jean-Pierre too."

"I can't believe they've been married for twenty-five years," he said.

"They got married so young. They were just kids, really."

"We all were."

"It was a lifetime ago, wasn't it?" she whispered.

Neither of them spoke again for quite some time. Tony finished his champagne and looked at Lily again, wondering if she'd finished hers. He chuckled, realizing that she'd fallen asleep. He studied her for a moment as she slept. It had been a long time since he'd seen that face so close up. It had a few more lines here and there, but it was still the most beautiful face he'd ever seen. He considered carrying her back to her room, but doubted he could manage it in his current condition. He resolved to give her another five minutes before waking her. He took his phone out of his pocket with the idea of answering a few emails, but the hour and the drink got the better of him too. Before he'd even finished reading the first message he was asleep.

7

SAY IT ISN'T SO

The sound of the shower woke Lily from her slumber. A smile spread across her lips as she stretched. It quickly faded when she tried to sit up. Her head was still spinning from the effects of the champagne. She took a moment to focus. Then, seeing the purple stripe on the wall, she realized she'd spent the night in Tony's room.

"Oh my God!" she said out loud and flopped back down. Before she'd managed to pull herself together her phone began to sing and vibrate in her purse on the table next to her. The sound was muffled, but she recognized the intro to "Dancing Queen". It was Danny. She hoisted herself up to a seated position and rifled through her purse to find the phone.

"Hey sweetie," she said, trying to force perky.

"Hey, Sissy."

"What's up?" she asked, closing her eyes and holding her head. It ached and her eyes hurt. The intense sunlight that flooded the room wasn't helping her condition.

"Isn't it insanely early there?" she said. "What time is it?"

"It's a little after five. I got up to work out and thought I should call and check on you. You sound tired. Were you up?"

"Yes... No. I just woke up. Oh, God. It's eleven already."

"How was the wedding?"

"Ah… it was beautiful. The whole thing was just perfect."

"How's Tony? Are the two of you getting along okay?"

"You might say that, yes. Strangely."

"You didn't do anything stupid last night, did you?"

"No. At least I don't think so. We had a lot of champagne. That's all."

"You sound strange. You didn't sleep with him, did you?"

She laughed uncomfortably. "Why on earth would I do that?"

"I don't know. Weddings have been known to make you hot. And no matter what you say, he is still dead sexy."

"Oh, God! Daniel, don't be an ass!"

"What?" he laughed. "Seriously though: Have you managed to get anything done on that Elvis routine yet?"

"No. Not yet. I've been thinking about…"

Their conversation was interrupted when the bathroom door opened. Tony came out wearing a pair of navy jogging pants that hung nicely on his hips. He was shirtless and still glistening from the steam pouring out of the small bathroom. Lily could only stare. Her mouth unintentionally dropped open at the sight of his chiseled abs.

"Lil. Are you there?" Danny called on the other end of the phone.

"Sweetie, I've gotta let you go. I'll take a look at Elvis on the plane on the way home, okay? I'll see you tomorrow."

"Lil—"

"Bye Danny."

She hit end and put the phone down on the table without ever taking her eyes off Tony.

"Good morning," he said, smiling as he finished drying his hair. He put down the towel and grabbed a t-shirt out of his suitcase. "How are you feeling?"

"I've been better. You're awfully pleasant this morning."

"Well, *you* are a very pleasant sight first thing in the morning."

He continued to grin in her direction.

"What's that look for?"

"Forgive me. I don't mean to stare," he said.

Just then there was a knock at the door.

"That'll be room service. You may want to cover up a bit." He strolled toward the door.

Lily looked down. She was wearing nothing but her black bra and panties. She quickly scanned the room. Her dress and pantyhose were lying in a heap on the floor next to the bed.

"Oh my God!" she muttered, frantically scrambling to pull the covers up around her chin.

Tony opened the door. A young man carried in a tray with coffee and croissants and set them on the tiny table in the corner of the room. Tony tipped and thanked him. The young man rushed out of the room, obviously making a conscious effort not to look in Lily's direction. Tony closed the door behind him.

"What the hell happened last night?" Lily asked, panicked.

"Do you mean you don't remember?"

"I remember you bringing me back here and a bottle of champagne, but did we…?"

"Sleep together? I'm afraid so."

"Sodding hell!"

He laughed. "No. Lil. I meant in the same bed. You didn't think that we…?"

"I thought—So we didn't?"

"No. Of course not." He saw her eying her dress on the floor. "For the record, I woke up fully clothed. And that—" He pointed and wiggled his finger around at the pile of clothing next to the bed. "That had nothing to do with me. You never could sleep if you were constricted. You must have taken it off in the night."

"Are you absolutely sure we didn't?"

"Darling, if we had, I should like to think you would remember it!"

Tony poured a cup of coffee and took a drink.

"Ah! Well, it's no vanilla latte, but it'll do." He looked pleased. "Care for a cup?"

"Please," she said emphatically. "Could you give me a second?"

"Of course." He picked up his towel and walked back into the bathroom. She hurriedly slipped out of bed and into his robe that he'd left on the end of the bed.

"Are you decent now?" he called.

"Yes."

He came back carrying a bottle of aspirin. "I imagine you could use a couple of these."

"Indeed. Thanks. How long do we have?"

"We should leave in about an hour I think, just to be safe."

Lily perched on a chair with her knees folded up in front of her pulling apart a croissant and sipping the strong, steaming, black coffee. Tony was just about packed by the looks of things, and she was thinking she ought to get moving herself. Then she noticed him looking at her.

"What?"

"Nothing. Just the way you're sitting there. I've never seen anyone sit like that at the table. Except you."

"Sorry."

"No need to apologize."

"Charles hates it. He says it's too unladylike. I thought he'd broken me of it. But I guess not." She laughed as she put her feet down and crossed her legs. "It is dead common, isn't it?"

"Does he expect you to be the perfect lady all the time?"

"Well, one never knows who's watching, does one?"

"Hmm. Still, there's nothing wrong with being a tad common. Keeps you from getting too stuffy. I fell in love with a common girl once. She was tons of fun with lots of moxie. And really sexy. Things went quite well for a while."

"Who was she?"

He turned back to his suitcase and resumed packing.

"Oh!" She blushed. She tore off another bit of croissant and popped it into her mouth as his phone rang.

"Hello Anna. How are you? Fine. I'm in Paris for a friend's wedding. No. I'm headed back to New York this afternoon. What? What happened? Oh my God! No. Of course. I'll be home as soon as I can. Call me if there's any change, okay?"

He hung up and sat down hard on the end of the bed with a terrified empty stare. After a moment, he started fumbling with the phone again.

"Tony, what's wrong?" she asked. He didn't answer. "Tony?" she asked again, walking over to him.

"Damn. I can't pay online. I'll have to call. I have to catch the next train through the tunnel. Can you get to the airport on your own?"

"Yes. Of course." She crouched in front of him so that she could get his attention. "But will you please tell me what's happened?"

He stopped what he was doing and looked into her eyes. She could see the fear in his. "It's my dad. They think it's his heart. They've taken him to hospital."

"Oh my God. I'm so sorry," she said, looking up at him. She no longer saw before her the ex-boyfriend she wasn't sure how to handle. She saw a scared little boy who had been her best friend throughout her adolescence and much of her young adult life. That boy had seen her through countless rough spots, and she was moved to help get him through this one. "When does the next train leave?"

"In about an hour."

"Okay. Just give me ten minutes." She stood and went to collect her dress and things from the bedside table.

"Why?"

"So I can pack up."

"The flight doesn't leave for another three hours. You have plenty of time."

"I'm not catching the flight. I'm going with you."

"You don't need to do that."

"I know I don't. But I'm going to just the same."

"Really. I can call you once I know something if you like."

"How long is the train ride?"

"About two and a half hours."

"Two and a half hours alone with your thoughts? You'll go crazy."

He sighed and nodded, knowing damn well she was right.

"Okay, then," she said with a reassuring smile. She gathered up her things and opened the door. "Ten minutes, love," she said, and out she went.

8

HOMEWARD BOUND

The high-speed Eurostar train soared out of Paris toward London. Lily watched Tony as he stared aimlessly out the window. His angst was almost tangible. He shifted in his seat and exhaled loudly through his nose without ever unclenching his jaw. Despite all they'd been through, or perhaps because of it, she wanted desperately to comfort him somehow. Without saying a word, she reached over and took his hand, weaving her fingers between his. He glanced at her for only a moment. Then he turned back to the window, giving her hand a gentle squeeze in silent affirmation that he knew what her heart was saying.

Knowing she was heading back to England for the first time in many years, Lily's thoughts wandered. Memories of her early years came to mind. Images flooded her brain.

She thought about the little maisonette in Landsdowne with the bright blue door that had seemed so warm when her mother was alive. How empty it became once she was gone. Lily's father was often absent, both physically and emotionally. When he was around, one almost wished he weren't. He was rarely sober and was not a friendly drunk. Without a wife or a mother to care for Danny, who was only an infant, he expected Lily to fill the void. She came to know far more responsibility and sacrifice than any ten year old girl should. She loved Danny dearly and never saw caring for him as a burden, but trying to satisfy her father's demands and deal with his volatile behavior took a toll on her. She grew to hate that house and all that came with it. She hated the mauve colored carpet, the hideous flowered wall paper, and the tiny, cramped room next to the kitchen that served as her bedroom. Even now, almost thirty years later the thought of being in that room made her shudder.

She remembered Aunt Sarah, her mother's older sister, with her kind face and loving eyes, who first taught her about the joys of dance in her tiny little studio over the pizza parlor. Sarah did what she could for Lily and Danny, but she certainly wasn't well-off and was never welcomed by their father. Lily wished she'd had more time with her before losing her to cancer.

Once again Lily remembered the day she first met Tony, when he came to Sarah's studio to pick up Anna after her first ballet class. She thought about the first time he'd held her hand so many years ago, and about the countless hours they'd spent talking on the swing in his parents' garden. They'd shared their stories, their plans, and their dreams on that swing. She'd spilled her share of troubles and tears there too. She couldn't count the number of times he and his family had been there to support and comfort her throughout her adolescence and young adult life. She recalled one night in particular: the night that her father brought home the woman who would be his second wife. She'd fought with him, telling him it was too soon after her mother's death. Angry and drunk, as usual, he had thrown her out of the house. Tony's family had taken her in that night.

In so many ways Maggie and Joe were like foster parents. After discovering her natural dance talents, they nurtured them, coached her, and taught her most of what she knew about ballroom dance. Maggie sewed her costumes for several shows and auditions, and bought her the only suit she owned, which she wore to every interview she ever had in those days. When she was accepted to the

Conservatoire National Supérieur de Musique et de Danse de Paris on scholarship, Maggie and Joe were the ones who paid for her living expenses and flights to and from, even when she wanted to come home on holidays.

At the time she didn't understand how they could afford to do everything they did for her. Being Latin dance champions couldn't have made them that much money. It wasn't until several years later that she learned of the family's previously existing fortune left to them by Maggie's parents. They never acted rich or lived extravagantly. They were kind, charitable, down-to-earth people who were wholesome, yet feisty and full of life, and they had friends everywhere. Their connections scored her the audition at Julliard, which eventually led to her joining the New York City Ballet and landed her a few parts on Broadway.

Lily had always regretted that she hadn't been able to keep in touch with them over the years. They had given her so much. They were the closest thing she had to a real family other than Danny. She hoped they knew how much their kindness and generosity meant to her. She'd told them as much in the letters she wrote to them after the breakup, but she'd never heard back from them. She always wondered if that had been their decision or if had been at Tony's request. She resolved to tell both Joe and Maggie how much they'd meant to her on this trip. She might not get another chance.

All of the memories brought tears to her eyes. She fought them, not wanting to cry. With her free hand she carefully fished a package of tissues from her purse, trying not to let Tony see her emotion. The last thing she wanted was for him to feel the need to comfort her. After a few deep breaths and what she hoped were inconspicuous dabs at the corners of her eyes she turned her attention back to him.

"Doing okay, love?"

He turned to look at her, shaking his head. He shrugged. "I've been better. I don't wait well."

"I know you don't."

"I just hate feeling…"

"Helpless? I know." She nodded sympathetically.

"What if he doesn't make it, Lil?" He threw his head back against the seat.

"He's gonna make it, okay?" She squeezed his hand. "Let's just get there and get off the train and we can call Anna back for an update. In the meantime, we should try to stay positive."

"Yes. You're right. I know. Maybe it would help if we talked about something else."

"Sure. Why don't you tell me about Anna? How are she and Gerald doing?"

9
YOURS, MINE, OURS

Their Eurostar tickets included taxi service, so Lily and Tony were able to bypass the lines of people trying to get cabs outside St. Pancras International. The cab driver opened the door and took their bags. As he hopped back into the driver's seat he asked, "Where to then, Guv'nor?"

"Wimbledon," Tony answered, handing him a business card with the address on it.

"Right," the driver said.

Lily was somewhat surprised. They had looked at a charming old house in Wimbledon called Matthew House on one of their trips home while she was dancing with the New York City Ballet. It was badly in need of repair at the time. They had talked about buying it and refurbishing it once she was able to secure a spot in the Royal Ballet. Sadly, that had never happened. She loved the area, but didn't imagine he would have bought a house there while he was still single.

When they pulled up in the circular drive in front of Tony's house, Lily could not believe her eyes.

It had a charming brick exterior with creamy yellow trim on a large lot. It had a wide front door made of solid oak and two dormer windows, one on either side of the second floor stone balcony. A six-car garage stood across the drive with guest quarters up above.

It wasn't just any house in Wimbledon. It was *the* house.

"Oh. My. God," she whispered.

He stepped calmly out of the car and began to walk to her side to open the door. "Oh my God," she whispered again as she climbed out.

"What?"

"This is our… This is your… This is the house we looked at that Christmas."

"Yes." He sighed.

"You bought it?"

He nodded, his lips pressed tightly together.

"Why?"

He didn't have the time or energy to come up with a convincing cover. "Because you fell in love with it. I wanted to remodel it and give it to you as an…" he stopped himself before revealing too much. "As a present," he finished.

"But you kept it."

"Well, by the time we split it was finished. Every bit of it was custom. I wouldn't have made half what I put into it if I'd sold it. It was a business decision, really. At that point. Can we talk about this later? Let's go in, shall we? See if Anna's here yet?"

As they stood on the doorstep he fumbled for his keys. "I don't understand why she wanted to meet us here. It would have been so much faster to meet them at the hospital. They should have a copy of the living will, for God's sake. They're the ones who drew it up in the first place. Damn it!" He dropped his keys. They both bent to pick them up at the same time, and the pain in his eyes brought tears to hers. Her stomach tightened.

He grabbed the keys and stood up again, still looking at the ground. She stood and reached out to touch his cheek. He looked up.

"It's going to be okay," she assured him with a gentle caress. "If he were in immediate danger she would have called again. No news is good news, right?"

"I hope so," he whispered.

"They'll be here soon," she said.

He closed his eyes and took a deep breath. "You're right." He forced a smile and turned back to unlock the door.

As they struggled through the door with their luggage, Lily's eyes were drawn immediately upward to admire the huge, bright, three-story entryway with a gargantuan sweeping white marble staircase.

She was so awestruck by the view that she hadn't even had a chance to notice what they were walking into until the shouts of "Surprise!" rang out and scared her half to death. Entering the foyer from all of the surrounding rooms were Maggie, Joe, Anna, and Gerald and about fifty other friends and family members including his dear old Aunt Edna and her socially inept son Rupert, who was currently picking his teeth and examining his findings. Everyone was dressed in semi-formal party-wear, cocktail glasses already in hand. Tony paused only a moment before rushing to Joe and throwing his arms around him.

"Christ, Dad," he said. "Thank God you're all right. What the hell is this?"

"Happy birthday, son!"

"That's what this was about? I thought you'd had a heart attack!"

"I'm sorry if we frightened you," Joe said.

"Mother, were you in on this?" Tony asked.

"No. It was my idea, Tony," Anna said, coming to her parents' defense.

"God dammit, Anna! What the hell were you thinking?"

"I wasn't thinking. It was stupid, Tony. I'm so sorry." She cringed. "I thought you were planning to come home today, and when I called and you said you'd changed your plans, I panicked. I said the first thing that came to mind and then I couldn't take it back. Mum wanted me to call you back, but—"

"Why didn't you?"

"I was afraid you'd be furious."

"You were right!" he shouted.

"I'm so sorry! I only wanted to surprise you."

"Well, you certainly did that. My God! I could—"

"It looks like you surprised us too." Gerald interrupted, nodding in Lily's direction.

"Ah...Yes," Tony said, pulling himself together enough to realize that it wasn't the best time or place to have it out with his sister. "Anna, we *will* continue this conversation later."

"Of course," Anna agreed. "Hello Lily," she said, walking toward a dumbfounded Lily and hugging her.

"Oh. Anna. Hi," Lily stammered. Her heart was pounding as one hundred eyes were suddenly focused on her. "Hi," she said again.

Lily watched over Anna's shoulder. Gerald nudged Tony and grinned. Tony tilted his head and smiled with raised brows in a "just-go-with-it" sort of way. Joe cleared his throat. He put his arm around Maggie and rubbed her shoulder. If he was trying to calm her, it didn't appear to do much good. Maggie only glared at Lily. Her lips were pressed together in a tight, thin line. She looked as though she might break free of her husband's hold at any moment and come straight at her.

"I take it this means you two have sorted some things out?" Anna asked.

Lily was still at a loss for words.

"Well, we managed to sit through a wedding together," Tony said, coming to her rescue. "Otherwise I'd say it's a work in progress. Anna, would you mind taking Lily up to one of the guest rooms so she can get settled?"

"Absolutely," Anna nodded. "Shall I take you take your bag up too?"

"Please," he said.

Lily smiled politely, but Tony could tell she was uneasy. He allowed Anna to get a head start. Then he took Lily by the arm and guided her through the crowd in the foyer.

"Don't worry, darling," he whispered, "I promise I won't tell a soul that we slept together last night!"

"Stop saying it like that!" She elbowed him. "Good Lord, what if someone were to hear you? What if Charles were to find out?"

"Well, he'd be pretty brassed off then, wouldn't he? But I'd tell him the truth."

"Which is?"

"That it didn't mean anything anyway because we were both completely pissed!" He gave her his most charming smile.

Lily couldn't help laughing at him. "You are incorrigible!" she said.

"Yes, but I thought you loved that about me."

"Was that what I loved about you?" she asked with an interesting twinkle in her eye.

He stared after her for a moment and then turned back to his party guests.

Anna was waiting for Lily by the small lift in the kitchen. She escorted her to one of the guest bedrooms on the second floor. Lily set her bag down on the bench at the foot of the bed and Anna went to open the heavy, lined drapes. The room was exquisitely decorated in various shades of blue with rich fabrics and classic furniture. It had its own sitting area, en-suite bathroom, and dressing room.

"This is a beautiful room. Very elegant."

Anna eyed Lily's clothes. "I imagine you'll want to change, since we have sprung a party on you. Not everyone travels dressed for business like Tony does," she laughed. "I'll leave you to freshen up a bit."

"Thanks, Anna."

"You're welcome. It really is nice to see you again."

"Somehow I don't think your mum would agree. If looks could kill."

Anna paused at the door. "Don't worry about her. She's not too thrilled with me at the moment either. Mothers are just a bit protective of the baby boys sometimes, aren't they? Speaking of which, do come back down when you're finished. I'd like for you to meet my boys."

Lily nodded and Anna left, closing the door behind her.

Twenty minutes later Lily appeared at the top of the stairs. Tony, who was talking with some friends near the entrance to the kitchen, noticed her immediately. He stopped speaking and stared as she glided elegantly down the staircase. His eyes started at her Casadei lace pumps and drifted up her long legs clad in black silk stockings. She wore a knee-length, form-fitting, little black number with an asymmetric neckline that puffed ever so slightly on the left shoulder. A diagonal panel wrapped around the hip to accentuate all of the right curves. Her hair cascaded onto her shoulders in soft curls and, when she smiled, her teeth looked as white as fine porcelain against her boldly painted lips.

He politely excused himself from the conversation and made his way over to take her hand as she reached the bottom. She accepted his hand and let him lead her a few steps to an out of the way nook near the stairs.

"Is everything okay?" she asked.

"It is now." His eyes fell to examine her more closely. "Wow. That is *some* dress."

"What? This old thing?" she said with a rather playful smile. "I meant, with you and Anna?"

"It will be. I still can't believe she would do such a thing, but I know she didn't mean to be hurtful."

"And she always did have an overactive imagination with an affection for the macabre."

"Yes. She did," Tony said. "Remember the time we went to Provence for the weekend and didn't tell anyone? By the time we came back she was crying her eyes out, convinced that we'd been in an accident and were lying dismembered in a ditch somewhere."

"Yes. Either that or laid up in hospital with amnesia," Lily said.

As they stood there, both of them laughing at the thought, a tall, thin girl with long blonde hair tied up in a ponytail approached. She had huge blue eyes with long lashes, and her smile was perfect. She was wearing a black skirt and a white polo shirt, a sort of casual uniform. She was a very beautiful girl, Lily thought, even in such simple clothes. Then again, she thought nearly all twenty-something girls looked beautiful.

"Can I get you drink, sir?" the girl asked.

"Oh, Miranda. Ah, yes. Thank you."

"The usual?"

"Yes. Please." He turned back to Lily, but noticed a moment later that Miranda was still standing there.

"Oh," he said, "Pardon me. Miranda Lucas, this is Lillian George. Lily is an old friend. We were in Paris for a friend's wedding when my sister called. Lily, Miranda is my... my housekeeper? No. That's not really it," he fumbled. "Well, anyway, she cleans for me once every couple of weeks and helps out whenever there's a party or something."

Lily found it curious that he was making such as effort to explain her presence to the young lady and vice versa. It was hard not to notice the way Miranda looked at him with those big eyes.

"It's a pleasure to meet you," Miranda said, stretching out her hand.

"Likewise," Lily said.

"Are you from round here?"

"Originally, yes. But I live in California now. Tony and I ran into each other in New York because I'm working on a show there."

"A show! Are you an actress?" Miranda asked excitedly.

"No, not really. I've done a few things on camera, but I'm actually a choreographer."

"Brilliant. Can I bring you something to drink as well?"

"I'd love a Manhattan if you can come up with one."

"Very good, madam."

Miranda scurried off, and Tony turned back to Lily. "No, by the way," he said, taking her arm and escorting her through the parlor and out a set of French doors onto a stone balcony that over looked the garden.

"No, what?"

"The answer to your question. About Miranda."

"I don't know what you're talking about. I didn't say a word."

"You didn't have to. You were thinking it."

"How do you know what I was thinking? All I was thinking was that she is a very pretty girl. A very pretty, very young girl."

"And you were wondering if she and I..."

"I was not."

"You were too. You can't fool me. You have a very expressive face when your guard is down. You'd better watch out, you know? All those questions last night and now this. If I didn't know better I'd think you were jealous!" He laughed.

"Oh!" She swatted at him and chuckled through pursed lips.

A moment later Miranda appeared behind them with their drinks and another girl in tow. The two girls were staring at Lily and chattering away. Lily was too busy admiring the garden, and Tony was too busy admiring Lily to notice until they heard one of them giggle. Lily turned around.

"It *is* her!" the second girl said. She smiled and squeaked, unable to contain her excitement.

"I knew I recognized you!" Miranda said. She held out her tray for each of them to take their drinks. "You're Lily Josephson! The one from *Last Dance*! You played Gracie Goodwin, didn't you?"

"I did," Lily admitted.

"We've watched it dozens of times! Oh, would you mind giving me—us—an autograph?"

"Not at all." Lily said politely. She looked at Tony. He picked up her cue.

"Be right back," he said.

"I just loved you in *Last Woman Standing*!" the second girl said.

"I haven't seen that one," Miranda pointed out.

"You should. It was quite good," said the other one.

"Thank you. And a tad more recent," Lily said.

By that time, Tony was returning with a pen and a couple of small cards. "My personal favorite was *Pieces Of Me*," he added.

"Thank you," Lily said, taking the cards. "What's your name, dear?"

"Sophie," the girl said, bouncing up and down a bit. "I'm her sister." She pointed to Miranda.

"Lovely to meet you, Sophie," Lily said.

Lily signed a card for each of them and handed them to the girls.

"Oh my gosh, thank you so much, Ms. Josephson. It's a pleasure to meet you, really. Come along, Sophie," Miranda said, still out of breath from the excitement. "We'd best get back to work." The two of them squealed and scampered off again.

"Do you still get that often?"

"Not too often. Charles usually attracts more attention than I do."

"I can't understand why."

"Thank you," she smiled. "Did you really like it? *Pieces Of Me?*"

"Absolutely. Maybe you can sign my copy later."

Lily looked out over the garden once more. It was lined with trees along the back and sculpted shrubs along the sides. Stone steps led off of the patio to a lighted stone path that cut through the grass. A swing sat in the far corner with pansies and wallflowers blooming all around it. "It's really warm for this time of year, isn't it?" she noted. "And the view is gorgeous."

"I'd have to agree with you there," Tony said, referring to an altogether different view. "Listen, Lily, I…"

"Uncle Tony," said a rather tall young man. He was peeking out at them from underneath his shaggy brown hair.

"Oh good Lord!" Tony grumbled under his breath at yet another interruption. "Hello champ! What can I do for you?"

"Mum wanted me to ask you if you could put on a movie downstairs."

"Of course. Where's your brother?"

"Right here!" called a voice from around the corner. A smaller boy with a sandy-blonde buzz cut appeared.

"Lily, these are Anna's boys: Edward and Harry. Boys, Lily is old friend of your mum's and mine."

"Hello," Lily said. The boys both smiled and little Harry, well trained, reached out a hand for her to shake.

"It's a pleasure to meet you," he said.

"Would you excuse us please?" Tony said.

"Of course."

Tony took off with the boys, and Lily leaned on the balcony rail, staring after them.

"Lily?" Anna's husband said as he came strolling out.

"Oh, hello, Gerald."

"Are you all right? You look as though you've just seen a ghost or something."

"Ah, yes. Fine. I can't believe how fast time flies though. I just met your boys. Edward must have been about two last time I saw him. He's practically a man."

"Yes. They grow up too quickly, don't they?"

"And Harry? How old is he?"

"Twelve. Last month."

"He's a very polite young man."

"I'll be sure to let his mother know." Gerald smiled. "Did Tony take them down to the media room, then?"

"Yes."

"I think I'll go and see if he needs a hand with them." He turned to leave and then stopped. "Good to see you again, Lily. You look lovely, as always."

"Thank you, Gerald. It's nice to see you too."

Lily waited a few more minutes. When Tony still hadn't returned, she decided to abandon the balcony and go looking for a refill on her Manhattan. She weaved her way through the guests still milling about in the atrium and found her way to the kitchen. She stopped in the doorway when she heard Tony with his mother and father. They were speaking in hushed voices, but it was obviously a rather heated discussion. As she'd suspected, while Anna and Gerald were pleased to see her, Maggie did not view her as a welcome guest.

"Joseph!" she said. She always used his full name when she was angry or disagreeing with him. "He's my son. I don't want to see him get hurt again. Do you?"

"Margaret, for goodness sake, they're both adults. If they've made their peace with it, whatever it is, I don't think it's any of our concern."

"I disagree. For one thing, I don't think he has a clear head when it comes to that woman and—"

"Mother!" Tony interrupted.

"Well, you don't, dear! You're obviously still smitten with her."

"Mother, I am not. And even if I were, it wouldn't matter. She's in a relationship."

"She was in a relationship with you too, wasn't she? And looked how that turned out. That woman!"

"Mother!" Tony shouted. "She's married! My God! And would you kindly stop referring to her as *that woman*?"

"Don't raise your voice to me, Anthony Francis! Why is she here anyway?"

"Because—"

Lily decided to intervene before things got any uglier than they already were. She took a breath and threw her shoulders back. Clearing her throat to announce her presence, she strode into the room.

"Hi. Sorry to interrupt." She walked up and put her hand on Tony's arm. "I just wanted to come in and say goodbye."

"Goodbye?" Tony said.

"Yes. It's a lovely party, but I really should be going. After all, your father is fine, so the reason that I came no longer exists."

"Where are you going to go? You're flight isn't until Tuesday."

"I can get a hotel. I can call Dilys. I haven't see her in ages. I'll be fine."

"You don't have to go."

Lily nodded. "Yes, love. I think I do. I don't want to cause you any more inconvenience than I already have." She turned to leave, then stopped and turned back to face Maggie and Joe. "But there is something I'd like to say before I go."

"And what is that?" Maggie asked.

"Joe, when I thought you were ill, I wanted to come so that I could see you one last time. To thank you. Both of you." She looked at Maggie. "I'm very well aware that I would not be who I am today if it hadn't been for everything that the two of you did for me. Everything you gave me. Without you, I might never have made it out of

Dalston. I'd probably have ended up working as a barmaid in one of the local pubs. Or worse. Just another nobody stuck in a dead-end job who used to dance when she was a little girl. But you changed all of that. You changed my life. You saw something in me. You all did." She paused a moment and looked at Tony and then back at his parents. "You gave me opportunities that I'd never have had otherwise. You were..." She fought the lump in her throat, trying to remain in control. "You were very important to me. I loved you very much. Whether or not I ever really told you that, I don't remember. You are both wonderful people. You have two beautiful children and two lovely grandchildren. You have a wonderful family. I'm actually sorry—very sorry—that I was never able to be a part of it."

She finished and looked at them. A single tear ran down her left cheek. She quickly wiped it away. When neither of them said anything, she continued.

"So, there it is. Thank you. And I'm sorry. And, ah... Goodbye. And Joe, I'm very glad that you're okay." She turned to Tony and smiled sweetly. "Tony, thank you for a lovely weekend. I'll see you back in the States in a few days, okay?"

"Yeah. I....Lil..."

She kissed him on the cheek and whispered, "It's okay."

"Can I walk you out? Call you a cab? Something?"

"No. Thank you. I'll be fine. I'll just go up and get my things."

* * *

Lily finished zipping up her cosmetic bag and was stuffing it into her suitcase when Maggie knocked on the open bedroom door.

"Oh," Lily said when she saw her. "If you've come to see me off, I'll just be another minute." She hoisted the bag off of the bench and pulled out the handle.

"Lily, before you go, I'd like to say something."

Lily turned to face her again. She could see Tony lingering just outside the door.

Maggie walked toward her, wringing her hands. She took a deep breath and started over again. "Lily, despite what you say, you were much more a part of this family than you ever realized. I think that's what made it all so difficult. It isn't easy for me to say this. But, I think Joseph may be right. If, after all that's happened, the two of you have found a way to be friends again, far be it for me to stand in the way of that. If Tony wants you to stay—if you want to stay—then you should stay."

Lily looked in Tony's direction, biting her lower lip.

He stepped into the room. "I'd really like for you to stay," he said.

She thought for a minute, looking again from him to his mother. Maggie's glare had finally melted into a very slight smile.

"Well," Lily said, "I guess it would be awfully rude of me to run out before you've blown out your candles, wouldn't it?"

10
MIDLIFE CRISIS

By the time the party wrapped up it was after ten o'clock. Lily returned to her room, anxious to find her pajamas and climb into bed. She rifled through the layers of clothing in her bag, unsuccessful in her quest.

She stood with her hands on her hips and looked around the room. "Damn!" She checked the dresser drawers. Nothing. She moved on to the closet and was pleased to find an assortment of suits and dress shirts hanging at one end. She grabbed a shirt and went into the bathroom to peel off her dress.

An hour later, Lily was still awake. She should have been tired after such a weekend, but somehow she wasn't. She dialed Charles. Her call went straight to voicemail.

"Hi, darling," she started in. "I thought I might catch you. I guess you're busy. I don't know if you heard from Danny, but we had a slight change in plans. Tony and I are in London. Wimbledon, actually. Anyway… I guess I told you that in my last message. I hope you're doing all right. Tomorrow is a big day for you. I'll be thinking of you. Good luck. Call me if you can. I love you."

She hung up and tossed the phone down on the bed with a sigh. She doubted he would call back. He was terrible about retrieving messages unless they came from business associates.

She climbed out of bed and left her room. Out in the hallway she noticed that the door to Tony's room was open, and the light was on. She stepped in. It was another spacious room, done in rich shades of brown and taupe with splashes of red for accent and a beautiful bolted fabric headboard. There was a huge custom-built dressing area and an impressive master bath, but no Tony. She crept down the stairs and saw a light coming from the small desk lamp in Tony's study. He was seated behind the oversized mahogany desk at center of the room in a red leather executive desk chair, turned away from the doorway with a drink in one hand and his phone in the other. She slipped in quietly and admired the room, thinking he hadn't noticed her. There were built-in floor-to-ceiling bookcases all the way around the room except for just to the left of the door. In that area, there was a mini fridge, a wet bar and an impressive array of alcoholic beverages. There were two gentleman's chairs and small table forming a conversation area near the bar. Two more small leather chairs faced the desk. It was another gorgeous room with a very regal feel.

"Hey, Lil," he said, as if sensing her there. He swiveled around to face her and put his phone down on the desk.

"Hi," she said, running her hand along the woodwork on one of the bookcases. "This house is really fabulous."

"Thank you." He stood and walked around to lean on the front of the desk, drink still in hand. "That's a pretty fabulous outfit as well." He laughed.

She smiled. "Yeah. Sorry. I hope you don't mind. I think I left my damn pajamas in the hotel."

He shook his head and took a drink, watching as she sat in one of the one of the gentleman's chairs and crossed her legs.

"Who did your decorating?" she asked, glancing around the room.

"I did, at least for the most part. Mum may have had a few suggestions here and there as you can imagine."

"She always did have great taste."

"And strong opinions," he chuckled.

"Hmm. Speaking of which, what exactly is it that she thinks I did to you?"

"Lil, I know this is going to sound odd coming from me, but I really don't want to talk about that right now. Can we please save it for another day?" He took another drink.

She nodded. "So, what are you still doing up?"

"Couldn't sleep. Too much on my mind."

"Must be big if you're still on the scotch at this hour."

"Hmm. Care to join me?"

"Why not?"

"Really?"

"I can't let you drink alone, now can I?"

"Well you could," he said, making his way to the bar. "But it's much more fun this way. The usual?"

"Please."

He mixed her Manhattan and handed it to her.

"Thank you."

He ambled back over to his desk and leaned on it again, pondering something for a while. Then he took a drink and started in. "I don't know," he sighed. "I honestly don't know. This whole weekend, what with Paris and thinking my dad was dying… My family. It's just got me thinking."

"About what?"

"Things. You know? Where I am. Where I'm going."

"And where is that?"

"Maybe nowhere. I don't know. Christ! I'm forty-five Lil."

"Oh! This is that kind of problem. I see. Come on. I'm gonna need reinforcements. By which I mean cake."

She took him by the hand and dragged him across the foyer into the huge modern kitchen with its white granite counter tops and chef's grade appliances. Everything was neat and clean as if there had never been a party.

"You don't mind, do you?"

"Be my guest." He sat on the stool on the opposite side of the island and watched her as she bent to pull the leftover cake from the refrigerator. He couldn't help but stare. There she was in his dress shirt with nothing but some skimpy, black, spandex panties underneath. He eyed her legs once more. He couldn't get over them. They were still beautiful, shapely, and they went on to Jamaica.

"What exactly are you wearing under there?" he finally asked.

"Dance pants," she said matter-of-factly.

"Dance pants?"

"Yes."

"Let me see if I've got this straight. You couldn't keep track of your nightgown, but you still have your spankies. Is that right?"

"What's your point?"

"No point. I just find your priorities interesting." He gave her a crooked smile.

"Hush up!" she said, trying not to sound amused.

"Oh, come now. Don't get your dance pants in a twist!"

"Tony Ward!" She picked up a dishtowel and threw it at him. He put his arm up to block it and caught it. Her excitement only made him laugh harder.

"Do you sleep in those things, or what?"

"No, I most certainly do not," she said. "I just didn't want to go wandering about the house with everything on display."

"So much for that!"

"Hey!"

"That's not a complaint, mind you. Just a casual observation."

"Good God! How many drinks did you 'ave before I came down?" she teased.

She brought her cake and sat down next to him on the other stool. Her bare leg touched his. He tried to pretend he didn't notice. He watched her as she took the first bite and then inverted the fork, pulling it out of her mouth again between closed lips, licking it clean. Somehow it seemed just a touch provocative, but maybe it was just the scotch.

She heard the grandfather clock at the far end of the foyer strike twelve. "Okay," she said. "It's after midnight. Now you're forty-five."

"Oh, God!"

"Carry on."

"Yes. Okay. I'm forty-five."

"So?"

"What do I have to show for it?"

"Oh, go on! What the hell do you mean? You're a rich, successful businessman."

"Not that rich."

"What?"

"I'm not as rich as your husband."

"No, but who is? Except maybe Spielberg. And just think about what he's had to do to get where he is. Charles, I mean. Not that I don't understand his motivation. But that's another story."

"What is his story?"

"Charles?"

"Yes."

"He was an Iowa farm boy whose parents thought he would grow up to be an Iowa farmer. They didn't understand his dream. They didn't support it. So he set out to prove to them and to the world that he could be a rich, successful film maker. He crawled his way to the top and stepped on whoever he had to in order to get there. He can be sweet and funny once you can get past his 'can't touch this' exterior. But you..."

She jammed another fork full of cake into her mouth. He just sat there shaking his head at her.

"Is this what a mid-life crisis feels like? Should I just go and buy a motorcycle or get a tattoo or something?"

"Please. Listen to me. You have a successful business, you're well invested. You have a fabulous home."

"Which I don't need," he interjected.

"You're independent, strong, smart, witty, but you have a very sensitive, romantic side that—need I really go on?"

"If you want to. I quite like your version of me so far."

"What is it you want that you don't have?"

"Do you suppose it's too late to be thinking about marriage and family?"

"No. Of course not. It's not as if you're past it, for Heaven's sake. And men can have children whenever they want. I'm sure you wouldn't have any problem. Especially considering your propensity for younger women!" She took another bite.

"You shut your cake hole!" he said jokingly.

She covered her mouth as she laughed for fear she had cake in her teeth.

He went on. "I'm not? Past it, I mean?"

"Hardly! You're as fit as ever."

"Fit? Is that in British English or American?"

"Well you're just fishing now, aren't you?"

He shrugged.

"You know, maybe you've been searching too hard," she went on. "All these women in your life. Trying to make it work. Maybe you just need to stop looking."

"Hard to find it if you're not looking, isn't it?"

"Not necessarily. It's like when you're looking for your keys and it's making you crazy. Then you stop looking and give up, and there they are right on the counter. Sometimes once you stop searching, you find that the thing you were searching for was right in front of you the whole time."

"Hmm. Maybe you're right." He took another drink. "Can I ask you something?"

"Sure."

"Are you happy?"

"With what?"

"With your life? Your career? Everything? Are you happy with it?"

She thought for a few seconds then said simply, "Yeah. Sure."

"Yeah, sure?"

"What? Things don't always turn out the way we expect, do they? But overall, I'd say I'm pretty damn lucky."

"Do you like choreography?"

"Sure," she said again.

"Do you like it as much as performing?"

"It's different, but it's enjoyable, yes."

"Enjoyable?"

"Enjoyable," she said firmly.

"If you could choose, would you stick with choreography or would you rather be performing?"

She tilted her head and looked at him as if to say, "This is pointless."

"Humor me. If you could do anything you wanted— if there were no 'issues', as your husband says— which would you rather do?"

She was quiet for a minute. She looked down and scraped at some leftover frosting on her empty plate. She did the inverted fork move once more and looked at him. She licked her lips.

"If I could do anything I wanted?"

"Anything."

"I'd rather be dancing."

"I knew it!"

"It doesn't really matter though, does it?"

"Why not?"

"Cause I can't do it."

"You don't think you can."

"Tony…"

"I think you can."

"And what makes you so sure?"

"Because I know you. You're strong. Dedicated. You can do anything you put your mind to."

"Well, unfortunately my mind and my body do not always see eye to eye anymore."

"If you say so." He took another drink. "What about your husband?"

"What about him?"

"Do you ever dance with him?"

"Ha! No. Charles doesn't dance."

"That's too bad. It almost makes me feel sorry for him."

"Why?"

"Because watching you dance—dancing with you—it's magical."

"Thank you. That's very sweet." She fiddled with her empty glass.

"Can I get you another?" he asked.

"No. Thank you. I don't think my liver would appreciate it. It's been a rough weekend already. We should probably try to get some sleep, don't you think? I've heard that old people get up really early." She stood up and stretched.

"Is that a joke?" He smiled and grabbed her wrist as she turned to walk away and pulled her back.

"Yes. Of course it is," she answered, laughing. Without thinking, she stepped between his legs as he sat on the stool and threw her arms around him.

His arms naturally wrapped around her waist.

"Good night, love," she said. "Happy Birthday."

"Thank you. For everything," he whispered so close that he could smell the familiar scent of sweet almond oil and aloe from her shampoo. They lingered there for a minute. Then she pulled away and stepped back. She eyed him, half smiling and half biting at her lower lip.

He was wondering if he ought to say something, but she spoke first.

"Do you have plans for tomorrow?"

"Anna's bringing the boys round in the morning."

"What about school? Hasn't autumn term already started?"

"Yes. But as luck would have it, there's an issue with the heating system at their building."

"Goodness, I bet they're really chuffed, aren't they? Well, what about plans for the evening?"

"None that I know of."

"Then you'll have to let me know what you'd like to do. If you'd like to go out, then I'd like to take you out."

"You want to take me out?"

"Well, I can't very well leave you sitting around here wallowing in self-pity. Of course if you'd rather stay in, I can cook for you."

"Since when?"

"Oh, Tony! I've learned a lot of things in the last twelve years. You'd be surprised."

"Oooh! I bet I would."

"Mmm hmm. So, you think about it and let me know."

"I was planning to go for a run in the morning if you'd care to join me."

"Ha! I don't run, Tony. And you know this!" She flashed him a coy smile and sashayed out of the room.

"Oh yeah!" he called in a way that was more like "look at that body" than a statement of agreement. He turned back and threw down the last swallow of his scotch.

11
HOME

Lily woke the next morning to sunlight flooding her room. She rubbed her eyes and looked around. On the bedside table was a note. She yawned as she opened it.

Dear Lady Churchill,

Thank you for the company and the chat. I do hate to drink alone. I hope you slept well. Breakfast will be waiting.

He had signed with a "T" and doodled a small picture of a fancy dress hat like the one that Eliza wore to the races at Ascot in the upper right hand corner. Typical Tony. There was some sort of doodle or drawing on every letter he'd ever sent her.

When they were kids he would send notes for Lily with Anna when she went to ballet class. The notes always had a flower or a dog or cat, something cute drawn on them. While she was away in France at the Conservatoire they wrote to each other faithfully. In those days they still wrote everything by hand. Lily's letters were usually short and sweet, jotted down between classes and mailed as she rushed to the next dance rehearsal. Tony's were longer and more formal, almost poetic, and he included beautiful sketches of gardens and fountains or city scenes. Later, when he started studying architecture he would include elaborate sketches of buildings he would build some day.

When she was seventeen and he was nineteen, he joined her in Paris to study at L'École d'Architecture de Paris on a one-year exchange program. Their relationship had not started out as a romantic one, but after that year in Paris together, there was no way to avoid it. Surrounded by the magic of that city, they could no longer deny that there was more than just friendship between them. Though, truth be told, Lily knew Tony was ready to admit it a lot sooner than she was.

"Ah, Paris," she said to herself. She lay in bed, daydreaming about that enchanting place for quite some time, the old memories mixing with a few new ones, until finally she heard rumblings from downstairs. Tony must have come back from his run. She knew she should get out of bed, but it was far too comfortable at the moment. She wondered where on earth he'd bought his bedding. It was more comfortable than anything she'd ever slept in. She stretched and sunk back in for a bit longer. There was a slight nagging in her head telling her that she should probably try to call Danny to check in, or Charles, for that matter, but it was the middle of the night in New York and midnight in LA. She took her phone off of the nightstand and sent Charles a quick text.

- **Are u still up?**

She closed her eyes for another minute while she waited to see if he would answer. When no response came she sent another one.

- **Big day 4 u tomorrow. Good luck! XO**

Then she remembered that Tony's note said something about breakfast and was at once motivated to get up. She peeled herself out of the bed and headed downstairs, phone in hand just in case Charles should happen to call.

* * *

She paused in the doorway to the kitchen. Still in his form-fitting Underarmour shirt and jogging shorts, Tony was hard at work.

"Good morning, love," he called over the snapping and sizzling going on in the pans.

"That's Lady Churchill to you," she called back.

"Ha! I thought you'd like that. It was either that or Sexy Knickers, but the latter seemed a tad over the edge."

"Maybe." she laughed. "How do you do that anyway?" She sat on one of the stools and watched him.

"Do what?" he asked, turning to smile at her.

"Speak to me before you ever turn around to see if I'm there? You did it last night too. Come to think of it, you've always done it."

"I don't know. Must be my sixth sense."

She laughed. "It smells wonderful in here. What are you making?"

"Eggs, potatoes, fried bread, sausage, bacon, beans—the full monty."

"Ha! You're kidding!"

"No, madam, I am not. Welcome home!"

"Brilliant! I'll need a workout after, but I love it."

"I know. So will I. It's a heart attack waiting to happen, but it's so damn delicious! You're welcome to use the gym downstairs, by the way."

He moved gracefully from one pan to another.

"Do you need any help?"

"I think I've got it. Coffee's ready if you want it, or there's juice." He nodded toward a pitcher on the counter. "Help yourself."

"Fresh squeezed?" she asked, pouring herself a glass of juice.

"Just this morning."

"How *did* I ever let you go?"

"That, my dear, is a very good question."

By the time they'd finished their full breakfast it was nearly nine thirty. Anna was supposed to drop Edward and Harry off any minute. Lily hurried upstairs to dress so as not to be caught in Tony's dress shirt when they arrived.

She showered, put on fresh makeup, a bra, and panties, then checked her figure in the mirror. She looked fine for the moment, but if she didn't get a workout in soon, things would start to take a turn for the worse. She was used to getting up by six every day and doing at least an hour of combined cardio, weight training, and yoga. Some days she did more than that, in addition to dancing. Since she'd left L.A., her routine had fallen woefully by the wayside. Any day now she would start to see the pounds appearing on her hips. If only she could tell them where to go, it wouldn't be so bad. An extra pound or two up top might actually be appreciated. She'd always wondered what it would be like to have larger breasts, though she wouldn't have wanted such pendulous ones as Mrs. Moretti, their former housekeeper. She was a robust Italian woman who made delicious meals, but she was lucky not to have set herself on fire the way her bosom hung over the stove when she cooked.

Lily sighed. She supposed the state of her breasts didn't matter much at this point. Charles never seemed to pay them that much attention. She seemed to remember that Tony had, and he never seemed to mind their modest size.

* * *

Lily took her laptop into the sitting room to work on the dreaded Elvis number, but she soon grew tired of the routine and of work in general. She could hear faint indications of Tony and the boys fooling about downstairs, and she was distracted by the sunlight flooding in the French doors. It seemed like such a rarity in England that she longed to get outside and enjoy it. She put down her tea cup, left her laptop on the sofa, and went looking for the others.

She followed the noise through the kitchen and down the stairs to the media room. There stood Edward and Harry with cue sticks in their hands as dear old uncle Tony attempted to teach them how to play a game of Eight-ball. They must have inhibited Tony's sixth sense because Lily was able to sneak up on him. As he leaned over the table taking his aim and explaining how he planned to sink the ball in the corner pocket, she came up behind him, leaned in and whispered, "Aim low or you might scratch."

Startled, he jumped, hit the cue ball before he was ready, and bounced it across the table. Lily started to laugh.

"Aren't you supposed to be working?" he asked.

"I was, but it's such a nice day I thought perhaps you all might like to go for a picnic and some fresh air."

"Not a bad idea, but it's a bit chilly, don't you think?"

"If we take a couple of blankets and our jackets we'll be fine. I could pack up a lunch."

He thought for a moment then put down his cue stick. "Edward, did you bring your football?"

* * *

Half an hour later they were munching sandwiches and crisps on Wimbledon Common. Afterward, Tony told Edward to grab his football, and he and the boys were soon wound up in a two-on-one game. Lily watched them from the blanket. Seeing Tony with them, remembering watching him play as a boy, she couldn't help but smile.

"I hope you weren't too bored over here by yourself," Tony said, returning to sit on the blanket next to her while Edward and Harry continued kicking the ball around.

"Not at all. You looked like you were having so much fun out there I almost thought about joining you."

"You?"

"Well, I'm no expert of course, but I learned a little practicing with Danny when he was a kid, and I'm still fairly quick on my feet most days. But I don't suppose you can take the three of us."

"Lillian Michelle, are you challenging me?"

"So what if I am?"

"Bring it on!" he taunted.

"All right. Let's see what you got, hot stuff!"

With that, Lily hopped up and jogged over to Edward and Harry. Tony played hard, but eventually the pressure of keeping up with all of them got to him. Lily and the boys were able to dribble and pass their way across the common until finally, Edward sent the ball whizzing past Tony. The trio shouted and gave each other high fives.

"Very nice," Tony called out. "You got lucky, but can you do it again?"

"You'll never know," she said, patting him on the shoulder on her way back to the blanket.

"What? Now you're going to quit?"

"Yes. The thought did cross my mind that I should probably check out the shops for a new pair of pajamas. Not that your shirts aren't lovely."

"Why don't we gather up these things, and then we can all take a walk through the village."

"Okay. If you like. I'll get this. You go wrangle those nephews of yours."

* * *

Lily was quiet as she and Tony walked down High Street arm in arm, watching people scurry from one shop to the next or hustle onto the red double-decker buses. Tony pointed something out, and when she didn't respond, he said, "You haven't said a word since we left the common. Is everything all right?"

"Hmm? Oh. Yes. Just taking it all in. It's such an interesting place. I mean, just a few blocks away you have this great open green space for picnics or riding. Now here are all these trendy boutiques, cafés, and galleries right in the middle of some charming old nineteenth century buildings flying the Union Jack. It's absolutely fabulous. I should have liked to live here."

Tony smiled, thinking he should have liked for her to live there too. They walked on a ways without speaking.

Edward and Harry were ahead of them playing games or texting on their phones. Every once in a while Harry would turn back to look at them until finally Tony asked, "Hey sport, whatcha gawking at up there?"

Harry just shook his head, smiling, and went back to his game.

"Hang on a minute," Lily said, slowing to look in the window at a women's fitness store.

Tony looked up at the marquee. "Good Lord. Sweaty Betty. I think that's my cue," he said. "You go on in. Text me when you've finished. We'll meet you at the electronics shop or somewhere slightly less threatening to our masculinity."

"Okay," she said. He turned to walk away. "Oh, wait." She fished her phone out of her handbag. "I don't have your number."

"Sure you do. I took the liberty of adding it to your contacts this morning."

"No. It's not here," she said, thumbing rapidly through the W's.

"Keep looking. You'll find it. You used to be a pretty good detective." He grinned mischievously and sauntered off. The two boys were walking along in front of him shoving at each other and laughing in typical teenage fashion.

Lily shook her head. How very odd, she thought. She tossed the phone back into her bag, figuring she would decipher his clue later.

She visited several shops before she found what she was looking for. She ended up with a pair of Juicy Couture Angel lounge pants and an Angel camisole with a short, cream terry robe to match. Once she'd completed her purchases she sent Tony a message.

- **Finished.**

- Took u long enough.

- **Sorry. Had to crack your code. Spike! :-)**

- Your skills are rusty, Lulu. :-)

- **Where r u?**

- Was dragged 2 Pizza Express 4 round of dough

  balls.

- **Delicious!**

- Edible. 84 High St

- **Copy that!**

Lily walked into the pizza parlor just in time to catch an interesting conversation between Tony and his nephews.

"All right you two," Tony said, "You'd best finish up. Lily will be here any minute, and your mother just texted me. She's done in court much earlier than expected. She'll be here in a bit to pick you up."

"Are you sure she's not your girlfriend?" Harry wanted to know.

"Don't be ridiculous," Tony joked. "Your mother is my sister."

Edward grinned, but kept quiet. Harry giggled.

"Not Mum. Lily," he said.

"Ha! No. Lily is absolutely not my girlfriend."

"Too bad."

"Why is that?"

"Because I think you like her. And I think she's very pretty."

"Well, you're right. I do like her. But she's just a friend."

"That's it?"

"That's it." He paused and leaned in closer. Harry followed suit and leaned in too. "She is pretty though, isn't she?"

"Quite," Harry said.

"For her age," Edward said, looking up from his phone for a very brief moment. At that Lily walked up and took the empty chair next to him.

"Coming from a strapping young man like yourself, I'll take that as a compliment," she said.

Edward blushed. The boys finished up their dough balls and soda while Lily and Tony laughed and shared stories about the detective adventures of Spike and Lulu that they used to make up when they were kids.

After Edward and Harry left with their mother, Lily turned to Tony. "Did you figure out what you'd like to do this evening?" she asked.

He thought for a minute and then declared, "Fish and chips."

"Fish and chips? That's what you want for your birthday dinner?"

"Why not? I'm a simple guy. Besides, fish and chips in the States—face it—it's just not the same."

"You have a point. Okay. Where to, then?"

"The Rose and Crown is just round the corner, but it's early. Let's take a walk through Cannizaro Park. Maybe stop for tea. Then we can end up there later. If you're feeling particularly saucy we could try for the Wimbledon Eight!"

"Ha! I'll pass on the pub crawl, thank you!"

* * *

As they walked through the Rose and Crown pub on their way to their table, Lily slowed. She eyed the colorful gold, burnt red, and olive green walls with dark wainscoting. The hardwood floors were covered with throw rugs. On top of them sat an eclectic mix of sofas and accent chairs clustered around mismatched bar and coffee tables. Light posts with decorative stained glass adornments rose out of the floor and stretched up to ceilings with exposed dark wood beams. A fire crackled in the fireplace at the center of the large room across from the bar.

They chose a small table in the corner. She sat on the red velvet Victorian sofa with her back to the wall so she could see the action in the entire room. He sat across from her in a cameo back, wooden chair. They each ordered fish and chips and a pint. The fish was delivered in the traditional newspaper wrapping, a touch that was usually overlooked with American imitations.

Lily inhaled deeply. She smiled as she took in the scent of the beer batter and the paper wrapping mixed with grease. She took the first bite and washed it down with a swallow from her pint of Young's London Gold.

"Home."

"Hmm?" Tony said, his mouth full.

"I hadn't really thought about it until now, but today, what with breakfast, the village tour, sitting here now, I feel like I'm… home. I haven't been back in so long I'd almost forgotten what that feels like."

"It was a nice day, wasn't it?"

"Very. Edward and Harry are such nice boys. Handsome too. Edward reminds me a lot of you at that age."

"Does he?"

"Absolutely. He's got dark hair like his father, but he has the face of a Ward. And Harry is…" She trailed off and looked down.

"What?"

"He's… very sweet. I'm glad I got to meet them."

"I think they rather liked meeting you too."

"You're really… really great with them. It's a shame you didn't have children. You'd have been a wonderful father," she said, clearing her throat as her voice cracked.

"Blimey, don't go getting all choked up about it. Last night you tried to convince me that it wasn't too late."

"Oh, it's not. Not for you. There are a couple of young blondes at the bar who can't take their eyes off you. They might be willing candidates."

"Where?"

"Really?"

"You brought it up. No harm in checking out the talent, is there?" he teased.

"Too late for me I expect," she went on, unmoved by his attempt at humor.

He wondered why she didn't have any children. She used to talk about wanting them someday, but he could tell by the sound of her voice and the way that she was prodding at her food that it was a sensitive subject and decided to avoid further questions.

"I think you've about dissected it," he said. "Aren't you hungry?"

She smiled weakly. "Sorry."

"It's all right. If you don't want it—"

"Do you want it?" she asked, nudging it in his direction.

"Not if you're going to eat it."

"I don't need it, do I? I've done nothing but eat this weekend. But yes. I am going to eat it. Every bite!" She dug back in, grateful that he hadn't pressed the previous topic. After finishing her fish and chips and the second pint, she moved on to her standby. They laughed and chatted for some time.

Half way through a second Manhattan Lily shouted, "Oh! I almost forgot." She pulled a box out of one of her bags and handed it to him.

"What's this?"

"Your present."

"Present? Goodness. That's a surprise."

"Open it," she said.

"Okay. Okay." He took off the lid and peeled back the tissue paper. He pulled out a pale blue V-neck Sweater.

"Oh, how nice. Is that cashmere?" he asked, holding it up.

"Yes. Do you like the color?"

"I do. I don't know that I would have chosen it on my own, but I like it. It's different."

"Well, you seem to wear so many dark colors. I thought a change would be nice. I mean, not that you need to change. I just—I thought it would bring out your eyes."

Tony chuckled.

"What?"

"It's just funny. If someone would have told me two weeks ago we'd be sitting here like this, I never would have believed them."

"It's nice though, isn't it?"

"Very."

"Happy birthday," she said, raising her glass.

"Thank you." He lifted his too, then looked around and noticed that the crowd in the pub was starting to thin. "It's after eleven," he said, consulting his phone. "Looks like we'd better be getting home. Why don't you finish up that drink and we'll get going. If you'll excuse me a moment…"

He stood up and walked to the restroom. She watched him move calmly and confidently through the room. It was no wonder women found him attractive. He had such finesse. He returned from the restroom and went to the bar. He took care of the bill and came back to the table.

"Are you ready?" he asked as she fumbled in her purse, trying to hide the fact that she'd been staring.

"Sure." She slipped on her coat and attempted to stand up. Either due to the drinks or to the fact that her body was still tired from so much travel and several long, emotional days, she didn't quite make it. She fell back into her seat and laughed heartily. "I guess I didn't need that last one, did I?"

"I wouldn't have needed the first one. I don't know how you can drink that stuff. Blah!" He wrinkled his nose. "Come on, Mrs. George. Let's go home." He took her hands and pulled her up, escorting her out with his arm around her waist.

* * *

Tony walked slowly across the drive and up to the door with the packages on one arm and Lily on the other. Once inside the house, she hung up their coats and Tony started up the stairs. Lily paused a moment at the bottom of the stairs watching him.

"Are you all right?" he asked, turning around halfway up.

"I'm fine. I'm just coming, love," she said, hoping he hadn't noticed that she was enjoying the view again. By the time she reached the top of the stairs, Tony had deposited all of her packages outside of her room and was waiting for her.

"Thank you for a lovely day, " she said.

"Thank *you*."

"You're not on the verge of a mental breakdown now, are you?" she said.

"I don't think so. But if I have any trouble, I know where to find you. I'll see you in the morning."

She hugged him. "Good night," she whispered.

As they stood there in the hallway, Lily couldn't help but think again how alluring he was. She could feel his taut body underneath his thin sweater. There were no love handles on him, not quite the same as what she was used to by now. Charles was a nice looking guy and a sharp dresser, but working out was not his idea of a good time. Feeling Tony's body against hers, his cheek on her cheek, the smell of his cologne, she found it difficult not to respond.

Tony felt her arms tighten around him and her lips brush softly across his cheek. He lingered there for a moment, wondering if he was reading her right. Either way, despite his attraction to her, he wasn't about to do, or let her do, anything that either of them might regret in the morning. He let go of her and reached back to take her hands from around his waist. Still holding on to one hand, he bent over and picked up one of her bags. He held it up for her to take.

"Your pajamas, my lady," he said courteously. She took the bag. He gently kissed the hand that he was holding, and said goodnight.

"You really are something," she said.

He paused a moment, then gave her a gentle smile, turned, and walked down the hall to his room. She picked up her packages and went into her room, closing the door behind her. She leaned on it a moment, took a cleansing breath, and made her way over to the bed.

12
WHERE DID THAT COME FROM?

Lily was wakened by a noise in the middle of the night. Without thinking, she climbed out of bed to see what it was. She opened the door and found Tony standing just outside with his hand raised to knock. They stood in silence, staring into one another's eyes. Without a word, he took her into his arms and kissed her. She melted in his arms like butter on a hot potato. Before she had time to question what was happening, they were falling onto the bed. His strong arms were wrapped around her. His magnificent, sculpted body pressed against her. The old feelings were impossible to deny. She abandoned all reason and let him take her. Making love to him was both wildly exciting and oddly comforting.

Then, as if struck by a wave of sheer panic, she sat up like a shot. She opened her eyes and blinked them rapidly. Her heart was racing. She was short of breath. She scanned her surroundings and was relieved to find that she was still in the guest room, alone.

"Oh thank God!" she said out loud and flopped back down. She rubbed her eyes in an attempt to erase the X-rated images of Tony that lingered in her subconscious.

"It's not like that," she reminded herself. She took a deep breath. "It was just a dream. You dreamt about Michael Marinello once too and you wouldn't be caught dead with him." She shuddered at the thought.

After another hour of lying awake unable to settle her mind, she threw back the covers and climbed out of bed. She put on her new robe and snuck quietly down the stairs for a glass of water. Seated at the kitchen counter, she dialed Charles.

"Hey," he answered.

"Hi. Oh. Hi!" she fumbled. "I didn't know if you'd pick up. How are you?"

"Fine."

"Good. I'm glad I caught you."

"Lillian, I'm a little busy at the moment. Did you need something in particular."

"No. I just wanted to talk to you. I'm in London. We had a slight change in plans."

"So you said in your messages."

"Yes. I guess I did. Anyway, everything turned out okay with Tony's dad. So, I'm flying back tomorrow."

"Good."

"How is the first day going?"

"We had a few good takes earlier. Unfortunately, McCormick is now locked in his dressing room pouting because he doesn't like the damn tie that wardrobe picked out for him."

"What? Ridiculous! What are you going to do about him?"

"I'm going to have wardrobe get him a new tie. What else can I do. I swear—he's a pain in my ass."

"But he *is* brilliant."

"True. But he's still a pain in my ass. Listen, I should get going. I'll see you soon."

"When?"

"End of the week."

"Okay. Charles…"

"What?"

"I love you."

"I… I love you too," he answered hesitantly.

"Bye, darling," she said, as he hung up.

She put the phone down and smiled, pleasantly surprised that he got those words out.

With nothing better to do, she decided to go on a self-guided tour of the rest of the house. There didn't seem to be any end to the wonder of it. She crossed the kitchen and entered the huge media room again. Charles would like it, she thought. It had a full-sized movie screen, dark red velvet sofas all the way around the room, and tons of floor pillows for lounging in the center. It would be great for work or entertaining. She eyed the billiard table where the boys had been playing earlier and chuckled as she recalled Tony's missed shot.

She wandered down a short hallway searching for light switches as she went. She found the fitness room and an indoor pool. Across the hall from that was a full-sized dance studio, complete with mirrors, barres and a floating floor. At the far end of the room was a large portrait of Maggie and Joe in their Latin costumes. They were a stunning couple. It was easy to see where Tony got his looks.

As the show he was watching ended, Tony turned off the television in his bedroom, hoping he would finally be able to fall asleep. The house was not silent as he'd expected. He closed his eyes and listened. A faint hint of Tchaikovsky wafted its way into his room from somewhere down below.

He found Lily in the studio working her way through Swan Lake. Lost in her own world, she didn't notice him come in. It felt strange, like an invasion of her privacy, but he couldn't resist watching her. As he'd suspected, she was still a consummate dancer, as enchanting as ever, capable of captivating a man's heart and moving him to emotion with her movements. Seeing her like that gave him pause, just as it had the first day he met her.

* * *

His mother had sent him to pick up his sister from her first ballet class. He walked into the studio looking for Anna. There was Lily, helping one of the younger girls. Her dark hair was wound into a tight little bun on top of her head. She was tall and delicate-looking with long, thin legs. After class, the other students left the floor, and Anna went off with the teacher. While Tony waited patiently, Lily put on another record and began dancing, unaware that he was watching her. She floated across the floor with such grace and confidence that a part of him fell in love with her in that instant, before she'd even spoken a word. When the song was over, she sat on the bench to change her shoes, and they finally engaged in a short conversation. She was shy and somewhat awkward, but he was intrigued nonetheless. As he and Anna left, he turned back just for a moment, long enough to see her flash him a shy smile. Her face lit up when she smiled. He couldn't quite explain it at that moment, but he was already anxious to see her again, to see if he could make her smile once more.

* * *

The music wound down and she stopped. When she finally opened her eyes and came back to reality, she caught his reflection in the mirror. He was leaning on the door frame, hands in his robe pockets, one ankle kicked over the other with a sort of wistful smile on his face.

"How long have you been standing there?"

"Long enough."

"I'm sorry if I woke you."

"You didn't."

"I hope you don't mind. I couldn't sleep. I thought if I could work out a bit it might calm my nerves. I didn't mean to go snooping but…"

"No. It's okay."

"This is really a spectacular space."

"It should be. It was built for you. I'm glad you finally got a chance to use it."

Lily didn't know how to respond to that. She started for the bench to pick up the robe she'd left there.

"I figured out something else I want to do tonight," he said, pushing off of the doorway and strolling into the room, hands still stowed nonchalantly in his pockets.

"Oh? What?"

"I want to dance with you."

"No. Sorry."

"Come on! What do you mean—no?"

"I mean—no. I don't dance anymore. I told you."

"Yes you do. I just saw you."

"That was different. That wasn't really… I was just… You weren't supposed to see that."

"But I did. And you looked… fabulous. Your extension is incredible."

"Oh. Is it?"

"Come on." He nodded toward the center of the floor.

"No. Really. I don't think so."

"I'm not asking you to perform in public. It's just me. We're here alone. No one's going to see us. Why not give it a shot."

"I just don't trust my body anymore."

"Then trust me. If you fall, I'll catch you."

She bit her lower lip and shifted her eyes. He could tell she was starting to crack.

"Tony…"

"Lily, I'm pretty sure you have to honor my request. It's my birthday!"

"Not anymore."

"Close enough."

"I can't."

"Why not?"

"Because."

"What's the matter? Don't have your dance pants?"

"No. It's not that. I don't have my dance shoes."

"I can fix that." He went over to a small closet and took out two pairs of shoes. "Size eight American, right?" he asked, dangling the ladies' shoes by the straps from his finger as he walked back across the room.

"Yes. You keep extra dance shoes on hand for just such an occasion?"

"These are my sister's, you goof. You're the same size. Now, are you going to put them on or not?"

"Fine!" she said, snatching them out of his hand. She plunked down on one of the benches and began to buckle them.

He sat down next to her to put on his shoes too. Then he turned on the stereo and selected a Sarah McLachlan song.

"'Angel'? Interesting choice of song," she said.

"It's a nice Viennese." He took his robe off and tossed it on the bench. "So, are you going to sit there all night or what?"

"I might. Perhaps if I wait long enough you'll get tired and go back to bed."

"Not a chance!"

She sighed. "I'm not promising anything, you understand." She stood and took her robe off again, too.

"It's just me," he reminded her.

She approached him. He held out his arms in proper frame. She slipped her body into it, took his left hand, and tilted her head into proper smooth dance posture with full body contact. He could feel the nervous energy coursing through her body. He waited a measure or two to capture the rhythm, and they started off around the floor. He felt her tenseness subside as the dance continued. When the song ended, they slowed to a stop, and he dipped her. When he pulled her back up, she threw her arms around his neck and hugged him, only slightly out of breath.

Lily couldn't believe it. She and Tony hadn't danced together in years, but the way their bodies moved together it was as if they were still a perfect fit. It felt like the most natural thing in the world. She couldn't imagine that it would have been that easy with anyone else. With anyone else she wouldn't even have tried.

"I knew you could do it," he whispered.

"I don't know that it really counts as performing, but thank you. It's been a really long time since I've felt what it feels like to do that. I just figured that that part of my life was over. It was lovely. Thank you."

"Lil, you were wonderful. Your form was exquisite. You were smooth, fluid, fantastic. You just did a perfect Viennese waltz with a partner you haven't danced with since… since the Wonderbra was re-launched in the U.S.!"

"Good Lord, how random!" she interrupted, laughing. "Why do you know that?"

"I couldn't sleep. I was watching some damn retro special about the nineties—come to think of it, that's not entirely accurate—since Ginger Spice left the Spice girls is more like it."

The Spice Girls reference only made her laugh harder. "Did it say whether or not I can still get one of those?" she asked.

"What?"

"A Wonderbra."

"Why?"

"Isn't it obvious?"

"Please! Your body is perfect. Who needs large breasts when you've got a bum like Baryshnikov?"

"Why, exactly, are you so familiar with Mikhail's backside?"

"That was purely for alliterative purposes darling. Although, he does seem likely to be a nice one, don't you think?" His words came out rapidly. He was filled with excitement.

"I think you really need to get some sleep. That's what I think."

"No. Lily, will you stop changing the subject? My whole point was that your performance was incredible— especially considering the fact that we haven't even practiced together in over a decade. Don't you see? The only thing keeping you from really dancing again is the fact that you're self-conscious."

"I don't know about that, but it was nice," she said, smiling at him. "You've certainly kept up on your technique as well."

"Well, you know, the ladies do like a man who can dance," he laughed.

"Oh!" She shoved him playfully.

Suddenly she had an idea. "Tony, this is a bit of an odd question, but would you consider helping me with a bit of choreography sometime?"

"Really?"

"Yeah. Well, this show of my brother's—it's a really bizarre collection of music. I can't imagine anyone but Danny putting together Elvis, Marvin Gaye, and Mac Davis in a musical and getting away with it. Anyway, he's been after me about this Elvis number. I really want to spice it up, you know? But I'm having trouble visualizing some of it. Maybe when we get back we can take a look at it?"

"Sure. If you think I can help. What's the song?"

"'A Little Less Conversation'."

"Seriously?"

"I know! Believe me. I know."

As they stood there talking Tony fumbled with the buttons on the stereo remote. Another song came on. It was "Crazy Love" by Michael Bublé.

"One more?" he asked.

"Why not?" she said, with a tilt of her head.

They danced a bolero, like a rumba, but slower. Sexier. He ended the dance with her in a cradle hold, spinning her around. As he slowed to a stop, she gave him the most amazing smile. He bent slightly and put her down carefully, making sure she had her footing. Their eyes met. They froze there for a moment, their gazes locked as in some romantic scene from an old black and white movie.

"That was wonderful," she said in a breathy voice. She couldn't take her eyes off him.

"Beautiful," he whispered in a way that suggested he was no longer talking about the dance. He tucked a stray strand of hair behind her ear. Then he slipped his hand around to cradle the back of her head and, ever so slowly, he leaned in and kissed her. With the other hand still on her back, he pulled her closer. The kiss, though soft at first, deepened. Her hands instinctively moved from their place on his shoulders. She began to wrap her arms around him, running one hand up the back of his neck into his hair. Then, as if waking up from another dream, she abruptly broke free and backed away.

"Oh my God. Tony. What the hell are we doing?" she asked, breathing rapidly.

"I think it's called kissing. Or snogging, if you prefer." He laughed nervously.

"Don't. I'm serious. We can't do this. Fuck!" she cried, putting her hand to her mouth as if she were trying to hide it.

"I know. I'm sorry." He shook his head, confused. "I shouldn't have... I mean... That was never my intention. I guess I just got carried away in the moment. I'm sorry. Forgive me."

She nodded, cautiously moving her hand away from her face. "I guess I got caught up in it all as well."

They stood there for a moment staring at each other as if they knew they should walk away, but neither of them wanted to. Finally, he spoke. "Right. Well, you probably have to finish packing or something, don't you?"

"Yes. I'm sure I do."

"Well, good night then."

"Good night. Sleep well," she said.

She threw her robe on and scurried out of the room without stopping to take off her dance shoes.

"Yeah. Ah… you too," he called, staring after her.

13
GOOD-BYE AGAIN

The following morning there was no breakfast. There was no kitchen chat. Lily was nowhere to be found until it was time to leave for the airport. Tony loaded her things into the car and opened the door for her.

"Thank you," she said quietly. It was the only thing she said. Neither of them spoke during the drive, though each was dying to know what the other was thinking. He pulled up to the passenger drop-off area and got out to get her bags. She had more than she'd come with due to multiple shopping trips. She stood silently on the curb with her hands in her coat pockets, the wind blowing her hair. He put her things down on the sidewalk. He had to say something before letting her walk away.

"Lily," he started.

"Tony," she said at the same time. They both laughed.

"Go ahead," he said.

"About last night..."

"Awkward, right?"

"A little. No. Very, actually," she said.

"I'm really sorry about that. I..."

"No. It wasn't just you. I didn't exactly stop you, did I? But you know, I was thinking. This whole weekend the nostalgia was really intense, and it was all sort of romantic, what with the wedding, and Paris, and dancing at two in the morning in our pajamas. And I'm sure that's probably all it was. Don't you think? Nostalgia?"

"Yes. You're probably right. It's not as if there's actually something between us after all this time. Is there?"

"Of course not," she said with as much sincerity as she could muster. "So let's just put it behind us and move on, okay? Friend."

"Sure. Good. Okay."

"Great. So, I'll see you back in New York in a couple of days, right?"

"Yes. I'm going check on a few business items and catch Edward's football game as long as I'm home and I'll see you back there on Saturday."

"All right. Take care of yourself."

"I will. You too."

"And we can take a look at that routine when you get back?"

"Absolutely."

"Okay. Well, call me if you have a crisis of any kind. You know—if you should get any more sudden urges to buy a sports car or something," she teased.

She hugged him and he kissed her on the cheek. They said goodbye and she picked up her bags and turned to go inside.

"Lily," he called after her, "I'm glad we had this chance—to start over."

"Me too." She smiled sweetly, then walked inside.

He got back into the car and sat for a minute, hesitant to leave, until the other cars started honking and he was forced to drive off.

As she sat on the plane preparing for takeoff, she was surprisingly optimistic about going back to work. She was relieved that Joe was never really ill. She was happy that she and Tony were able to be on friendly terms again. She forced herself to concentrate on those feelings rather than acknowledge the other one: the funny, anxious flutter in the pit of her stomach.

14
BACK TO REALITY

On Wednesday morning, Lily's first stop was her chiropractor's office. After the third plane ride in two weeks it was absolutely necessary. By the time she arrived at the theater, the gang was already hard at work. She slipped off her coat, left it in the front row, and jogged up onto the stage. Nina was already rehearsing with the chorus dancers.

"Lookin' good, girl!" she shouted.

"Thanks, Lil. Welcome back!"

Danny came strolling up. "Hey, Sis!"

"Oh, hi, Sweetie. How are you?" She hugged him.

"Doing well. How was your trip?"

"Good. Emotional, but good." She felt slightly uncomfortable discussing it, seeing as how she couldn't seem to stop thinking about that kiss.

"How's Tony?"

"How should I know?"

"Because you just left him twenty-four hours ago."

"Oh, right. Fine. Good. Tony's great. He'll be back in a couple of days, I think."

"Great, because Tracie's about to begin construction on the Paris set and she wanted to run a few things by him first."

"Sure. I think he flies back on Saturday."

"Lil, is everything okay?"

"Yeah. Why wouldn't it be?"

"I don't know. You seem… distracted."

There wasn't much that she kept from Danny, so it was tough not to blurt out the truth, but telling him about the kiss would only give it more merit than it deserved. She bit her lip as her mind raced to come up with a plausible diversion. "Well, maybe it's because I'm trying to watch my dancers and catch up on what I've missed, while you're still waffling on."

"Sorry," he said sarcastically. "I'll let you get back to work, then. Hey, how's Elvis?"

"I have a few new ideas. I'll run them by Natalie and Hank later on."

"Great! Thanks." He took off to find Tracie and let her know when to expect Tony.

Lily gave Nina her updated notes on several routines and settled in to watch Nina go through the changes with the troupe. By the end of the day, Lily was relatively satisfied with the Marvin Gaye number. Mac Davis was coming along too, but she still hadn't shown any of her Elvis changes to the principals. She wanted to hold off a while longer. She just wasn't satisfied with it in its current state. She resolved to wait for Tony to return before tackling it again.

* * *

Charles flew in on Friday night and took Lily, Danny and Steven out for a late dinner. She told the three of them all about the trip, at least the parts that she intended to share. Steven asked all sorts of questions about the wedding and the dresses and the shops in Europe. Danny was dying to know how Maggie had aged and what the house looked like. Charles nodded occasionally as if he were listening, but didn't hesitate to excuse himself when his phone rang.

Sometime during dessert, he grew tired of pretending, to care and cut her off as she was about to launch into another story.

"Well, I hope you're not too exhausted from gallivanting around Europe to enjoy our anniversary party tomorrow night."

"What?" she asked, more surprised by the suggestion of a party than by the interruption.

"Tomorrow is our anniversary, remember?"

"Of course I remember. But I wasn't expecting—you planned a party?"

"Or at least his secretary did," Danny chimed in.

Charles shot him a look and then turned back to Lily. "All you have to do is get ready for a night out."

"I think I can do that." She smiled. "Thank you." She hugged him.

He smiled at her but gave Danny a death stare behind her back. Danny rolled his eyes.

* * *

The following evening, Lily dressed for her anniversary date with Charles. She wasn't entirely sure what to wear, since he wouldn't tell her where they were going. She'd chosen a Chado Ralph Rucci cocktail dress in emerald satin, which she'd found at Bergdorf Goodman earlier that day. She wasn't sure that it was worth thirty-seven hundred dollars, but it was beautiful with a high round neckline, A-line silhouette, and banded shirttail hem. The clean front resolved into a cutout, folded back which was revealing enough to be sexy, but still covered certain areas that she wished to keep hidden. She figured she could get away with wearing the Manolo Blahnik flower-toed suede pumps that she already had. She covered her shoulders in a black cashmere wrap with faux mink trim and was ready to go.

When they pulled up outside of Sardi's, Lily was not overly impressed. They had been there before. But when Charles escorted her through the restaurant and into the back room, her opinion quickly changed.

He'd rented the private dining space, installed a small temporary dance floor, and assembled most of the cast and crew and a few old friends to celebrate the occasion. She was certain that Danny had been right. Cora was probably mainly responsible, but the fact that he went through with it was exciting.

"Oh!" she said. "This is fabulous. Thank you so much, darling!" She kissed him on the cheek.

Someone came up behind them and took her wrap, and they began to circulate among the crowd, greeting and thanking their guests.

After about half an hour, Lily looked up to see Tony standing in the doorway. She excused herself from Charles, Hank, and Natalie and worked her way toward him.

"Hi!" she said when she reached him. "How are you?"

"Fine. You?" he answered with a smile.

"Very well, thanks," she said. "I'm a bit surprised to see you here, though."

"Well, I had a message from Tracie saying that most of the gang was here. This looks like one hell of a party. What's the occasion?"

"Do you mean you really don't know?"

Tony shook his head.

"It's our tenth anniversary party. Charles threw it as a surprise."

"Jesus. I'm sorry, Lil. I didn't mean to crash the party. This is awkward."

"Well, you didn't know. Tracie probably should have realized."

"God bless her, she is talented, but not necessarily all that bright. Listen, I'm going to take off before she notices that I'm here. I'll just text her later and tell her my flight was late."

"Well, you can stay if you want to. You are technically part of the company, after all."

"That's very hospitable of you, but your husband may not agree. I think I'd best take off."

"Tony!" Tracie shouted from across the room. She was jiggling her way toward them.

"Damn!"

"Don't worry about it," Lily assured him.

Tracie reached them and threw her arms around him. Lily's guess was that Tracie had already had quite a few drinks.

Charles came strolling up about that time. "Hey, Tony. Glad to see that you made it back safely. Lillian said you had a great time in Paris."

"Ah…"

"Better you than me. Having to sit through a wedding with her blubbering the whole time. She didn't embarrass you at the reception, did she? She has been known to hit the champagne pretty hard."

Tony's brow wrinkled. "Certainly not. Lily was her usual charming self," he said.

"Glad to hear it. Can I get you a drink?"

"Well, actually, I can't stay. I—"

"What do you mean you can't stay?" Tracie pouted.

"I'm not sure if I should be here. I mean—"

"Nonsense," Charles said. "The whole gang is here. Stick around. Unless you two are on the outs again or something?" he asked, trying not to sound too hopeful.

"No," Tony said, glancing at Lily.

"Okay, it's settled then. Grab a drink and pull up a chair." Charles snapped his fingers in the air to call over one of the servers. He took Lily's hand and dragged her back into the crowd.

An hour later, Tony found himself in a corner with Danny and Steven, while Tracie went off in search of yet another glass of champagne.

"Wow, she's drinking like she's never seen champagne before, isn't she?" Steven asked.

Danny nudged him. "Quiet!"

"No, he's right," Tony said. "I don't know what her problem is."

"Maybe she's jealous that you went off for a weekend with Lillian," Steven suggested.

"I hardly think so," Tony said.

"Why not? For that matter, maybe Lillian's jealous that Tracie's been hanging on you all night."

"Steven," Danny cautioned.

"What? Haven't you seen the way Lillian's been watching him all night?"

"Here, how much have *you* had to drink, then?" Danny asked.

"I'm just saying, he's had two dames staring at him all night. If Hank's not careful, his girlfriend might be next. Or I might be," Steven joked.

"Ha! Not much danger there, chap!" Tony said. "I wouldn't want to upset your beau here. He's a scrappy fellow. You know, he used to plan guerrilla attacks and leap out at me from behind furniture when he was a kid, right, Danny?"

"Yes. And just because he and Lil are friendly again, I hardly think that means she's interested in him," Danny said.

"Hardly," Tony repeated, clearing his throat and slipping his hands into his pockets.

By that time, the party was in full swing and most of the cast had had enough alcohol to really let loose. Someone got the idea that they should do karaoke and dance to some of the songs from the show. They weren't doing the choreographed moves, just playing around, but it gave Tony an idea. He was convinced that Lily needed to get over her stage fright and he was also convinced that he was going to have to be the one to help her do it. He excused himself from the conversation with Danny and Steven and went off to find Charles.

Charles was standing near the dance floor surrounded by a group of the younger cast members—mostly females. He was showing off pictures of himself with various Hollywood actors and actresses he'd been privileged to work with—or who had been privileged to work with him. Tony put a hand on his shoulder to get his attention, and Charles stepped out of the circle.

"Charles, sorry to bother you. Are you having a good time?"

"I was. What do you need?"

"Do know where Lily is?"

"She's in the ladies room. Why?"

"Okay. Hey, listen, I'd like to ask for your permission to dance with her."

"Maybe you didn't hear, but she doesn't really dance anymore."

"Yes. I have heard. But if I can convince her, do you mind?" he asked, sounding impatient.

"What's the rush?"

"Well, she was talking a lot about this Elvis number for the show, and I'd like to see if I can get her to test it out while everyone is just fooling around and having a good time."

"Ha! Good luck with that. She's not going to get up there."

"Well, it can't hurt to try, can it? As long as it's all right with you?"

"Go ahead and try."

"Thanks!" Tony said.

Charles waved him off with a laugh and returned to his band of admirers.

Tony rushed over to one of the guys who was selecting the music and said something to him. Then he headed Lily off at the pass as she returned from the restroom. Charles glanced up and shook his head at the sight of Tony trying to persuade her.

"Lil, come on. Everyone is just having fun. Now would be the perfect time to mess with that Elvis routine you were telling me about."

"What? Tony—"

"Come on!"

"Tony, that's crazy. We haven't even had a chance to look at it."

"So, we'll make it up as we go along. It'll be fun. Spontaneous. It's perfect. And your husband has already given me his permission."

"What?"

"I asked him if I could dance with you to test it out and he said yes, but he didn't believe you'd do it."

"He was right. I can't!"

"You can. I know you can. You were fabulous the other night. You can do it."

"I don't know. Dancing alone with you was one thing. This is something else."

"Lily, do you trust me?"

"Tony..." She paused, her mouth still open as she searched for a good excuse.

"Do you trust me?" he asked again. He stared into her eyes and she stared back.

The voice in her head was screaming, *"This is a ridiculous idea!"* But something in his eyes said, *"You know I'd never let anything happen to you."*

"I trust you," she answered.

"Good!" He held out his hand and she took it. "Have you got your spankies on, then?"

"Of course. I never leave home without them," she laughed.

"Thank God!"

He turned and headed for the floor, pulling her behind him. He moved quickly so as not to give her time to rethink her decision. Half way there she shouted, "Tony!"

He stopped. "What?"

"Listen, we've got a twelve-measure intro. Well, it's cha-cha, so, six counts of eight, you know?"

"Got it."

"I want you to do a dip and then drop me on the downbeat of the fifth set. Then we can—"

"Hey, Lil..."

"What?"

"Are you going to lead or should I?" he teased.

"Sorry! Force of habit. I just—are you really sure about this?"

"Hey." He took both of her hands and gave her arms a shake as if trying to work out the tension in them. "No worries, all right? We can do this. *You* can do this. Now let's go!" He turned back and pulled her the rest of the way.

Those who were on the floor naturally separated and made room, shocked to see her standing there.

"Is she actually going to perform?" someone whispered. Nina, also surprised, shushed them.

"I'll be damned," Charles said, walking over to where Danny and Steven were standing. "Can you believe this?" he asked.

"No, I really can't," Danny said.

Lily was stuck. She couldn't escape now. "You do realize if this doesn't go well I'll be forced to kill you?" she said to Tony through her teeth while putting on her stage face.

He just smiled and nodded for someone to start the music. Then he leaned in and whispered, "I'll catch you. I promise."

During the intro he tore off his jacket, twirled it over his head, and threw it into the crowd. She threw her head back and laughed. Then she pulled the clip out of her hair, tossed it away, shook her hair so it fell to her shoulders, and gave him a come hither look. He dipped and dropped her as instructed, and she worked her way back up his leg and into frame. He did a cross-body lead and the dance was underway.

They started with some traditional cha-cha: Cuban breaks, chassé steps, underarm turns, and the like. Tony managed to work in a bit of freestyle with some hip rolls and pelvic thrusts for entertainment's sake. Lily followed suit and the crowd reacted. As he started into a chase turn at the refrain, she stopped and playfully tapped him on the shoulder. When he turned to face her, she kicked her leg up onto his shoulder and leaned back so he could drag her across the floor. The crowd let out a collective, "Oooh!" As the music ramped up again he nodded to her and she nodded back. The next time they broke apart she ran toward him and leapt into his arms, wrapping her legs around his waist. She let go and leaned backward. He spun her in a circle, holding her by the waist. Again the crowd cheered. By the last verse of the song he was sliding across the floor on his knees and flipping up the hem of her dress with his hands as she spun in a circle in front of him. Then she stopped in front of him, sexily stretched out her leg, and planted her foot on his shoulder. She pushed him over with her heel, spun one more time, and dropped. When the music ended she was kneeling over him as he lay on the floor. They both turned to face the audience with flirtatious smiles on their faces and the room exploded with applause and whistles. As they stood up, Lily's eyes were filled with tears of joy. She was laughing and crying all at the same time. She threw her arms around Tony and he lifted her off of the ground, beaming.

"I don't know what to say," she whispered.

"You don't have to say anything." He put her down carefully. "The look on your face is enough."

"I do have one thing to say."

"What's that?" he asked.

"Your Cuban motion is really... It's really incredible," she said, still trying to catch her breath. "Your parents must be so proud," she kidded.

"Lillian!" Nina shouted from the crowd.

Lily turned to look at her, then turned back to Tony, hesitant to walk away.

"Go." He smiled. She kissed him on the cheek and ran off into the crowd to receive hugs and accolades.

Nina hugged her and said, "Lady, I am so proud of you. Congratulations! That was awesome! I have just one question."

"What's that?"

"After a breakthrough like this, do you think you will be doing more of your own demos? And if so, does that mean I'm out of a job?"

Still a bit stunned and out of breath, Lily answered. "First of all, that's two questions. Second, you will always have a job with me as long as you want it. But good Lord... don't get too far ahead of me, girl!" She kept moving through the crowd to get to Charles and Danny. She saw Tracie push past them and head for the door.

"Now that's what I call a show-stopper, Lil," Danny said, hugging her.

"Thanks! I think we're going to have to cut out a few measures of instrumental, though. That song's way too long. It damn near gave me a heart attack!"

"Yes, well, I wouldn't worry about it. Natalie's a bit younger than you are."

"You do make a cogent point, darling." She laughed.

"It was a bit risqué."

"For the show?"

"No. For your husband. He turned about the same shade as your dress. As for the show, if you can reproduce that with backup on stage, you'll bring the house down."

"Right on. That was hot!" Steven said, giving her a high five.

Charles came strolling over with a fresh drink in his hand. "That was really something. I can't believe you did it," he said. He put his free arm around her shoulders and gave her a half-hearted squeeze.

"I can't believe it either, actually," Lily said. "I hope it wasn't too strange for you."

"Well, if it ends up on Twitter or YouTube, we might have to deal with some fall-out."

"Right. Sorry," she winced.

"Too late now," he said, sucking on an ice cube.

"How long have you two been practicing that?" Steven wanted to know.

"We haven't."

"Come on. How can you possibly dance like that without practicing?"

"I don't know. He's a strong lead and we've been dancing like that since we were kids, thanks to Maggie and Joe. Would you excuse me? I think I'd like to see what Hank and Natalie have to say about the whole thing."

Lily walked off toward Hank and Natalie, but what she really wanted to do was find Tony. She looked around, but didn't see him anywhere.

"Well, boys, I think that explains a few things," Charles announced.

"What?" Danny asked.

"Well, I was wondering if I should be concerned about anything that might be going on between Lillian and him, but clearly there's no issue."

"Why is that?"

"Oh, come on. She would never talk about why exactly they split, but now it seems pretty obvious, doesn't it? He never married. Doesn't sound like he can keep a steady girlfriend for any real length of time. And a guy who dances like that with that kind of hip motion—come on! He has to be, doesn't he?"

"Has to be what?" Steven inquired.

"Gay!" Charles laughed.

It was all Danny and Steven could do to keep from laughing out loud. They looked at each other and rolled their eyes in disbelief.

"I'd better go check on that guy serving the cake," Charles went on. "He's cuttin' it like he's sellin' it. I'll see you boys later," he said as he walked away.

"Stereotype much?" Danny asked after Charles was gone."

"Sometimes straight guys are so clueless," Steven said.

Lily never did find Tony that night. He must have slipped out somehow. Maybe he went looking for Tracie, not that it was any of her business. The party lasted until almost two in the morning. When most of the guests had gone, Charles stepped out to settle the tab and send for the car. Lily found her wrap and purse. When she opened her purse to find a tissue, she found another note from Tony tucked inside. The doodle: dance shoes and a bottle of champagne.

My dearest Gracie,

Congratulations! I knew you could do it. Don't ever sell yourself short again. You are an amazing woman.

Thanks for a lovely weekend. I haven't enjoyed Paris that much in years.

Yours,
-T

"Lily?"

"Oh, good Lord, Danny. You scared me. Do you always sneak up on people like that?"

"Lily..." he said with a disapproving tone.

"What?"

"What are you doing?"

"I'm just getting my purse."

"No, I mean with Tony. What are you doing?"

"Nothing. What do you mean?"

"Is there something going on between you two?"

"Absolutely not. Why would you say that?"

"First of all, I don't believe for a minute that the length of the song was the only thing that had you out of breath tonight. I had my eye on you as he walked into the room tonight. You practically stopped breathing. Then you went out on that floor and danced the world's sexiest cha-cha, which in and of itself is a minor miracle, and it took him to get you out there. Now you're reading a note from him, rosy-cheeked and glowing like a school girl after her first kiss. I'm just guessing."

"Hush. What were you doing anyway, reading over my shoulder, you weasel? There is history, okay? We do have a connection. It doesn't have to mean that there is anything going on between us."

"What exactly happened last weekend?"

"We agreed to start fresh. As friends."

"And?"

"And what?"

"Are you still attracted to him?"

She delayed answering, folding up the note and putting it in her purse.

"Lil?"

"He's an attractive guy."

"Who could have any woman he wants?"

"I suppose so."

"Including you?"

"No! First, I'm a married woman. Second, he doesn't want me."

"Are you sure about that?"

"Danny, *he* left *me*. Remember? He had me. He didn't want me anymore."

"Time can change a lot of things."

"Daniel," she said sternly, "enough already."

"I just think you should be careful, Lil. I'm worried about you. I don't want to see you get hurt again."

"Well, there is no reason for you to worry. Tony and I are friends again and that's nice, but that's all. As for me,

I'm fine. In fact, I've never been better. I danced tonight!" she said happily.

"Yes, I know. With Tony," he teased.

"Oh, for Heaven's sake! Daniel, you make me tired! Come on then, let's get out of here," she said, picking up her things.

They put their arms around each other's waists and walked out.

"You really were awesome tonight," he told her as they walked. "You looked beautiful up there."

"Thanks," she said, resting her head on his shoulder.

They found Steven and Charles waiting for them outside. They bid each other a good night and went their separate ways.

* * *

Lily crawled into bed, exhausted, but still energized. She felt renewed, with a whole new sense of accomplishment and confidence. It was an amazing feeling. She looked over at Charles. He was already asleep. She didn't dare wake him.

She took her phone off of the bedside table and texted Tony.

- **Are you still up?**

- Yes. ???

- **Nothing. Just had to talk to someone.**

- R u ok?

- **More than. Never better. I am liberated.**

- I'm proud of you.

- **Couldn't have done it w/o u. Thank u is not enough. U really r something. :-)**

- So are you. Good night, Gracie. :-) Sleep well.

She put the phone back on the table, snuggled down into the comforter, and drifted off to sleep, still smiling.

15

TURKEY

During the week following the anniversary party, things went well at the theater. Lily was quite proud of the fact that she and Nina had gradually begun to swap roles. Nina now took a few more notes, and Lily did more training and one on one work with those who needed it. It felt good. Things were going well between her and Tony as well. They seemed to have successfully put the awkward kiss behind them. Danny had stopped staring every time he saw them together. Tony still came around the theater each evening after work, but he didn't stay too long most days. He and Tracie were still friendly, but she seemed different with him. She was more serious, or at least less flirtatious.

That Thursday was Thanksgiving, and Danny and Steven had invited Lily, Charles, Tony, and a few other cast members and friends who didn't have family in the area or weren't going home over for dinner. Danny put Steven in charge of the meal, since he claimed he still didn't have the knack for cooking a true American Thanksgiving feast.

While most of the men entertained themselves with the pre-game festivities on TV, Danny's friend Monica took a break from Twitter and Facebook on her phone long enough to discover a Cosmo quiz online. She convinced Danny to answer the "how well do you know your mate?" questions about Steven. He was doing well, getting most of the answers right. But when they came to the question about favorite flowers, Charles decided to object. "Okay, haven't we had enough of this? Some of us are trying to watch the pre-game show, and you two are interrupting with the breaking news as to whether or not cupcake one and cupcake two know each other's favorite flowers. Come on!"

"Charles!" Lily shouted from her post at the kitchen counter.

"What?"

"You can't talk to my brother or to Steven like that."

"I wasn't talking *to* them."

"Oh for God's sake! To them or about them, either way, I won't let you talk like that. Since when do you watch football, anyway?"

"Since I have money riding on it."

"Oh good Lord." She turned back to the guys. "I'm sorry about him."

"Oh, Lil, it's okay. He's just jealous cause he knows that he wouldn't do half as well if we asked him the same questions about you," Danny said, talking loud enough that Charles was sure to hear him from the sofa.

"Danny," Lily said in a cautionary tone.

"Well, he wouldn't."

"Is that a challenge?" Charles wanted to know.

"Yes."

"Fine."

"Okay. Fine. So, what's her favorite flower?"

Charles thought for a moment. "Roses. Every woman loves roses." He looked at Lily for confirmation. She tilted her head and raised her eyebrows at him with a half-smile.

"I don't think so," Danny said. "Next. Favorite take-out food?"

"Easy. Italian."

Lily reached for the bottle to pour another glass of wine, shaking her head.

"Favorite beer?"

"Dumb question. She never drinks beer."

Lily was watching the embarrassing event from her spot at the counter, debating whether or not she should stop it, when she noticed her phone vibrating. There were three text notifications from Tony.

- **Daisies**

- **Chinese**

- **London Gold :-)**

She answered.

- **Well done.**

"Favorite ice cream flavor?" Danny asked.
"Butter pecan," Charles bellowed.
Another text came in from Tony.

- **He got one.**

She answered.

- **:-) Finally.**

Danny pressed on. "What kind of shampoo does she use? What perfume does she wear?"

Charles was quiet for a moment, texting someone from his spot on the sofa. If he was trying to hide it, he was unsuccessful.

Tony engaged Lily in another exchange.

- **Still Gilchirst and Soames.**

- Damn. You are good.

- **Azure?**

- Yes again. Do you buy a lot of perfume? ;-)

- **Wouldn't you like to know?**

Charles spoke again, still fumbling with his phone. "Ah... I think the perfume is Azure. The shampoo—"

"Wait a minute," Lily called, walking toward the sofa. "Please tell me you didn't just text your secretary to ask her what kind of perfume I wear."

"Assistant," he snapped.

"Whatever!" She grabbed the phone from his hand. "Oh my God! Too bad. She couldn't remember the shampoo!"

"Lillian, give me the phone back."

"Hang on a minute. Shall I ask her the next question?"

"Give me the God damn phone!" He slammed his hand down on the back of the couch.

"Sorry." She tossed it down on the cushion next to him and walked back to her place near the wine bottle, feeling as though she might need to refill in the very near future.

"Here's one I don't think Cora can answer for him," said Danny. "Favorite position?"

"Oh, God! Danny, I think that's enough," Lily said, before it could get any worse.

"Thank you!" Charles shouted.

Her phone buzzed again.

- **I'm not going to answer that one either.**

- Why stop now? You were on a roll.

- **5th? :-)**

- LOL

Things quieted down after that as the big Thanksgiving Day face-off between the Packers and the Lions got underway. Dinner was served at two-thirty in the afternoon, which Lily thought odd, but Steven said that was the way it was always done at his house. Besides that, they were apparently trying to place it strategically during halftime of the game. They had so much food that it didn't even fit on the large dining table. They had to put some of it on the counter like a buffet and then either get up for it, or pass it around and return it when finished. Lily didn't think they'd had that much food at the last Oscar party she'd gone to. She could feel her skirt beginning to cut off the circulation to her ankles just looking at all of the turkey, stuffing, potatoes, and yams. There were three different types of cranberry jellies, homemade rolls, and some green bean casserole concoction that all of the Americans were drooling over, but that Lily did not find particularly appetizing.

Steven started the meal with a prayer of thanks. Afterward, Charles led with his patented line, "Here's hoping we have more next time!"

Lily nudged him. "You sound like an old grandfather when you do that."

Tony coughed, trying not to laugh.

"Steven, Danny, thank you both so much for having all of us. And Steven, thanks for putting together such a wonderful meal," Lily said. "Now, pass those rolls this way please. I'd like to be sure I get one before my brother eats them all."

They all laughed and started passing. The sound of clinking plates and spoons erupted as they piled their plates high with food. Twenty minutes, later most of their plates were empty. Their stomachs were anything but. Lily was thankful that she'd worn a skirt with a little give to it. She was fairly certain that she saw Smith, one of the young dancers, unbutton his jeans. "Who does that?" she thought.

Steven got up to take a phone call from his parents and when he returned Danny clinked his fork on the edge of his glass to get everyone's attention. "Everyone, Steven and I would like to thank you all again for coming and sharing this wonderful day with us. It's great to have such wonderful friends and family with us. We have so much to be thankful for, with a show opening on Broadway and fabulous people to experience it with. But we have even more to be thankful for this year." He took a breath and smiled widely. "Steven and I are adopting!"

"You're what?" Smith asked.

"We're adopting a baby. We are so excited. We talked to a number of agencies and now that we've gone through the review process we have been matched up with an expectant mother who has agreed to give us her baby. So, when the baby is born we will fly to Russia to pick him or her up, and by this time next year, we will have another family member at our Thanksgiving table!"

"Isn't it wonderful?" Steven asked, clasping Danny's hand.

"Cool," Smith said.

"Great. Good for you," Charles said, jamming another fork full of stuffing into his mouth.

"Congratulations," the others chimed in.

Tony watched Lily from across the table. When she spoke, it was obvious she was trying not to let herself get choked up. "I am so happy for both of you!" She closed her eyes, trying to keep back tears. "Sorry, I feel like such a turkey," she said, carefully touching the edge of her napkin under each eye. She stood up and walked around the table to hug both of them. "This really is fantastic news. You're going to make wonderful parents."

Her words were sincere, but Tony got the distinct feeling that her smile was forced. No one else seemed to notice, but Tony had seen that look before.

She'd often had the same look as a teenager. The day before she left to begin her studies in Paris he'd asked her

148

how things were going at home. She'd smiled in much the same way and said, "Fine. Thank you for asking." When he went round to her house later that evening to say one last good-bye he found her sitting out in her father's car crying. Her father had thrown her out along with all of her luggage. He'd told her if she was going to abandon the family to run off to France, she might as well get going a day early. Tony took her home with him that night. He and his parents took her to the airport the next day. The old man never even showed up to see her off.

After dinner everyone adjourned to the living room to finish watching the big game. Lily stayed behind and started to clear the table. Danny followed her into the kitchen as she carried some of the plates to the sink.

"Are you okay, Sissy?" he asked.

"Fine, darling. But I think maybe I should have skipped that last glass of wine. Or the second round of stuffing."

"Are you sure?"

"Absolutely, love. Now, go ahead and watch the game."

He hesitated.

"Go on." She looked at him sternly. "Get out of here and let me get these dishes started. There's hardly room enough in this kitchen for the both of us."

"You're going to wash all of these dishes?"

"Yes, I am. Now scoot."

"It's a shame you don't have an assistant here for that!"

"What exactly are you trying to imply?"

"Well, most of my house guests don't travel with an entourage, and it's been a long time since I've seen you get your hands dirty. That's all."

"Daniel Christopher! Don't be cheeky. Just because I don't normally have to do my own washing up doesn't mean I can't do it. I didn't need an assistant to change your nappies and I won't need an assistant to kick your ass!" She smiled at him. "What I don't do is watch American football. I'd much rather be in here than stuck in there with you lot. Now get out of here and let me get this mess cleaned up, hmm?"

"Thank you," he said, giving her a kiss on the cheek.

"You're welcome. Enjoy the game. But Danny…"

"Yes?"

"Do try not to agitate Charles, please."

"Yes, mum," he chided.

"Oh, you!" She snapped him with the dishtowel and he ran out of the kitchen laughing.

Once she finished the dishes and had all of the leftovers put away she slipped out the front door to get some air. Tony noticed her leave. He waited a few minutes. When she didn't come back in, he quietly got up and followed her out.

He found her sitting on the steps of the brownstone. When she heard the door open and close she peeked up and saw that it was him. She tried to hide the fact that she was crying, but she couldn't fool him. He sat on the step next to her, taking off his sport jacket and putting it around her shoulders.

He stared across the street. "A dry cleaner, a shoe repair shop, and a massage parlor. Nice. But something tells me you're not just out here for the view."

She shook her head.

"So, what's up?" he asked calmly.

"It's nothing, really. I'll be fine. You go on back in. The game must be about over by now. Don't you want to see who wins?"

"I'm neither a Detroit nor a Green Bay fan. I'm more concerned about you."

She couldn't speak. She just leaned on him and started to sob.

He held her, rocking her gently. After a good five minutes, she finally started to calm down. Once she'd pulled herself together, she wiped her eyes and apologized for crying all over him.

"Do you want to talk about it?" he asked.

"No. Thank you, but I can't. I wish I could, but it's too complicated to get into here." She rested her head on his shoulder for a minute longer. Then she stood up and said, "We'd better get back in there."

"Are you sure?"

"Yes. Thank you," she said smiling and handing his jacket back to him.

Green Bay beat Detroit, which pleased Smith, but not Steven. After some heated discussion about incompetent refs and a phone call from Steven's sister, the group settled back down to watch the Cowboys play the Dolphins.

"Well, on that note..." Charles said, standing and stretching. "Are you ready to go, hon?"

"Where are we going?"

"A buddy of mine—you remember Tom Dubecki—he invited us to his place for dessert. I thought we'd swing by since we're rarely in this area."

"Oh. Would you mind terribly if I didn't go with you?"

"I'm sure he and his wife would love to see you."

"I'm just not feeling very well. I think I'd like to go back in a bit and lie down."

"So, do you want me to drop you off first or send the car back for you?"

"They're in Long Island, aren't they? Don't make the driver come all the way back. You go ahead. I'll manage on my own."

"Okay. I'll see you later, then."

She nodded. He sent a quick text and slid his phone back into his pocket.

"Don't forget to call your sister and wish her a happy Thanksgiving."

"Yeah. I'll call her from the car."

"Bye, Charles," Danny called from the sofa.

"Later." He waved to the crowd, gave Lily a peck on the cheek, and took off.

"Well, who wants pie?" Steven asked, jumping up during the next commercial. Lily couldn't even conceive of eating dessert. She sat in the armchair and sipped a glass of water, trying to decide how long she should wait before taking her leave.

As the others buzzed about gathering their dessert dishes and coffee, Tony made his way over to Lily. He sat on the arm of the chair.

"Why don't you let me take you home?" he asked.

It was a welcome suggestion. She nodded. "Are you sure it's not a bother?"

"No bother."

He found their coats and her handbag in the pile on the bed. They congratulated and thanked the hosts again. Tony shook hands with everyone. Lily kissed them and they left. They drove the entire way back to the Plaza in silence.

16
HOW COULD I?

When they pulled up in front of the hotel, Tony wasn't sure if he should drop Lily off or escort her back to her room. Then she turned from the window and asked, "Do you have time to come up?"

He consented and asked the valet to park the car. The doorman opened the door for them.

"Good afternoon, Mrs. George."

"Hello, Albert."

"Happy Thanksgiving."

"Same to you, Albert."

"Sir," Albert nodded as Tony passed by. Tony nodded back.

He walked her up to the room and she invited him in. It was an Edwardian suite decorated in the rich style of Louis XV. Most of the room was neat and tidy, except for the desk area, which was covered with papers, books, and Charles's computer.

"You know, I've never actually been in one of these rooms. They're quite nice," he noted. "Do they really have 24 karat gold fixtures?"

"Yes."

"Hmm."

She took off her coat and hung it in the closet. She paused with the closet door open. He took his off and handed it to her.

She headed straight from there to the butler's pantry and her electric teapot. She turned on the water and let it run for a moment.

"Are you going to want a cup of tea?" she asked.

"No, thank you."

Lily filled the pot and plugged it in. She checked her phone. No messages. She set it down on the counter.

"Do you mind if I change into something more comfortable?"

"Not at all. I'll just... have a seat."

"Thanks. Be right back."

He sat down on the sofa. She walked through the bedroom into the master bathroom and closed the door. She came back a few minutes later wearing a pale pink track suit and white fuzzy slippers, pulling her hair up into a high, messy pony tail. She was the only woman he knew who could make that look sexy. Then again, he thought she could make just about anything look sexy

"Nice fuzzies."

"Thanks," she smiled weakly. She sat down next to him, one foot folded underneath her, and turned to face him. He shifted a bit to face her too. Her eyes were still wet. She was far from over her emotional outburst. Tony wasn't sure exactly what to expect, but he could tell she had something she needed to let out.

She took a deep breath. "Thanks again for the shoulder to cry on."

"No problem."

"I'm very sorry about your shirt," she said, acknowledging the black smudges she'd left on his shoulder. "I guess I really should stick to waterproof mascara even when I'm not on camera," she said with the tiniest chuckle. "I'm happy to replace it if it doesn't come clean."

"What? The shirt? Don't worry about it. You can't even see it with the jacket on." He smiled, trying to put her mind at ease.

"It was nice of you to bring me back."

"Any time."

"I'm sorry you missed dessert."

"Are you kidding? You saved me. I didn't need it anyway. I missed my workout twice this week." He patted his middle as if he were getting fat.

She smiled, knowing that his abs would have survived a slice of pie with no trouble at all. Her smile soon faded back into a pained expression.

He put his hand over hers. "You can tell me, you know? Whatever it is."

She nodded and took another deep breath before she spoke. "I am so happy for Danny. Really... I am." As soon as the words came out of her mouth she started to choke up all over again. "But for some reason, when he said that they were going to get a baby, it just... hit me somehow. It felt like somebody punched me right in the stomach."

"Why?"

"I can't even believe that I'm going to say this and I swear, I'll never say it out loud again, but I was angry. Or jealous. Or something. I don't know what to call it."

"Why?"

"I've wanted a baby for so long. But no matter what I tried, I never... And now my brother and his—what— partner are getting the chance that I never got?"

"And you feel like you deserved it at least as much as they do. Is that it?"

"Yes."

"Especially when they aren't even living a conventional lifestyle?"

"Yes! No! I... I hate myself for even thinking that. I've never cared about that. It doesn't matter if he's gay or straight. I want my brother to be happy. It doesn't matter to me if it happens to be with a man. I love him. Okay...

I'm certain my father would have had a problem with it if he hadn't run off before it could come to light. The rest of the family—if you can call them that—was none too happy about it. Hell, apparently even my husband has a problem with it. But I didn't. I don't!"

"Well, then don't worry about it."

"How can I not worry about it? How can it possibly be okay for me to feel like this?"

"I just meant that jealousy sometimes rears its ugly head when you least expect it. I think it's the way you choose to react to it that matters."

"You don't think it makes me a terrible person to have these thoughts?"

"Do those thoughts really reflect the way you feel?"

"No. Absolutely not. Danny is the sweetest, funniest, most deserving person I know."

"Would you be equally as upset if someone else you knew announced they were having a baby?"

"Probably. Like Tracie."

"Oh, God, do we have to use her as an example? Please!"

"Sorry. She just came to mind."

"Why?"

"I don't know why. But I would be terribly jealous of her. You know, there's just something about her I don't like. I'm sorry."

"Don't be. For the record, we are not actually dating. Or anything else. Anymore."

"Oh? Why not?"

"It doesn't really matter. You said you would be upset if anyone you knew were having a baby, because it would remind you that you've never had that chance. I don't think the issue has anything to do with Danny and Steven, does it?"

"No. Still, I feel just awful, thinking about myself instead of just being happy for them."

"Lil, it's okay. Sometimes you can't control those feelings. They just happen. You can't beat yourself up over them. Let yourself have a good cry—another good cry—and then move on. Before you know it you'll be taking them shopping for nursery items or some other baby paraphernalia."

Lily nodded. Noticing that the hot water was bubbling madly in the little pot, she stood up.

She'd forgotten how easy it was to talk to Tony. He was so understanding. It was almost like talking to a girlfriend. Charles certainly didn't reason things out or discuss things at length the way he did. Perhaps it was a learned skill from all of his years of trying to understand the different women in his life. Maybe it was just because he had amazing parents who taught him to listen and think before speaking. She didn't care. She loved the fact that she could share things with him and he never seemed to be judging her.

"Are you sure you don't want any tea?"

"No. Really, I'm fine."

As she prepared her cup, she started in again. "Charles and I tried, you know? But we couldn't. I thought it was either because I'd already lost one baby, or because of the accident, or because I was already pushing forty. No matter. After that, I wanted to adopt, but he didn't. He was already over fifty. He said it would take too much time and besides that, you never knew what kind of problems you might inherit if you adopted. Too many chances for unknown genetic issues or social issues, special needs." Each phrase came out between sniffles.

Tony reached for the box of tissues on the end table and handed it to her as she made her way back to the sofa.

"Thanks." She stopped and blew her nose.

"I didn't realize you'd ever lost a baby. I'm sorry."

She nodded and looked down at the floor as she sat back down. She hadn't meant to mention that, but words seemed to be flowing out of her mouth faster than she could control them.

"I would have adopted a baby with you."

"You wouldn't have had to."

He looked at her, puzzled. "What?"

She paused for a few moments, sipping her tea, as she tried to work up the nerve to continue. "As it turned out, I wasn't the one who couldn't have a baby. It was Charles. Some rare complication of the mumps that he had when he was a kid."

Tony shook his head. "I don't understand."

"Well, I don't know exactly what causes it, but the virus—"

"No, not that. I don't understand—if he couldn't have children—you said that you'd had a miscarriage."

Lily put her cup down on the coffee table and stood up. She walked to the window and gazed out, now cursing the fact that he was such a good listener. She swallowed hard, trying to figure out how to say the words she needed to say.

She sat back down next to him.

"Tony, the baby that I lost... was your baby."

He slumped back against the couch. His mouth hung open, but he said nothing. The silence seemed to last forever.

"Tony, say something. Please?"

"I don't know what to say." He shook his head. His brow furrowed.

"Say something. Anything. Are you angry or upset?"

"I'm confused. Surprised, or... stunned. When? How? Why am I just now hearing this? Why didn't you ever tell me?" he asked, leaping up off of the sofa.

This type of conversation was precisely what she had been trying to avoid all along. There was too much in the past, too much pain that could be drudged up.

"I wanted to."

"But you didn't."

"No."

"Why not?"

"Because I never got the chance!"

"What the hell does that mean?"

"Tony," she said, trying to remain calm, "will you please just sit down and let me explain?"

He sat, reluctantly. "Go ahead."

"We spent the year in L.A. together, right? Then you came back here to New York for work, and we tried to make things work long distance. I came back to visit you in February to celebrate Valentine's Day, remember?"

"Of course I remember. That was the last time that we... were together."

"Yes. Before everything went wrong. It was such a beautiful week. We were so very much in love—at least I thought we were. Anyway, I flew back, and several weeks later I found out I was pregnant. I was so happy. I couldn't wait to tell you, but I wanted to tell you in person. So, I thought I would wait until you came out to California at the end of April, even though I could hardly stand it. But, the day you were supposed to arrive, you called and..." she trailed off, trying in vain to fight back the tears.

"And said I wasn't going to make it."

"Yes. I should have said something on the phone that day, but..."

"Why didn't you?"

"You said maybe the following week, so I kept waiting."

"For what? Why?"

"Because I wanted to..." She was crying harder. "I wanted to see the look on your face when I told you that we were going to have a baby." She continued to cry for a few minutes before trying to finish her story. "When you didn't come back, I wanted to see you to tell you, but—"

"But what?"

"You were...Oh, God," she cried. "It doesn't matter, does it? You were gone. We were finished. I didn't know how to tell you at that point and before I could figure out what to do it was too late. I'd lost it."

He had no idea what to say. He pulled her to his chest and held her. Looking out the window over her shoulder he cried too.

"Why didn't you tell me afterward?" he finally asked.

"What difference would it have made? If you didn't want to stay with me, I didn't want you to change your mind just because you felt obligated to take care of me. Again. I never saw you after that."

He sat there staring at her. The look in his eyes told her he had something to say, but he was silent. Then suddenly he stood up again.

"Tony, what is it?"

"Lily... I... I have to go."

"What?"

"I'm sorry, but I can't stay. I need to get home."

"Tony, don't go yet, please."

"I have to." He turned to leave.

She followed him. "No, please. We can sort this out, please!"

"There's nothing to sort out, Lily."

He was already headed for the door. He grabbed his coat from the closet, threw it on, and rushed out the door, leaving her standing there, speechless. She sunk to the floor in the middle of the room and sobbed with her head on her knees and her arms wrapped around herself.

She heard a text message come in a while later. She grabbed for the phone, praying it would be a message from him. It wasn't. It was from Charles. He was on his way home. She had to get out of there. She was a wreck. She couldn't let him find her like this. She ran to the bedroom for a pair of tennis shoes. She grabbed her coat and purse, put her phone in her pocket, and left without any idea where she was headed.

For lack of a better place to go she went down the street to the Paris Theater. She was surprised to see that it was open on a holiday. She bought a ticket for *Young Goethe in Love*, probably not the best choice given the circumstances. Once inside, she sent Charles a message so he wouldn't worry.

- **Out for a walk. Be back in a bit.**

In the darkened theater she checked her phone several times. No messages. She wanted nothing more than to call Tony, to text him, to try to explain further. Apologize. Something. But she knew she couldn't. She had to give it time. She waited until the movie was over and then stopped in the ladies room to see how terrible she looked. Her eyes were red and puffy from crying. She pulled out all of the makeup tricks she had in her purse. She looked somewhat more presentable. At least she could blame the movie for her tears if she had to. Charles already thought she was an emotional basket case where movies were concerned anyway. When she was convinced that it was as good as it was going to get, she walked back to the hotel.

"There you are," Charles called from the sofa. "I was starting to wonder where you were. That was a long walk."

Lily closed the door and opened the closet to put her things away. "I'm sorry. I didn't mean to worry you."

"You didn't. I was just wondering."

"Well, I went out for a walk but I—"

"Shhh! Hang on a minute." He grabbed the remote and turned the volume up to catch some news piece on CNN. "What were you saying?" he asked when it was over, eyes still glued to the TV.

"I ended up at the theater round the corner. They were showing *Young Goethe*."

"Ha! Too bad I missed that," he said.

"How are Tom and Jaimie?"

"Fine. Tom just closed a great deal. Jaimie went on and on about their kids. Their daughter got accepted to Brown on scholarship, and their son made the varsity golf team as a freshman."

She cleared her throat and nodded. "That's great. Really great."

"See. It would have been nice if you could have come with me. You're much better at pretending to care about that stuff."

"I'm sorry. I just wasn't feeling up to it. Next time."

"Sure." He flipped through the channels.

"If you don't mind, I think I'm going to go to bed and read a while."

"Good idea. You look tired."

"See you in a bit."

"Mmm hmm. Goodnight," he said as he settled back on CNN.

In the bedroom, Lily called Danny to thank him for a lovely afternoon. She congratulated him again and told him that she was sure they would make fabulous parents. She offered to help them with anything they needed. They wished each other goodnight, said they loved each other, and hung up.

17
WHAT CAN I SAY?

The long weekend came and went without any word from Tony. Tuesday morning as Lily dressed to go to the theater, her stomach was doing flip-flops. She hoped he would be there, but was afraid that he would not. As she feared, he did not show up that morning. He did not show up at lunchtime or that evening, either.

Lily looked for Tracie before she left that night. She found her with some of the set builders, supervising the final touches on her café scene.

"Hey, Tracie."

"Hello, Lillian."

"How are you?"

"Fine. What do you need?

"Ah, well, I was just wondering if you'd by chance heard anything from Tony in the last couple of days."

"No. I haven't talked to him much since that party. Not that I expected to. He came by and took a look at some of the sets, but that's about it. I would have thought you'd be more likely to know where he is than I would."

"Why?" Lily asked.

"Well, you two seemed pretty chummy the other night is all."

"What's that supposed to mean?"

"Nothing. Should it mean something?"

"I guess not."

"Okay," Tracie said.

Okay, then. Have a good night," Lily said.

"Yeah, you too."

"Stupid cow," Lily whispered to herself as she walked away. She dialed Tony on her walk back to the hotel. It went straight to voicemail. She left him a message.

"Tony, it's Lily. Listen, I feel terrible about the way we left things the other evening. Can you please give me a call when you get a chance? Thanks."

When she got up to their room Charles had the table set with wine, pasta, and salad from La Tratoria. Lily knew what that meant. They had a nice quiet dinner with chitchat about the day's happenings. Afterward they adjourned to the bedroom. Lily did her best, but her heart was not in it. In fact, when she heard her phone ding out in the other room, it was all she could do to keep from getting up to see who was messaging her.

Afterward, she put her robe on and said she was going to make a cup of tea. She asked Charles if he needed anything from the other room.

"No thanks," he said, reaching for his phone. "I have a few emails to send."

Lily rolled her eyes as she walked out of the room. She picked up her phone on the way to turn on her teapot. The ding was only a message from a friend in L.A. Still no response from Tony. She sent him a text.

- **Thinking of u. Hope u r okay. Pls call me.**

Lily made her cup of tea and then turned on the television. She selected the Hallmark channel. She didn't much care what was on as long as it wasn't CNN or another documentary. Had they been at home, she probably would have gone downstairs to work out or run over some routines, but she didn't feel like getting fully dressed to go to the hotel gym, and she certainly wasn't going to go back out to use the theater space.

She finished her tea and checked her messages. Ten o'clock. No new messages. She grabbed a blanket and curled up on the sofa. There was no point in trying to go to bed. Charles was blathering away on the phone. From the sound of it, it was important business. She would never get to sleep in there.

Charles flew home the next day, promising to be back in two weeks. Lily kept busy and tried not to worry about him or Tony for the remainder of the week. She worked the troupe hard during those few days, telling them that they had a lot of work to do before out of town tryouts in Toronto that were now less than a month away. That part was true, but it may also have had something to do with working out her frustrations over the current situation.

Danny caught her at lunch time one day and questioned her about it. She wasn't even sure how to explain what she felt, except to say that she was upset that he wasn't speaking to her, and yet she was angry at herself for being upset.

* * *

By Friday, neither Lily nor anyone else in the company had heard anything from Tony. It had been more than a week, and Lily was really starting to get worried, not just about the status of her relationship with him, but about his well-being. She asked Tracie for Tony's address, which Tracie grudgingly surrendered.

Lily stopped at China Moon for takeout on the way to Tony's apartment. She told the doorman that she was there to surprise Mr. Ward and asked him to let her in. Apparently he was used to this type of request from women because he let her in without any question.

She knocked on Tony's door. She could hear him walking toward it. Her stomach was in knots again. She didn't exactly know what she was going to say to him, but she'd figure it out. She took a deep breath and put on a smile. He opened the door.

"Oh, hello," he said, completely straight-faced.

She looked him up and down. He was well put together, wearing his typical business casual slacks, collared shirt partially unbuttoned, and sport jacket.

"What can I do for you, Lily?"

"Nothing. It's about what I can do for you."

"And what is that?" His tone was quite cold.

She held up the bag. "Egg rolls, pot stickers and moo goo gai pan," she said. "You haven't eaten, have you?"

He shook his head. "Smells good," he finally allowed.

"Can I come in please? Or is this a bad time?"

"Suit yourself," he said. He stepped aside to let her pass and closed the door behind her.

"Thanks." She walked into the loft-like living and dining room and set the bag on the long, glass-topped dining table. She watched him walk across the room. It was another well decorated, tidy space with dark hardwood floors and crisp white walls. Oversized windows that wrapped around the room on three sides offered panoramic views of Central Park and the city beyond. "This is a very nice place. How many floors is it?" she asked, eyeing the large wooden staircase to her left.

"Three," he said as he turned off the local news.

"Really? Is that a terrace out there?" she asked, starting to unload the bag.

"Yes. And there's one off of the kitchen and another off of the master," he snapped. "Lily, what is this?" he asked, walking into the kitchen.

"Dinner. What do you think it is?"

"I haven't the slightest idea. It seems I never know what kind of surprise you have in store for me these days."

166

He returned with some plates and set them down on the table.

"Ouch. Look, Tony, you haven't returned any of my calls or messages. I didn't like the way we left things and I—"

"I've been busy, Lily."

"Is that all?"

He didn't answer. She knew it wasn't.

She started in again, "I was hoping we could talk about...what happened the other night."

"I don't know what I could possibly say," he said, throwing his arms up in the air.

"Okay, then don't say anything. Let me." They sat down at the table and she began to put food on their plates. "Tony, I'm sorry. I'm sorry if you feel I betrayed you by not telling you about the baby. I wasn't trying to hide anything. I just didn't see why I should put you through all the pain of it for nothing."

"Well, for one thing, you wouldn't have had to go through it alone. But then, I guess since you had him you no longer needed me."

"That's not true."

"Isn't it?"

"No."

She handed him a pair of chopsticks. They sat in silence for a few minutes, pushing food around on their plates and taking occasional bites.

"Tony, is there some other problem?"

"There's no problem."

"The hell there isn't. You've been avoiding me all week and now you're sitting over there—you can barely stand to look at me."

She stood and began to pace about. "I don't know what else to say except, I'm sorry. I mean, if things had turned out differently, I would have told you eventually. I know I should have told you on the phone that day. I just didn't know what to say. I needed to process everything. I needed time. But I would have told you. I would have wanted you to be a part of his life."

"His life? Did you know that it was a boy?" he asked.

"No. It was too soon. But I always imagined it was."

She made her way across the living room to the windows overlooking Central Park. Looking out at the fall-colored treetops, she struggled to keep it together.

"I've wondered so many times... what he would be like. Would he be athletic or musically inclined? Would he have your smile or your eyes? And when I saw Harry..." She took a breath. "He looks so much like Anna. Like you. They would have been about the same age and I..."

She felt his hands on her shoulders. She closed her eyes, breathing deeply, trying to avoid another complete breakdown.

"Maybe *she* would have had your eyes. Maybe she would have been a dancer like her mother." She heard his voice crack and she couldn't fight the emotion anymore. She turned to face him, buried her face in his neck, and cried as he held her.

"I'm so sorry," she said again. "God! If I had done something differently— if I had told you—maybe our baby would be—"

"Don't." He cupped her face in his hands, gently wiping the tears from her cheeks with his thumbs. "Don't do that to yourself. It's not your fault."

Part of him wished only to comfort her as a friend. Nothing more. But as he stood there holding her, another part of him had the overwhelming urge to do more than that. He stared into her eyes. They were still moist and filled with anguish, and he wanted to kiss her—to kiss away her tears. She stared back at him, her breaths growing quicker under the heat of his gaze. Then, with a jerk, he pulled away and walked back toward the table.

"Christ, Lily!" he said, shaking his head. "I can't do this."

"Tony, what's happening between us? What is *this*?"

He threw his arms up. "This! You. Me. Us. I thought I could handle it. I thought we could just be friends. But now… It's just too much."

He picked up his plate and carried it into the kitchen. She followed him.

"Why?"

"I just don't think I can do it. That's all. It's too much."

"Why? A week ago we were just fine and now…"

He shook his head and brushed past her as he walked back into the living room. He stood staring out the window with his arms folded.

"Tony, talk to me, please."

"I can't."

"You can't? Or you won't?"

"Lily, please."

She hung back a moment, trying summon up the courage to continue, then walked in after him. She moistened her lips and swallowed before speaking again. "Tony? What happened to us? Where did we go wrong?"

"How can you ask me that?" he asked, turning to face her. He looked for a moment as if he might cry.

"Because I don't understand why—"

"You know damn well what happened!"

"No! I don't know. I've wondered for twelve years now just what exactly it was that I said or did—or didn't do—that made you stop loving me."

"Lily, I didn't stop loving you. I've loved you since the day I met you. I've never loved anyone but you. But you broke my heart."

She stared back. "I broke *your* heart?" she shouted in disbelief. "Surely you're joking."

"I wouldn't joke about this."

"Forgive me, Tony, but you're going to have to explain yourself because I'm not following you."

"You're not? Really?"

"No. I'm not!" Her voice continued to elevate as she got more and more worked up. "Do you have any idea how much I cried over you? I couldn't eat. I couldn't sleep. I couldn't function. You were the only man I'd ever loved. You were the only man... No. The only person that I ever gave myself to completely, because I thought you truly loved me. Unconditionally. I trusted you with my heart and you walked out on me without even so much as a goddamned face-to-face conversation. So yes, I would like you to explain just exactly how the hell I broke *your* heart!"

"Are you quite finished?"

"No. While you're at it there is one other thing you could tell me."

"And what, pray tell, is that?"

"How long were you with her before you finally decided to leave me?"

"What are you talking about?"

"Please, Tony. I was naïve, but I wasn't stupid. I know what I saw."

"When?"

"When you cancelled your visit and then you called and told me it wasn't going to work, I thought you meant because of the distance. Well, the following week I decided to go back to New York. I wanted to tell you that I was moving back. When I got to our apartment you weren't home yet. I thought maybe you were just working late, so I went across the street to Ming Dynasty to pick up dinner. I stopped at the market for wine for you and candles. God, I was still ridiculously hopeful. I thought we would have dinner and I'd tell you I was coming home. Then I'd tell you about the baby and we'd make love." She paused, pressing her lips together. "To think I actually considered asking you to marry me. God! No. Instead, I came up the stairs and found the two of you together."

"Christ, Lily! It wasn't what you thought."

"Bullshit! You had her backed up against the wall, coiled around you, kissing her, one hand on her ass while the other hand searched frantically in your pocket for your keys so you could take her in and finish the job. Don't tell me I don't know what I saw. Don't you think you had me in that position enough times that I ought to know?"

He fell on to the sofa and covered his face with his hands. "What did you do then?"

"What do you think I did? I left. I dumped everything in the bin outside and took a cab back to the airport."

"God. I'm sorry. I had no idea that you ever knew about her."

"Who was she?"

"Her name was Tricia. She worked in my office."

"Ha! Classic! You left me for a slapper named *Tricia*? What the hell did she have that I didn't?" She wiped at her eyes. "Oh, what am I saying? A tall buxom blonde, she was everything I wasn't. I should have known it was only a matter of time until I just wasn't enough for you anymore."

"Lily, stop it! For God's sake! You were everything I ever wanted. The only thing I ever wanted. I didn't leave you for her. She didn't mean anything to me. She was just a... a rebound. A distraction. One stupid night of drinking and sex to make the pain of losing you go away. And you're right about one thing. She was nothing like you. I wanted the farthest thing from you. I wanted to forget. Only it was a horrible mistake. When I woke up the next morning and found her lying next to me... Christ. I would have given anything in the world for it to have been you instead."

"Tony, *you* left *me*. It was your choice. If you still wanted me, why——?"

"I was hurt, Lily."

"What could I possibly have done to hurt so badly? Can you please tell me that?"

"You mean other than move halfway across the country, move into another man's house, and fool around with him while you were supposed to be with me and while, as I now realize, you were pregnant with my child?"

"Tony, I moved to L.A. for the film. You know that. Landing that role in *Last Dance* was an incredible opportunity. And to be fair, you did agree to it. I did move into Charles's guest house when the lease was up on our apartment. That's true. You and I hadn't decided what our next move was going to be yet. It was supposed to be a temporary situation. But as for fooling around with him... I have no idea what you mean. I don't think it's any secret that he had a thing for me, but I didn't want him. I wanted you. I certainly never—"

"I saw you kissing him, Lily!"

"When?"

"That day in April."

"That's not possible."

"I got there early, so I thought I'd surprise you. When I pulled up outside the house, I saw the two of you along with another couple strolling down the front walk. You were all laughing and seemed to be having a marvelous time. He had his arm around you, and then I saw him lean in and kiss you. I drove away and called you from the airport. I just told you that I was stuck in New York on business because I couldn't stand to face you."

Lily shook her head, "I don't believe it," she muttered.

She knew exactly what he was describing, but she remembered the situation very differently.

"Tony, that other couple that you saw us with—they were Brenda and James Bartlett. They were investors in the next film that Charles was planning to do. They were all pressuring me to get involved. I was protesting. Do you know why I was protesting? Because I was trying to decide if I wanted to continue working there or if I was going to give it all up in order to move back the East Coast and marry the man of my dreams, with whom I was expecting a baby. Not that they knew that. Christ! As we were walking them out I finally agreed that I would at least think about it. Charles said—and I quote—'If it weren't politically incorrect I'd kiss you right now!' Then he said, 'Ah, what the hell!' and he leaned in and kissed me. That's what you saw, and if you had stuck around a minute longer you also would have seen me slap him across the face for doing it!"

"And that's it?" he asked doubtfully.

"Yes. That's it. He even told that story in his autobiography."

"I've never read it," he said sharply.

"My God, Tony, did you seriously think that I was having an affair with him? Based on that? Did you honestly think that I would do that to you? How could you? After all that we'd been through. Everything we meant to each other." Her voice shook with anger. Tears were welling up in her eyes again.

"You looked awfully happy with him."

"Did you happen to think that perhaps I was happy because you were supposed to arrive that day? I was miserable without you."

"Every time we spoke, all of your letters, you always said that everything was fine."

"That's what I wanted you to believe, but I would have thought that you knew me better than that. I was terribly depressed, but I didn't want you to know that. I didn't want you to stop doing your work, work that you loved, just to come back and rescue me. When you left to go back to New York I was alone for the first time in years. I hadn't lived without you since I was nineteen. I was lost. I needed you desperately. I was thirty years old and I had no idea how to deal with life on my own. I didn't know how to be me without you. I lived for your letters and phone calls."

"Then why did you start sending them back?"

"What?"

"As soon you moved in with him all of my letters started coming back labeled 'Return to Sender.' I called several times and left messages, but I could never seem to catch you and you never called me back."

"I never got them."

"You cancelled your trip home in March."

"Because I was ill and exhausted and I didn't even know why at the time."

"Then I saw you that day, kissing him, and the reason for the returned letters seemed fairly blatant."

"Except that it couldn't have been farther from the truth." She shook her head again and wiped her eyes. "Tony, when you left me, I had a breakdown. It was a big break. I'd lost you. I'd lost your baby. I damn near lost my mind. My life shattered around me. Charles was there to help me pick up the pieces. What we have grew out of that. Now, I can't explain what happened, but please believe me when I tell you that I never got any of your messages, and I never sent back any letters. And I never slept with him. Not until long after you and I were over."

He left the room and came back carrying a shoebox. "I found these as I was going through some of my old albums after my birthday. I don't really know why I kept them all of these years, but…" He handed her the box.

"What's this?" she asked.

"See for yourself."

She sat down on the sofa with the box on her lap. and lifted the lid to find dozens of letters postmarked before and after the breakup. Every one of them was marked "Return to Sender". Lily pulled the first few envelopes out and stared at them. She immediately recognized the capital "S" in "Sender" as the same one her husband used for his middle initial in his signature. "Oh my God," she whispered. "He sent them back."

"I always assumed that you put him up to it."

She shook her head and swallowed hard. She was mortified. "I can't believe he would… Why would he?"

She stared blankly for a few moments. He wondered what she was thinking. Finally, she spoke again. "May I read them?"

"Go ahead. They're yours if you want them." He walked over to the wet bar and poured himself a scotch. "Drink?" he asked her.

"Please," she said, settling back. She pulled the first letter from the front of the box and opened it. He put the drink on the table in front of her as she read. She immediately reached for it and took a sip. By the time she was finished with the third letter, she had finished most of the drink. Tears were rolling down her face. She put the box down, stood up, and walked over to the chair where he was sitting. She knelt down and looked up into his eyes. "I'm so sorry. If I had only known..."

"No. Don't apologize to me, Lily. I don't deserve it. I'm the one who's sorry. I was a fool. A complete fool."

He held her face gently in his hands again. "All of these years I blamed you, and it was no one's fault but my own. If I hadn't jumped to conclusions...Can you ever forgive me?" She put her hand over his hand and held it, turning her head to kiss his palm. She reached up and hugged him tightly around the neck. He leaned into the hug with his arms around her waist. She could feel his body shake as he started to cry.

"Tony, it wasn't all your fault."

"Yes, it was."

"No. I should have fought harder for you. For us. I should have confronted you. I should have questioned you instead of running from the pain. If only I'd been stronger. We could have talked about all of it the way we're talking right now. Maybe then we wouldn't have had to go through half of our lives each thinking that the other just... stopped loving them. Instead, I fell apart. There you were, heartbroken, thinking that he and I were living happily ever after. Meanwhile, I was destroyed because you didn't think our relationship was worth fighting for anymore."

"I guess we both made a real mess of it then, didn't we?"

"Or he did. I don't even know what to think about that. I've always known him to go after what he wants, but I never thought…" She stood and turned her back to him, trying to gather her thoughts. Tony stood too. After a minute she turned and embraced him again. He held her close, one hand placed tenderly on her head, as she rested it on his chest. They stood there holding each other for quite some time, neither of them wanting to let go. After a long while he felt compelled to break the silence. "So now what?" he asked.

She backed away slowly. "Now what?" she repeated. She shook her head and shrugged her shoulders.

"What do we do? Where do we go from here?"

"I don't know," she said. "Did you mean what you said before? Do you really still love me after all of this time?"

"Finish reading those letters and I think you'll have your answer. The bigger question is how do you feel?"

"I honestly don't know what to feel right now, Tony. I know that I was crazy this week when you wouldn't answer my calls or messages. I know that for whatever reason, God has brought you back into my life, and I can't seem to imagine going back to a time when you weren't in it. Honestly, I do still have feelings for you…"

"But?"

"But he's my husband. I'm angry with him right now, for what he did, but I can't just ignore everything else. What you and I had was like a fairy tale. It was perfect. At least I thought it was. But then one day the fairy tale ended as all fairy tales do. Everything just went up in smoke, because… well, life just doesn't end with happily ever after, does it? What I have with him… it's not perfect. Far from. But it's real. We've had our issues, but we've always worked them out. He's the one who has loved me and supported me even when the going got tough, the one I've built my life around all these years. He's not the one who..."

She let the thought drop and gazed into his eyes once more, her lip quivering as she fought the tears again. He stepped closer and caressed her cheek, wiping away the lone teardrop that had escaped with his thumb again.

"He's not the one who left, is he?"

She shook her head apologetically

"Then again," she sighed, "I'm not even sure now how much of our relationship was built on a lie. Maybe it's not so real after all. It's all very confusing at the moment."

He took her hands in his. "Well, you don't have to decide anything tonight," he said, knowing it would not serve him well to push her. "So, let's go back to where we were a few weeks ago. Let's not *do* anything. Let's just let it be and see what happens. Take some time to figure things out."

"Are you sure you're okay with that?" she asked. "You said earlier that you didn't think you could handle being just friends."

"I meant that I couldn't go on pretending that I didn't have feelings for you. But now you know. So... I may have to control my feelings, but at least I don't have to lie about them."

"Are you sure you can control them?" she smiled.

"I can if you can." He smiled back.

"What time is it?"

"About ten."

"I should really get going. We've got an early call tomorrow."

"Sure."

Still holding her hand, Tony walked her toward the door. He helped her on with her coat.

"Lily, thank you for coming here tonight. I'm very glad that we had this talk."

"Me too."

"And I'm very sorry. That I didn't have more faith in you. In us."

She nodded, biting her lip to hold back more emotion. "I'm sorry too." They hugged each other tightly and said good night.

"Oh," Tony said suddenly. He ran back over to the coffee table and picked up the box of letters. "Take these with you," he said, handing them to her.

She took the box and smiled ever so slightly. "Thank you."

"Let's keep in touch, then."

"Okay."

She opened the door and walked out. He closed it behind her.

* * *

Once back at the Plaza, she put her coat in the closet and kicked off her shoes. She looked at her phone. It was almost eleven. Only eight in LA. She stared at Charles's name in her favorites list. There was a part of her that longed to ring him up and lay into him about what he'd done, but she couldn't bring herself to do it. Not yet. She needed time to sort out the mess in her head before confronting him. She changed into her pajamas, poured herself a glass of wine, and sat down on the sofa with the box of letters. She thumbed through the stack of fifty some envelopes. Most of them were postmarked the year of the breakup. The last few were in unaddressed envelopes as if they were never meant to be sent. Curled up in a blanket, Lily began to read.

18
TO LILY WITH LOVE

1 March 1999

Dearest Lily,

How did the move go today? Well, I hope. I'm sorry I couldn't be there to help you. I suppose we're very fortunate that your friend was able to offer you a place to stay until we can figure things out, but I must admit that I will be much happier once you and I are able to settle under one roof again. I miss you terribly. I love New York, but the apartment just isn't the same without you. Nothing is the same without you.

I can't wait to see you on St. Patrick's Day. It'll be nice to be home with family again, even for a few days. Anna says she has a surprise for us. She won't tell me what it is, but I suspect she may be pregnant again. She says Edward is talking up a storm. She sent me some pictures. You won't believe how much he's grown.

Have you booked your flight yet? I'll be in London by the 14th. I have a few things to take care of before you arrive. Anna's not the only one with big news. I have several surprises in store for you, my darling. I'm looking forward to your reactions. That's not all I'm looking forward to. No fair making any big plans for the first two days at least, as I don't plan on letting you out of my sight or out of my bed.

I'm counting the days, lover.
-T

P.S. We will NOT be staying with mum and dad this time.

17 March 1999

My Lily,

For some reason the last letter that I sent was returned. I hope I have the correct address and that this one finds you.

I'm so sorry that you're ill. It must be quite bad for you to cancel your trip. I hope it's nothing serious. I know traveling is hell when you're miserable, but I can't tell you how disappointed I was when I heard your message. I was looking forward to seeing you more than you can possibly imagine. I had so many things that I wanted to tell you in person.

I hate to spoil the surprise, but you know I can't stand waiting. So, here goes nothing. I have good news. There will be no more nights spent in my old room at my parents' house while we're in London. From now on we will be able to make as much noise (and as much love) as we want in our own bed at our own house! Do you remember the charming old house that we saw in Wimbledon? I bought it for you. For us. For what I hope will someday be our family.

That's it. I won't tell you anything more. You'll have to discover the rest of the surprises for yourself when you see it. I do hope you're going to love it.

I love you, angel. I miss you. I hope you feel better soon. Ring me when you have time. Day or night. I just want to hear your voice.

Always,
-T

1 May 1999

My darling Lily,

I pray that this letter reaches you. I don't know what else to do. You won't return my calls and you don't want to see me. Charles reminded me of that when I tried to visit you today. But I need to see you. We need to talk. There are things to sort out, things we can't say on the phone or in letters.

Putting distance between us was a mistake, especially with the added stress of career developments, moving, all of that. But we can fix things. I want to fix things. No matter what's happened, I don't want to lose you, Lily. I love you too much. I need you too much. If you no longer feel the same way, you can tell me. But I want to hear you say it, not him.

If you do get this letter, please ring me. I'll meet you anywhere you like.

Yours,
-T

14 July 1999

My Lily,

I don't even know why I'm writing this. It's likely to be returned just like the others. The house phone number you gave me has been disconnected and even the cell you kept for emergencies appears to be out of service. It is obvious at this point that you no longer wish to have any contact with me. Still, as I sit on this plane, I can think of nothing else to do but to write to you.

I returned to L.A. again today, still hoping to see you. As with the past three times, I was unsuccessful. Charles made it abundantly clear that you no longer wish to have anything to do with me. He was kind enough to remind me of your commitment to him just before he had me removed from the premises.

I hate feeling that so much is left unsaid. If only I could speak to you one last time.

Yours,
-T

P.S. Do you know what day it is? Do you remember the Bastille Day that we spent in Paris? I don't know which was more exciting, the citywide celebration, or you and I together in a passionate frenzy during the fireworks display. How I miss those days.

21 December 1999

Dearest Lily,

It snowed here today. Central Park was covered in a soft, white blanket of loveliness. I watched some young children catching snowflakes on their tongues. They were so playful and full of joy. It reminded me of the night that we walked through Covent Garden. You were spectacular in that red silk dress, your hair falling softly about your shoulders. It began to snow. I watched your face light up. You glowed with a childlike innocence as you spun about in the moonlight and the light of the lamps. The white flakes against your silken dark tresses... I have never seen anything so beautiful. You were my angel.

I miss hearing your voice and seeing your smile. I miss holding you in my arms. I miss having you in my life.

All my love,
-T

20 November 2001

Lily,

It seems congratulations are in order. According to the reports, you were married yesterday. Ridiculous, but I find myself wondering if you had made it home that St. Patrick's day, if I had been able to propose to you as I'd planned, would it have been me instead? I know it's silly, but until now I've held out some shred of hope that we would somehow find our way back to each other. Now that hope is gone. You have moved on with your life. I must find a way do the same.

It won't be easy. I've loved you for so long. It seems impossible to think about my life without you. I will never forget you, the gentle calm of your touch, or those beautiful chestnut eyes that could read my every thought and desire. I shall always remember the way your smile lights up a room and the swell of emotion that I felt the first and every time I watched you dance. It will take time, but perhaps one day I will be able to remember it all with fondness rather than pain.

I will not try to contact you again. You are his now. I pray that he can give you whatever it is that I couldn't.

Goodbye my friend, my love.
-T

1 November 2011

Lily,

It has been over twelve years since I last set eyes on you. Yet this morning, feelings that I thought I'd buried came flooding back to me like someone had opened the dam. I might as well have been fourteen years old again, seeing you for the first time.

The years have been more than kind to you. You are as exquisite as ever. I haven't the slightest idea how things are going to play out between us, but I pray that somehow we will, if nothing else, be able to be friendly again.

I have missed you.
-T

17 November 2011

My Lily,

I must thank you again for a lovely weekend. I haven't enjoyed Paris so much in years. You are an absolutely amazing person, to put aside whatever negativity existed between us in order to be there for Christine. Thank God my father was never really ill, but that doesn't change the fact that you were willing to be there when you thought I needed you. I shall be eternally grateful.

Of course, I'm now wondering if there may be more left between us than just negativity. I'll admit that I haven't been able to get last night's kiss off of my mind. I have never had the kind of physical connection with any one like the one I had with you. Last night I felt the same spark that I used to feel. Was it the same for you? I wonder.

After all of this time, I thought my heart had healed, but putting you on the plane today, sending you back to your new life, it opened up old wounds. I take some comfort in knowing that this time we are parting as friends.

I do hope that you are happy with Charles. I also hope that he knows how lucky he is to have you. You are truly a gift from God. You deserve to be treasured and adored like the rare jewel that you are.

Yours,
-T

P.S. You didn't imagine it. I was at the hospital the night before you woke up. I had to see you. I waited for Charles to leave for the evening before going in. He never noticed me in the waiting area. I spent the whole night talking to you, holding your hand, praying that you'd wake up and be all right. I slipped out before he came back the next morning.

24 November 2011

Dearest Lily,

I apologize for leaving you in tears this evening. It was not the most chivalrous thing to do. I didn't mean to make things any more difficult for you than they already were. I wish I could have explained to you how I felt, but honestly, I don't know if you would have been ready to hear it.

It wasn't only the fact that you hadn't told me that was so upsetting. Just as you felt knocked down by your brother's announcement, wishing that you had been the one to have a baby instead, I felt knocked down, too. Learning that you were pregnant but lost the baby, I am as crushed now as you must have been then. I wanted nothing more than to marry you, have children, and grow old with you. I imagined that we would get there one day, once we'd made names for ourselves in our respective businesses, but we never got the chance. It is heartbreaking, even though I'm only just now hearing it, to have that chance dangled out in front of me and then, in the same breath, have it ripped away again.

I can't help but wonder, if you had told me, would it have changed anything? It makes no difference now. It is all water under the bridge, but it doesn't make wondering "what if" any less painful.

Last week you asked me why I never married. I came close once. But I called it off just three days before the wedding. I simply could not go through with it. I couldn't explain it at the time, but the reason seems somewhat obvious now. You can't marry someone, promising to love, honor, and cherish her, when you're still in love with someone else. Can you?

Some people say that there is one true love out there for everyone. You were mine. You still are, whether or not the feeling is mutual.

I am, as I ever was, and perhaps ever shall be...yours,
-T

19
SIGNS

Lily put the last letter back in the box. She dried the tears from her eyes and finished the last swallow of her tea. It had taken her two weeks to get through the whole box of them. Some of them she'd read several times.

She sat staring at the box, teacup still in hand, debating. Tony had been her entire life, and in an instant, he'd been torn away from her without any warning whatsoever. Now, after so many years, they'd been thrust back together, and the bond that they once shared seemed almost as strong as ever. He very obviously still loved her. She definitely still had strong feelings for him, no matter how hard she tried to fight them, but she still had so many questions. Did she truly love him, or was she in love with the memory of him? Was she just longing to get back a piece of what she'd lost? Was it even possible to recapture what they'd once had? Had their relationship really been as wonderful as she remembered it, or was she just glorifying it in her mind the way people glorify childhood memories of favorite birthdays or family camping trips? Sometimes the passing years had a way of washing away the more difficult parts of the past and leaving you with only the good stuff. Maybe it really was just nostalgia as she'd been claiming all along. Or maybe Danny's suspicions had be right from the start.

She chuckled to herself, thinking back to Tony's recounting of the kiss on his birthday. He wrote that he'd felt sparks. She hadn't felt sparks at all. What she'd felt was more akin to a fiery eruption from a formerly dormant volcano.

As she sat pondering her feelings for Tony and Charles and Charles's involvement in the whole ordeal, her phone rang. She rushed across the room to the butler's pantry to pick it up, pulling the ties on her robe tighter as she walked.

"Hello, Cora. How are you, dear? Yes. I think everything is all set. What time is Charles supposed to arrive? Oh. I see. And he had you call me so that I wouldn't be angry, is that it? Is he sitting right there? Put him on please."

"Hello, Lillian," Charles said with a sigh.

"So you can't make it tonight?"

"No."

"When then?"

"By Christmas Eve at least. Maybe the twenty-third if we're lucky."

"Really? You promised you'd be here three days ago. Now it's not until Christmas Eve?"

"Lillian, you know I've had all sorts of issues with the shooting schedule. The interruptions have been ridiculous."

"Yes, I know. And your work always comes first."

"Don't start with me. You know how important it is that we wrap this up before the holiday."

"I understand that. I do. I'm sorry. It's just that…"

"What?" he bellowed.

"I think that *we* have some important things to deal with too."

"Well whatever it is, it's just going to have to wait." He could hear her exhale on the other end of the phone.

"All right. I'll see you next week. Can you give me back to Cora, please?"

He handed the phone back to Cora without another word.

"Will I see you for Christmas, or are you flying out to visit your family?" Lily asked her. "Okay. I'll send your gift back with Charles. See that he doesn't forget to give it to you. You know how his is. Bye dear."

Lily poured herself another cup of Earl Grey and wandered over to the window. She sipped the tea and stared out over the park.

"Dear God," she whispered. She shook her head. "If only you could tell me what to do."

A tri-tone text notification answered her plea. She picked up her phone and smiled when she saw Tony's name.

- **What's up Gracie? Haven't heard from you in a while. R u ok?**

- Ok. Lots of work to do. And lots of reading.

- **And?**

- We'll talk later. Going to the party tonight?

- **Yes. U?**

- Of course. Bringing anyone?

- **No. Single these days.**

- Snap! :-)

- **Oh? What about Chuck?**

- Charles? Too busy. Still in LA.

- **Too bad.**

- Is it?

- **Not really. Just being polite.**

- Smart ass. :-) C u later.

- **Looking forward to it. ;)**

Lily put her phone in her robe pocket and the lid back on the box of letters. She stashed the box on the top shelf of the coat closet. Filled with anticipation about the evening to come, she headed into the bedroom, tossed her robe on the bed and went into the master bath to begin preparation for the festivities.

20
HAPPY HOLIDAYS

There wasn't enough money left in the production budget or in Danny's personal budget to throw a huge holiday Party. So Lily volunteered to take it on, with Cora's help, knowing full well that Charles's personal budget had room in it for just about anything. They booked the West Side Loft in Manhattan. Lily was sure to arrive before the other guests to check things out and make any last minute adjustments. The caterers buzzed about readying water goblets and appetizers. The room was beautifully decorated with garland swags, red bows and white lights. The tables were covered in white linens and each place setting had a gold napkin folded into the shape of a star. In the center of each table were several small poinsettia plants to be given as party favors.

The room was festive. The theme was fun. Lily had made sure to leave space for a dance floor. She and Cora hired a DJ who would play mostly old classics, Sinatra, Martin, and some holiday favorites during dinner. Afterward, he would take requests. He also promised a karaoke system, not that Lily had any intention of singing herself.

Danny and Steven were among the first to arrive. They were thrilled at the sight of the room and thanked Lily repeatedly. She told them it was nothing, kissed them, and wished them a Merry Christmas. Then she moved on to greet the other guests. By seven forty-five, Tony still had not arrived and dinner was supposed to be served at eight. Lily was starting to wonder if he'd decided not to come. Her phone was in her coat pocket. She was headed for the door, thinking maybe she should run to the coatroom to check her messages, when she ran into Danny who was coming back in with Natalie and Nina.

"Danny, have you by any chance seen Tony? He said he would be here tonight, but I haven't seen him. I'm hoping something else hasn't come up."

"Relax, Sis. I just saw his car pull up when I was walking these two in. He should be in any minute."

"Oh, was he the one with that sharp car?" Natalie asked.

"Yeah, the Infiniti G 37 coup," Danny said.

"Ooh, everything about that guy is sexy, even if he is older," Nina said.

"I know. Even his car is like sex on wheels!" Natalie said dreamily.

"I heard that!" Danny answered.

The girls shrieked and giggled, elbowing each other. Lily's mouth fell open.

"Sorry, Lil," Nina said, regaining her composure. "Hey, are you two going to dance again tonight?"

Danny just shook his head, threw his hands up, and smiled as he ushered them into the room. Lily stayed near the door, waiting for Tony to arrive, but trying not to make it too obvious. Unfortunately, one of the caterers beckoned her over to deal with something, and she was forced to abandon her post to see what was the matter.

When Tony walked in, he scanned the room for Lily and spotted her across the room talking to one of the event staff. He had worried that he was under-dressed, wearing slacks and the sweater she had given him for his birthday. He was glad to see that most of the crowd was dressed somewhat casually. Lily, on the other hand, was wearing an asymmetrical black chiffon skirt, knee-high boots with stiletto heels, and a spaghetti-strapped, form-fitting, black and silver beaded top. It was a look that not every woman her age could pull off, but on her, it worked very well. Her hair was piled up on top of her head in ringlet curls with just a few tendrils falling down for a bit of softness, beautifully displaying her long neck and strong, bare shoulders. Her large, dangling, teardrop diamond earrings were the perfect accent. Tony usually marveled at how elegant she looked. Tonight, only one word came to mind—sexy.

She looked up from her conversation with the caterer and smiled. He took a deep breath as she strode confidently toward him. He smiled back, trying not to expose his nervous excitement, not realizing that she too was covering up butterflies with a calm visage.

"Hello, darling," she said, kissing him on the cheek. "I'm so glad you made it. I was beginning to worry."

"Oh, sorry. I ended up talking on the phone to Anna for quite a while and got a later start than I'd anticipated."

"Well, no matter. You're here now. Dinner is about to be served. Why don't we have a seat? I hope you don't mind, but I seated you next to me, since neither one of us has a date for the evening."

"That's a real hardship," he joked, following her to their seats. "You look… gorgeous, by the way."

"Thank you," she said. A smile crept across her face again. That was just the reaction that she had been hoping for.

During dinner, Tony sat to Lily's left. As she reached for her napkin to put it on her lap, he couldn't help but notice something. Her nails were freshly manicured in a lovely cranberry shade to match her lipstick, but there was no bling on her finger. He leaned over and whispered in her ear.

"Where's your ring?"

"My ring?"

"The large rock you usually have weighing down your left hand. Where is it? It's at least ten carats. It's rather hard to miss, isn't it?"

"I... I left it in the safe."

"Why?"

"Because I didn't need the reminder. I don't want to think about him. Not tonight."

Tony regarded her curiously. Lily averted her eyes and took a drink of water.

During dessert, Lily accidentally stepped on Tony's foot under the table. "Oh, I'm so sorry," she said. She placed her hand on his thigh under the table in a comforting gesture and felt his body jerk. Her hand lingered there for a moment.

"No problem," he said. He cleared his throat and shifted in his seat, trying not to let his facial expression change as he continued his conversation with Nina. He finished commenting on her story and then shot Lily a look out of the corner of his eye. The twinkle in his eye told her that his reaction was one of excitement, not just surprise.

"Sorry," she mouthed to him. She moved her hand away, secretly amused by the fact that she could still have that effect on him. It had been a long time since anyone had responded that way to her touch.

When the meal was over, Danny and Steven got up to make a toast. They welcomed and thanked the cast and crew. They thanked Lily for putting the party together and everyone applauded. Then, Steven suggested it was time to get the party started. He nodded to the DJ, who revved up his karaoke machine, and Danny broke into his best Elvis impersonation with "Blue Christmas." The crowd laughed, hooted, and hollered. Next, Hank and Natalie did a foxtrot to Dean Martin's version of "Winter Wonderland." Natalie grabbed the microphone when it was over and announced that it was time for Lily and Tony to do something. Lily threw her head back and laughed politely.

"Oh, no thank you," she said. The crowd began to egg them on.

"I'm game if you're game," Tony whispered to her.

"No. She just wants you to go up there because she and Nina think you're dishy."

"Ha! Well, you know me. I always like to give the ladies what they want!" He stood up and grabbed her hand. She could hardly say no at that point without looking like an ass, so she stood up and followed him.

"What do you want to sing?" he asked her on the way.

"I don't sing."

"Well, you're no Julie Andrews, but you can carry a tune. Besides, you didn't dance either, until last month, remember?" He laughed.

"Oh, you!"

When they reached the front of the room, Natalie handed Tony a wireless microphone. "What's it going to be, Lil?" he asked her.

"Hmm, 'Je T'aime Moi Non Plus'?" She winked at him. She attached a battery pack to the waistband of her skirt and clipped the mic to her blouse.

"Ha ha! No. Too risqué," he said. "Ah… 'You're the One That I Want'?"

"Oooh! No. Too cliché." She thought a moment. "Well darling, it's quite cold outside," she smiled.

"Ah, Mercer and Whiting! Shall we dust off the old routine?"

"Why not?"

Tony said something to the DJ. "Comin' right up," the DJ said.

The music started. He stood behind her holding her left hand with his right hand on her waist.

"I really can't stay," she beamed.

"But darling, it's cold outside," he answered playfully. They continued, swaying to the music, dancing during the musical interludes.

"Are those the right words?" Steven asked as he approached Danny with fresh drinks.

Danny took his glass of wine and took a sip. "Ha! It's the edited version. Nobody calls Lily 'baby' and gets away with it, remember?"

"Why is that again?"

"Don't ask, don't tell, darling." Danny said. He gave Steven a look. Steven nodded knowingly and took a drink.

Lily and Tony harmonized the ending and finished with a dip. Their fans applauded wildly and they left the floor holding hands and smiling.

As they walked back to their seats arm in arm, Steven commented again, "Those two are absolutely fabulous together. Do you think she's sleeping with him?"

"I don't know," Danny said. "She hasn't been nearly as forthcoming lately, but I'll tell you one thing. If she's not, she wants to."

"Who doesn't?" Steven laughed.

When the party was over, Lily asked Tony if he would mind taking her back to the hotel.

"No problem," he said.

"Are you sure? Because I can get a cab if you have to get home."

"No. It's no trouble at all, really."

"Good. I'll just get my coat, then." She smiled nervously.

* * *

Tony pulled up outside the Plaza Hotel. Lily stalled. She fumbled in her purse for her room key. She cleared her throat. "Do you want to come up?" she asked.

"Sure," he said.

"Good," she nodded.

"Good," he mimicked. He helped her out of the car and gave his keys to the valet.

"Good night, ma'am," the doorman said. "Sir." He nodded in Tony's direction.

"Good night, Albert," they answered in unison.

* * *

"Thank you for bringing me home," she said, taking his coat. "Can I interest you in a nightcap?"

"Please." He took a seat on the sofa.

She took a bottle and two cocktail glasses from the butler's pantry. She poured and handed one to him. He eyed the bottle.

"Bowmore 25 year old. That's good stuff. Charles may not approve of you sharing it with me."

"Well," she said, strutting over to the lean on the desk, "First of all, I bought that bottle for you. Second, he's lucky I don't pull out his Macallan 1939 and give that to you as payment for damages the way I feel right now. Cheers!"

She held up her glass and then took a swallow. He smiled at her.

"What?"

"Nothing. It's funny to see you drinking that."

"Well, you've opened my eyes to a lot of new experiences lately. Why not one more?" she winked. She picked up the picture of herself and Charles that was on the desk and studied it. She sighed and laid it face down before joining Tony on the sofa. She took off her boots and tucked her feet up next to her as she began to pull the pins from her hair. "So, I read your letters."

"All of them?"

"Every one. Some of them three or four times."

"And?"

"And… They were beautiful. Sweet. Funny. Heartbreaking. All at once. Heartbreaking because of us. Because of him." She pulled out the last pin, shook her hair down around her shoulders, and ran her fingers through it. She took another drink and leaned sideways on the back of the sofa to look at him. "I'd forced myself to forget, you know? How much we meant to each other. How much we loved each other. But reading your letters…" She shook her head. "Everything was right there on the pages. And all over again I was hurt, sad, angry. What we had was so beautiful. I just don't know if we can ever get that back. No matter how much we might want to."

"Listen, Lily, I'm glad you read them. I'm glad you know everything. But, you should also know that I don't have any expectations, okay? I mean, I didn't give them to you just to stir things up or to drive a wedge between you and your husband."

"You mean like he did? I know that. But you didn't let me finish. I don't know if things can ever be like they were, but I'd like to find out. If there's even the slightest chance, I want to know. So the question is, are you willing to do what it takes to help me find out, even if I can't make any commitment to you right now?"

He put his hand on her cheek. "Of course. Anything you need from me. Just name it."

"Thank you."

"Only let's not mention any of this to my mother just yet, hmm?"

They both laughed. She picked up the remote and turned the Love Notes music channel on the television. She refilled each of their glasses and snuggled into the crook of his arm with her head on his chest.

"Right now, just hold me."

He put his arm around her and stroked her hair as she lay curled up on him. After some time, a song came on that she recognized. After only a few notes, she sat up and smiled at him.

"Do you remember this song?"

He nodded. "Our first night in the apartment."

"We had a picnic on the floor."

"We had no furniture."

"Except a bed."

"Priorities!" They chimed, laughing.

"After our picnic we danced to this song on the radio," he said, a sentimental, far off look in his eye.

"Dance with me now."

"Here?" he asked.

She nodded. "Just regular people stuff."

They stood. He took her hand and curled it in against his chest with the other arm around her low back. She wrapped her other arm around his neck and laid her head on his shoulder. Their bodies fit together perfectly. Their movements were smooth, natural. In his arms she felt safe. She felt needed. In his arms she belonged. Being near him only made her ache to get closer to him. As the song ended she looked up at him.

"Lost in love," she whispered. "That's how I always felt with you. Just like the song says."

"Me too," he mouthed.

His crystal blue eyes shined back at her, filled with such love and lust that she could no longer control herself. Her lips touched his softly on the corner of his mouth and then again as she gently caught his bottom lip with her teeth. She felt his breath catch. His arms tightened around her as she kissed him for the third time. He gave in and kissed her back, each of them enjoying it immensely. Then, suddenly, he broke free and rushed back to the sofa. He sat on the edge of the cushion wringing his hands, then picked up his glass and took a large swig.

"What's wrong?" she asked.

He stood again. "I think I'd better go."

"I think you should stay."

"If I don't go—"

She grabbed hold of the front of his sweater with one hand and pulled him to her, silencing him with another kiss.

"Lily," he said, so close to her lips she could feel it.

"Hmm?"

He gently moved her hair out of the way and kissed her shoulder. Working his way up her neck, he whispered, "I don't think this is a good idea."

"Don't you want me?" she breathed.

He looked at her longingly. "Of course I want you. My God, I've never wanted anyone the way that I want you at this exact moment. But this could turn your life upside down."

"You've already done that." She smiled and gave him a gentle push. He fell backward onto the sofa. She knelt over him with her skirt billowing around him.

"Oh. Yes. Well... I mean if he should find out. Wouldn't that make things a lot more complicated?"

She reached down and pulled off his sweater and t-shirt. She ran her hands over his bare chest, enjoying his muscular form. Then, running her fingers through his hair she leaned in and kissed him behind the ear. "Tony," she cooed seductively, "Kiss me."

"Are you sure?"

"Just… kiss me."

Her body pressed against his, the smell of her skin, her warm breath on his neck as she kissed it, he was completely mad with desire. He took her face in his hands and kissed her hard. She let out a soft moan.

His hands moved steadily under her skirt, up her thighs, stopping only a moment when he discovered the elastic of her thigh-high stockings.

"You are full of surprises, aren't you?" he managed between breathy kisses that traveled down the front of her neck.

"Keep going," she encouraged.

She smiled, as did he, when his hands moved over her hips and met with the bare flesh of her firm behind.

"Oh God! You are so sexy," he growled.

She arched her back and threw her head back as his lips moved across her chest. Distracted by her already racing heart and the brush of his soft lips on her quivering body, she struggled to get the words out, but her intent was clear. "I think... we should... into ... the bedroom."

She stood and took his hands, pulling him off the sofa. After another long and involved kiss, he asked her one last time, "Are you absolutely sure?"

"Tony, please," she sighed. "Make love to me."

His strong arms swept her up with such ease that she could have been a feather. He carried her into the bedroom and laid her across the bed. He inched up her skirt to reveal the lacey black thong and began slowly peeling the stockings off her muscular legs. He gently massaged the arches of her feet as he kissed every one of her toes. Then he kissed his way up each leg, giving special attention to the soft skin on the backs of her knees and inner thighs, enjoying the sounds she made each time he touched her. Once confident that she was as ready as he was, he removed everything else.

She was pleased to find that his stamina had not decreased over the years. If anything, his skill level had increased. She hadn't even thought that possible.

He was equally pleased to find that she was still as fit, flexible, and energetic as ever, despite any earlier claims to the contrary.

"My God, you are beautiful," he said, examining her lying next to him.

Still slightly out of breath, she looked into his gorgeous baby blues and smiled. "I'd almost forgotten how fabulous you are."

"Mmm, thank you," he laughed. He was propped up on one elbow, smiling, tracing the curves of her body with his other hand, either reminiscing or memorizing them all over again.

"I'm a little worse for the wear since the last time you saw me," she said as she felt him moving over the scar on her abdomen. It wasn't the only one she had.

"Hush. You are perfect."

As he leaned back in and kissed her again, her phone rang out in the other room. She ignored it, much more concerned with what Tony was doing with his hands, but the xylophone ringtone sounded again almost immediately.

"Ugh! I'm going to have to answer that," she groaned, turning away from him and sitting up.

"Are you serious?" He flopped back down on the other side of the bed.

"I'm so sorry, darling. It's Charles. He won't stop until I pick up."

She climbed out of bed and grabbed her plush, white Plaza robe. She walked into the sitting room, but Tony could still hear her end of the conversation.

"Hi. I'm surprised to hear from you. I thought you'd be busy. No. We were still up. Yes. Tony's here. We were just having a nightcap. He brought me home after the party. Yes, it was lovely. Oh, all right, put her on then." She walked back in, paced a bit, then walked out again. "Hello, Cora. Yes. Thank you. The evening was a smashing success. Yes. Thanks again for all your help. Okay, well, keep him out of trouble then. Yes, you too. B'bye." She returned with their glasses and the bottle of scotch.

"I'm sorry about that. Where were we?" she asked. She sat next to him on his side of the bed, refilling the glasses and handing one to him.

"Christ, Lil, did you have to tell him I was here?"

"It's not exactly secret, is it? The valet and the doorman know it." She took drink.

"Yes, but don't you think—"

She gave him another intense, whiskey-coated kiss. "Let's not talk about that, hmm?" She stood up, emptied her glass, and set it back on the nightstand. "I have a better idea," she said, dropping her robe onto the floor. She slid back into bed next to him and wrapped herself around him with a feisty look in her eyes, as if challenging him to another round.

He fought to hold his glass upright as she began to work her wiles. "What, again, you little vixen?"

"Well, if you're not interested…" she said playfully, rolling back over to her own side of the bed.

"Oh, don't go putting words in my mouth, now. I'm a little surprised, that's all."

"You try cubed steak for twelve years and see what happens when someone finally gives you filet mignon again."

"Interesting analogy. Are you telling me that Sir Charles is not, in fact, the world's greatest lover?"

"That is exactly what I'm telling you. And that's if he manages at all."

"What's his problem? I mean other than the fact that he's almost sixty, of course."

"I told you, he's only fifty-six."

"No matter. It's the wrong side of fifty-five. I'm just saying, he's past it!"

"Yes, well, I don't think age is the issue. It's not exactly a recent development. For one thing, he has no rhythm. That's why he can't dance. You, on the other hand…"

"Ha! Maybe it's the name. *Charles*," he said in a haughty tone as if imitating the queen. "It doesn't exactly scream excitement. C.S. George. What's his middle name? Maybe he should go by that."

"I don't think so."

"Why not? What is it?"

"Sherwin."

"What?"

"Sherwin!"

"Oh, right. That's not exactly one you want to scream out in a moment of passion, is it?" Tony asked, struggling to keep a straight face.

"Definitely not. Not that I'm accustomed to screaming."

"You could've fooled me."

"Well, I wasn't accustomed, but I think I could get used to it again," she laughed, moving back in for another kiss. After a moment she stopped. "My guess is he's already used it up banging his assistant."

"Really?"

"No. I don't know. I mean I asked him once. He swore there was nothing between them. But if you ask me, there's something. Whether or not he's ever acted on it is another story. Do you know he came home on her birthday, at two in the morning, smelling of perfume? He said it was a stripper, but come on! Hell, he's with her right now. It's a bit late to be working, don't you think?"

"So is that what this is about? Evening the score?"

"No!" She propped herself up so that she could look into his eyes and caressed his cheek. She kissed him softly and moved her hand slowly down his neck and over his bare chest until it came to rest over his heart and she could feel it beating. "This is about me…wanting to be with you, wanting to figure out if this thing between us is real. This might seem strange, but here's the way I see it. We've been on this rollercoaster ride for weeks, you and I. At first, I tried to put on the brakes. To stop the train. But after all the ups and downs, the force of it is too strong. I don't know where the train is headed or if it'll derail completely. But either way, there is no stopping it. So, tonight I finally decided to throw my hands up and just… enjoy the ride."

He was quiet for a moment. Then he took a drink and put his glass down. "Well, then…" he began, kissing her passionately. "Buckle your seatbelt my darling, because this wild ride is only just getting started."

"Oh!" she cried as he shifted to face her and threw her onto her back with the weight of his body.

He made his way under the covers and went to work. By the time he finished with her there was not an inch of her body left untouched nor a single urge left unsatisfied.

She would have liked to have him stay all night, but decided it might make things even more obvious than they already were. Around two a.m., she kissed him goodbye and sent him home, promising to call him in the morning.

21
CAN YOU KEEP A SECRET?

The next morning Tony and Lily arranged to have breakfast at Fluffy's. Not long after she hung up with him, Danny called, wondering if she wanted to have breakfast while Steven was out running errands. She thought Danny would find it more odd if she turned him down than if she told him that she was meeting Tony, so she invited him to join them.

Danny arrived first and was already seated inside waiting for the two of them. They arrived separately. He watched them walk in together. The two of them sat down next to each other across the table from him. Lily said good morning. Tony said good morning. Tony asked Danny how things were set for Toronto.

"Fine. I think we'll be ready."

"Good. That's good," Tony said.

"So, Tony…" Danny paused, taking a moment to salt his eggs. "Care to tell me how long you've been shagging my sister?"

"Jesus! You told him?"

"Oh! Fuck it, Tony! I didn't tell 'im anything," Lily said. "But you just did!"

Danny sat across the table laughing. "You two are really going to have to work on your responses if you're going to get away with this for any length of time. You look like goddamned deer caught in headlights, for Christ sakes."

"Daniel! Shut it, will you!"

"Now, Lil, don't go getting your knickers in a twist! That is if you're wearing any!"

"If not, she probably has a pair of dance pants handy," Tony chimed in.

"Don't you start with that again," Lily said, smacking him on the arm. "Seriously, Danny, how did you know?"

"You know I already suspected there was something going on, but today it was much more obvious. It's all in your body language. I watched you when you met each other on the street just now. You kissed him on the cheek, but it was a little too close to the lips to be platonic. He hugged you, but his hands were too low. If you don't stay above the small of the back it immediately says, 'we are more than just friends'. Besides that, you were wearing your sex kitten boots last night with no wedding ring and then you asked him to take you home. I could have been wrong, but I thought I'd ask and gauge your reaction. It was even better than I imagined. So, how long has this been going on?"

"Just since last night," Lily admitted.

"Really? Just the one time?"

"Well, one night," Tony said.

"Damn, Tony, I knew you were a stud!"

Tony laughed.

"Danny, keep your voice down," Lily pleaded.

"Sorry."

"Danny, do you think Charles will know?"

"Ha! No. For that he would have to pay you some attention. Besides, he seems to be laboring under the illusion that Tony is gay."

All three of them laughed out loud at the thought of that.

"For Heaven's sake, why?" Lily asked. "That's the most absurd thing I've ever heard."

"I know, right? Apparently his dance moves are too impressive for a straight guy."

"Un-fucking-believable," Tony muttered. "Well, if that's what saves us I'll play along."

"Excellent!" Danny remarked with a twinkle in his eye.

"For the record, Danny, I said I'll play along, but even I have my limits. Don't go thinking you have a chance now."

"Damn!" Danny said.

"Anyway, I think Steven is more my type," Tony said, faking the stereotypical lisp when he said Steven's name.

"Bastard!" Danny said jokingly.

"You won't tell him, will you?" Lily asked.

Danny thought about it for a moment. He watched the two them squirm. Finally he answered. "No."

"Oh, thank God," she said. Tony exhaled, relieved.

"I know that probably doesn't say much about my character," Danny said, "but I'm a sucker for true love or hot sex, whichever is your reason. And... I'm reasonably certain I'm going to hell for any number of things, the least of which is whether or not I blow the whistle on the two of you. I just have one question."

"What's that?" Lily asked.

"How was it?"

"Damn!" Tony laughed. "On that note, I have a few things to take care of, if you'll excuse me." He stood to leave.

"Wait. Will I see you later?" Lily asked.

"I certainly hope so." He gave her a peck on the cheek. "Why don't you ring me when you're finished for the day."

She nodded and watched him walk out. Then she turned back toward Danny, fiddling with her coffee cup and smiling but unable to look him in the eye.

"I thought that would get rid of him," Danny laughed. "I knew it! I knew you still wanted him! How was it? Seriously?"

Still fiddling, she half smiled and bit her lip, peeking up at him with a look that said, "Too good for words."

"Damn! So what does this mean?"

She shook her head. "I don't know yet."

"Do you love him?"

"I don't know. Maybe I do. Maybe I always have. I'm not ready to put that label on it just yet, all right?"

"All right. So? What are you going to do now?"

"I'm going to spend some time with him and see where it all leads."

"Well, it's no secret that I'm not your husband's biggest fan—"

"Danny!"

"Well, I'm not, but still... After the way things ended with Tony the last time, do you really think it's wise to get mixed up with him again?

"That's the thing, Danny. There's a whole hell of a lot more to the story. I don't know if we've got the time."

"We'll make time. Do tell."

22
AN AFFAIR TO REMEMBER

During a break from rehearsals that afternoon, Lily sent Tony a text.

- **Can I make dinner for you tonight?**

- I'd like that. My place?

- **Obviously. :-) How do you feel about Wellington?**

- Love it.

- **Great. I should be done in a couple of hours. I'll be over as soon as I've finished shopping.**

- Send me your list. I'll have what you need when you get here.

- **Thnx. But r u still talking about groceries? ;-)**

- LOL. Aren't you?

- **Just checking. C u soon.**

- Can't wait.

* * *

"Hiya," she said, smiling as he opened the door.

"Hi yourself," he said. "What's that?"

"My overnight bag. Just in case."

"Oh."

"Albert was very curious about it."

"The doorman? What did you tell him?"

"That I was visiting a friend."

"I see. Well, is that what we are, then?" he asked, taking her coat.

"Yes. Aren't we?"

"Definitely, but…"

"You were hoping for something more?" she asked with a flirtatious gleam in her eye.

"Well I thought that—"

"Tony…"

"Yes?"

"I'm just pissin' around!" She laughed.

"Oh, that's bloody harsh!" he exclaimed, taking hold of her.

"You can kiss me now."

"Thank God," he whispered, enveloping her in his arms and laying one on her.

"Mmm. I should get dinner started," she said, peeling herself away from him. "It takes an hour or more to prepare. If I let you get started we won't eat until midnight. May I?" She asked, motioning toward the kitchen.

"Please." He gestured for her to enter and followed her in.

"Wow. This is gorgeous!" She ran her hand over the solid surface counter top on the island as she looked around the bright, windowed room. All white cabinets lined both sides and a good-sized table was situated at the far end near the door that led onto the terrace. "A double range and double ovens. Nice!"

"It's great for entertaining, though I still don't use it as much as I would like."

"Well, let's put it to use now then," she smiled.

"Right!" He opened the fridge and began handing her the ingredients she'd requested.

"Thanks. Did you get the wine?"

"One dry white," he said, pulling a bottle of Sauvignon Blanc from the wine fridge. "I've got a nice Saint Emilion Bordeaux to go with it once it's done."

"Perfect."

While Lily prepared the entrée, Tony made the salad and used the leftover puff pastry to make a heart-shaped tart for two.

She put the beef Wellington in the oven and poured two glasses from the remaining Sauvignon Blanc. She gave one to him.

"Santé," she said, holding up her glass.

"À la tienne," he answered.

"Cute," she said, smiling at his dessert as he put it in the second oven.

"Are you making fun of my culinary skills?"

"Not at all. I think it's adorable. You—are adorable," she said. She put down her glass and moved closer to him. He took her into his arms again, and with one ardent kiss the fire between them was ignited. He lifted her up onto the island so that she was sitting on the edge with her legs around him. He deftly removed her blouse and threw it to the floor. One hand slipped into her bra to massage her breast. The other held the back of her head as he eased her onto her back.

"Tony…" she struggled to speak as he kissed her stomach. "Shouldn't we go upstairs?"

"Why waste time and energy taking you upstairs when I can take you right here. Right now."

Twenty minutes later the oven timer sounded. Lily stumbled to the stove, half-dressed. As she bent to take the tray out, Tony came at her from behind. His hands, still eager, glided over her body as he kissed her neck.

"My God, you are insatiable."

"I can't help it. I can't get enough of you."

"Well I hope your appetite is as healthy as your libido," she laughed. "Come on, darling. If you don't want it to be overdone you have to let me get it out. Besides, the pastry is done!"

"Oh, all right!" he moaned. He turned off the second timer and moved to get his tart out. As he took a bowl of berries from the fridge, his muscles peeked out from under his open shirt. Lily shook her head and smiled at him, licking her lips.

After dinner Tony brought out a small artificial Christmas tree. He put on a collection of Old English carols, and they chatted and laughed as they decorated the tree with lights and ornaments. After placing the star on top, they sat down on the sofa with the rest of the red wine from dinner and admired their work.

"Well, it's not a huge tree, but I think it does the job," Tony said, putting his arm around her.

"I think it's lovely." Lily slouched down a bit and put her head on his chest.

He kissed the top of her head.

"It's nice. Decorating the tree for a change," she said.

"Don't you decorate for Christmas in LA?"

"Oh. Yes. We do. Well, I do. I doubt if he's done it this year. I don't get to do it myself though. I just... supervise. Charles would rather I don't interfere. He says that's why we pay decorators. And gardeners. And housekeepers. So we don't have to waste time on all of the boring details. The only thing I get away with is cooking."

"He'd be a fool not to let you do the cooking. Your Wellington was cracking!"

"Thank you," she smiled. "I shall tell Gordon you liked it. You know, he's really quite a good teacher."

"Gordon?"

"Ramsay."

"That's a load of codswallop!" he laughed.

"No. Really. You don't believe me?"

He couldn't decide if the grin on her face was because she was teasing or just happy, but he didn't really care. He was just content to see her smile.

They sat for a few minutes without saying anything. Then she spoke again.

"Tony?"

"Hmm?"

"Am I a terrible person?"

"Why would you say that?"

"This. Us. I know it's wrong. I'm not proud of myself. But right now, all I feel is... happy. Everything with you is so..."

"So what?"

"Easy."

"And here I thought you were going to say exciting." He poked her in the ribs until she giggled.

"That too." She half smiled as she bit at her lip. "I never thought of myself as unhappy with him, but I never felt like this either. Am I a terrible person for allowing myself to feel this way?"

"Lily, you are not a terrible person. I find it amazing that you turned out as well as you did."

"Why?"

"Well, let's see. Your mother died when you were ten years old leaving you to care for your infant brother. Your drunken father blamed everyone but himself for everything that ever happened to him. You took every bit of abuse that he put you through, some of which I can't even bear to think about, and I don't know how you lived through it. When you finally decided to go off to school and save yourself from the whole mess, he made you feel guilty about it. On top of that, years later, the only man you'd ever loved abandoned you because he was too proud or stupid to realize that you were both victims of another man's schemes to claim you for his own. Throw in a miscarriage and a drunk driver who could have left you paralyzed—you have quite a few reasons to be bitter, to be angry at the world, and yet here you are. You're still the most beautiful, loving, forgiving creature. Call me crazy. I don't know about Charles, but I think God may forgive us for this. I suspect he's the one who brought us back together in the first place."

"But what if he's just testing us?" she asked, sitting back up to look at him.

"I've got a test for you!" he teased, leaning in to kiss her.

"What are you testing? My ability to resist you? Because I'm doomed to fail if that is the case."

"How about your endurance?"

They made love on the living room floor by the light of the tree. It was only the second time she'd made love outside of the bedroom in twelve years, which made it all that much more exciting. They finished the bottle of wine wrapped in nothing but a blanket and then went up to bed.

Lily couldn't get over how different everything felt with Tony. Even going to sleep was different. Charles clung to his side of the bed as if there were barbed wire down the center dividing the two of them. Tony's body moved with her, no matter where she went. She liked the closeness. It was a beautiful feeling, warm, familiar, and safe. They drifted off, entwined with one another. Lily slept more soundly and peacefully than she had in a long time.

The next morning Lily awoke to Tony's kisses on her neck and shoulders.

"Good morning, darling," she said. "Mmm. That is better than any alarm clock I've ever had. What time is it?"

"About nine-thirty," he answered, nibbling on her ear.

"Don't you have to go to work today?" she asked, picking her phone up off the nightstand and fumbling with it.

"In theory, yes. But Monday is your day off, isn't it?"

"Yes."

"Well then, why don't I just play hooky?"

"Are you sure you can do that?"

"I can do whatever I want. That's the beauty of being the boss. So, what do you want to do today, gorgeous?" he asked, between kisses.

"I can think of one thing."

"What's that?"

"You," she laughed. She selected a playlist on her phone and put it in the iPod dock, hitting play.

"I'm serious."

"So am I," she said, turning to face him. The music came on and he recognized it immediately.

"AC/DC's *Back In Black* album?"

"Yes. Do you remember?"

"How could I forget?" He smiled mischievously. "How many copies of that album did we wear out?"

"At least two," she laughed. "And one cassette tape, I think! But good news—I bought it on CD and uploaded it. So this is digital. It can't wear out."

"If we keep up like this you're going wear me out!"

"Oooh, do you need to take a break, darling?"

"I'll manage," he said flipping her onto her back. He clasped her hands in his and pinned them over her head.

Tony collapsed back onto his side of the bed, satisfied but exhausted. "I think I may need to take tomorrow off as well, just to recover," he said.

"I've already scheduled an adjustment and a massage," Lily giggled, trying to catch her breath.

"Oh, God, I'm sorry. I hadn't even thought of that. Are you all right? Should I try to take it a bit easier on you?"

"Don't you dare!" she said, pulling him back into her embrace and planting another kiss firmly on his lips. They stayed in bed for another hour just holding each other before getting up to shower together. That was another hot and steamy adventure all on its own.

When Lily came out of the bathroom in Tony's robe he was nearly dressed. "I hope you brought along some warm clothes. You may need them today," he said as he pulled on his sweater.

"Why? Where are we going?"

"That's for me to know and you to find out." He gave her a quick kiss.

"But I thought we decided to stay in bed all day." She wrapped her arms around his neck.

"We'll get back to that, darling. I promise." He kissed her again. "But first we have someplace else to be, so you'd better get dressed." He gave her a tap on the behind and left the room smiling.

* * *

"That was a wonderful surprise. Thank you!" Lily gushed as they exited Radio City following the afternoon showing of the Christmas Spectacular. "I loved it. Didn't you?"

"I love that you loved it," Tony said. He checked the time on his phone. "It's later than I thought. We'd better get moving."

"Why? Where are we going now?" she asked, taking his arm as he turned left and headed down the street.

"That's the next part of your surprise. We have a five o'clock appointment for the rink at Rockefeller Center."

"You're kidding! I haven't been skating in years!"

"Neither have I. I guess we're going to find out if either one of us has still got it."

"Ha! Oh, you've still got it!" she said.

She looked up at him with a rather brazen smile on her face.

"My darling Lily, if we weren't in public right now I'd…"

"You'd what?"

"Never mind. I'll show you later."

* * *

They made it to the Igloo tent just in time for their appointment, put on their skates, and headed out onto the ice. They were both cautious at first, but soon enough they were back into the swing of it. Skating together wasn't all that much different than dancing together. It wasn't long before they attracted the attention of others with their skill and chemistry.

"That was so much fun!" Lily said. Tony squatted on the floor in front of her, unlacing and removing her skates. He looked up at her. With her hands wrapped around her cup of complimentary hot cocoa and her face lit up with a wide smile, she was like a girl again.

"You are is so beautiful when you smile," he whispered. "Do you know how much I want to kiss you right now?" he asked, gently caressing her foot as he put her boot back on.

"Stop." She blushed. "You know, Tony…"

She was interrupted by the voice of a woman approaching them from across the room.

"Excuse me, Ms. Josephson? I absolutely loved you as Gracie Goodwin. Would you mind giving me your autograph?"

Concerned about hiding her identity and their relationship, Lily shook her head and answered back in French, "Qui est-ce Gracie Goodwin? Je n'ai pas la moindre idée de ce dont vous parlez."

She stood, took Tony's hand, and they walked out.

"Nice save," he said once they were outside. "I thought you said that didn't happen much anymore."

"It doesn't normally. Still, we should be careful."

"Well it wouldn't be a problem if you could keep your hands off me," he teased.

"Oh!" She nudged him. "I will try. I swear I will," she snickered.

"Do you want to go for a walk?" he asked.

"I'd love to."

"Good. Just keep your hands in your pockets why don't you. You know, in case you should get the urge."

"Hush! You should talk. You're the one who's all arms. You're like a bloody octopus."

"I didn't hear you complaining last night—or this morning, for that matter," Tony laughed.

"Shhh!"

They walked fourteen blocks down 6th Avenue until Tony finally turned and headed west. Lily hadn't been paying much attention to where they were walking, but as soon as he changed direction she realized where he was going.

"You remembered," she sighed, admiring the miniature "Miracle on 34th Street" display in the Macy's window.

"We used to come down here at the start of the season every year." He stood behind her, hands in his pockets. She took a step back, trying to get close enough to feel his body against hers without being obvious. It brought back so many memories. She could have stood there for an hour just thinking about all of the happy Christmases they'd shared.

"Hey, are you hungry?" he finally asked.

"What did you have in mind?"

"Wait right here. I'll be right back." He returned a few minutes later with two items wrapped in foil. "New York's finest," he said.

She unwrapped one. "Hot dogs?"

"Mustard only. Just the way you like it."

"How do you stay so fit the way you eat? I've gained three pounds since I got here."

"I'll show you tonight," he promised.

Lily laughed and turned back toward the window. "I'd forgotten how festive New York is at Christmas time," she whispered. She took a bite of her hot dog. "To think, I wanted to turn Danny down. I would have missed it all."

After checking out all of the other displays at Macy's, they took 34th over to 5th. They walked up 5th past Tiffany's and the famed Cartier building, proudly displaying its mammoth Christmas bow.

* * *

"I suppose it's a good thing we came home when we did," Lily said as they arrived at the apartment. "It's getting cold out there."

"I'll take that as my cue to warm you up," Tony said, wrapping her up in his arms and kissing her.

"Mmm. That is wonderful," she said.

"There's more where that came from. But first, how about a drink?"

"Sure."

"What would you like?"

"Darling, why don't you sit down and let me get it?" She uncorked a bottle of Riesling, poured two glasses, and joined him on the sofa.

"Thank you."

"My pleasure. It's about time I did something for you."

"You do plenty. Trust me." He leaned over and kissed her again.

"Well, I do want to be sure I'm keeping up my end of the bargain," she smiled. She took a drink and set her glass down on the coffee table, then picked up one of the throw pillows and stood up.

"Where are you going?" he asked.

"Nowhere, darling." She took his wine glass from him and put it on the side table. "Don't you worry." She tossed the pillow onto the floor at his feet and dropped to her knees. She took hold of his legs and gave a swift tug, pulling his hips toward her. "You have been spoiling me all day, doing nice things for me." She reached for his belt buckle. "I think it's time you relax, and let me do something for you."

They spent one more blissful night together. The next morning, they said their goodbyes and went off to work, not knowing when they would see each other again.

Life continued as "normal" for the rest of the week. The only contact they had was an occasional sassy text or furtive phone call, usually in French, just in case.

* * *

Before they knew it, Christmas Eve was upon them. Charles flew in as promised with an added surprise. He'd stopped in Iowa to pick up his sister Gladys on the way. Once again Lily and Charles were invited to Danny's and Steven's place for dinner along with a few close friends.

Lily came through the door with a Fluffy's Bakery box in one hand and bag of gifts in the other.

"Hello, Lillian," Steven called from the kitchen.

"Hello, Steven darling. Merry Christmas," she said. "I thought you might be busy with dinner so I brought dessert. It's only a cheese...." She stopped short when she spotted Tony across the room. "Tony. What a surprise. I didn't expect to see you."

"A good surprise, I hope," Tony said, walking toward her.

"Oh, yes. It's a lovely surprise."

"Yes. Lovely," Charles said sarcastically. He squeezed through the doorway past Lily with one of the larger gifts in his hand.

Gladys charged in after him. "Well, hello," she said to Tony. Then she looked at Lily. "What's wrong with you? Your face is all red."

"Is it?" Lily asked. "It's a little warm in here."

"I'll take your coat," Danny said, dashing to her side. "And the cheesecake. Before the two of you melt the bloody thing," he said for her ears only.

Lily took the hint. She straightened her clothes, threw her shoulders back, and glided past Tony into the living room.

Tony spent most of the evening trying to fend off advances from Gladys. She followed him around the entire time, standing a little too close, making innuendos, and generally making it very clear that she found him quite attractive. When Tony politely pointed out that he wasn't interested she said, "I know. My brother told me all about you. What a shame. You're so handsome. You know, I think the love of a good woman could reform you."

Danny and Steven nearly peed themselves laughing. Lily laughed so hard at the look on his face that it made her stomach hurt and she had to gasp for air.

At one point, Gladys found herself standing behind Tony under the mistletoe and decided it was time to make her move. She tapped him on the shoulder and when he turned around she put her hands on his shoulders and hoisted herself up, clinging to him with her legs around his waist. She was surprisingly quick for sixty. Once she was up there, she planted a huge kiss on him. Tony, stunned and unprepared to be so unceremoniously accosted, stumbled backward and fell against the wall. Charles was forced to peel Gladys off in order to rescue him.

"Sorry, Gladys, darling," Tony said after catching his breath. "I'm still not interested. I guess if a kiss like that can't change my mind, nothing will."

While everyone was watching *A Christmas Story*, another tradition that Steven insisted on, Lily briefly considered cornering Tony somewhere and having her way with him. Seeing as it was Christmas, ravishing Tony seemed a rather unholy thing to do, so she banished the thought and resigned herself to watching the plight of Ralphie. But when he got up to use the restroom an hour later, she decided it was her best opportunity for a private conversation. The powder room was occupied, so Tony went in to use the master bathroom. Lily followed him into the bedroom at a safe distance and waited. It was dark except for the two electric candles burning in the windows and the sliver of light that shone through the cracked door.

"Oh, you startled me," he said, when he came out and found her sitting on the edge of the bed.

She leaped up and stood staring at him, biting her lip. She briefly considered leaving, but she was drawn to him as usual "I shouldn't have come in here," she said, approaching him and laying her hands on his chest.

"I'm glad you did," he whispered. He put his hands in his pockets, fighting the intense urge to wrap his arms around her. He teetered back and forth from one foot to the other, turning slowly with each step. She naturally turned with him until she ended up with her back to the wall.

"What are you doing here?" she asked. "I thought you were flying out last night." She smoothed out a bit of wavy hair near his ear with her fingers.

He braced himself with one hand on the wall near her head, and leaned into her as he spoke into her ear. "Change of plans. I'm leaving tomorrow instead."

She fussed with his collar and slid her hands down his shoulders, ironing out the non-existent wrinkles in his jacket. "You're missing Christmas Eve dinner with your family? Your mother must be terribly upset."

"Apoplectic," he said into her neck. "She thinks the plane had mechanical issues."

"Oh, Tony!" She sighed, nuzzling his cheek. "Lying to your mother—what have I done to you?"

"God only knows, but I'd love for you to do it again," he said invitingly.

In the darkness, Lily could only imagine the flirtatious smile that accompanied that remark, but even the thought of it stirred feelings within her that she could scarcely control, feelings that she'd forgotten existed until a few short weeks ago.

Tony felt her muscles tense and her sharp intake of breath. She wanted him, and he knew it. He was on the verge of insanity, about to kiss her with her husband less than fifty feet away, until Danny's voice boomed out over the sound of the television.

"I don't know. She must be waiting for the bathroom. There was a queue in there earlier."

Moments later, Charles appeared.

"Excuse me, Charles," Tony said, brushing past him in the doorway.

"Lillian?" Charles said, peaking around the corner.

"Yes, darling?" She had a hand on the doorknob, about to step into the bathroom.

"The movie is over. It's time to open presents."

"Okay. I'll be right there."

"Hurry up, would you? We have to finish this up and get out of here before Gladys eats the rest of your brother's booze-soaked fruitcake."

After they'd opened all of the gifts, Tony gathered his things and said goodnight to everyone. Lily offered to escort him out. She wanted to steal one more moment alone with him before he left the next day for his two-week holiday. She stood on the steps outside the brownstone preparing to say goodbye and was suddenly overwhelmed with emotion. All she could do was bite her lip and try to hold back the tears.

"Oh, come on now." Tony stood at the bottom of the stairs, looking at her. With her standing a step higher, they could see eye to eye. He tilted his head and gave her a debonair smile, which forced her to smile. "That's better," he said. "Okay, darling, let's do this. We don't have much time before they start to wonder what we're doing out here."

"I know. As it is, I practically had to arm wrestle Gladys for the chance to walk you out."

"She is a real treat, isn't she?"

"Well, if you weren't so damned sexy you wouldn't have so many women falling all over you all the time."

"Most of the time I don't mind, but she gives new definition to the term cougar," he said.

"At least she made herself at home and had a good time tonight. Even if she did have to sit on your lap most of the night to do it."

"Take it easy tigress. You're just jealous and you know it. There's plenty of me to go around."

"You'd best be careful about what you're spreading around. Let's limit it to holiday cheer, okay?"

"Don't you worry your pretty little head, my love. I'm all yours. Even if…"

"What?"

"Nothing."

"Even if I can't be all yours?"

"Yes. Even if." He reached into his pocket and took out a tiny, Tiffany blue jewelry box. He handed it to her.

"What's this?"

"Your Christmas present."

"But I don't have anything for you."

"You've already given me the greatest gift I could ever hope for," he smiled.

She opened the box. Inside was a tiny diamond-crusted charm in the shape of a key on a delicate silver chain. She took it out and he fastened it around her neck.

"Now you hold the key to my heart," he said.

"It's beautiful."

"Happy Christmas, darling." He hugged her. He would have loved to kiss her, but there was no way to tell who was watching, and they had flirted with danger once already that evening.

She wanted more than anything to tell him she loved him, but somehow it didn't seem like the right time or place. The only thing she got out was, "Have a safe trip tomorrow. Text or call me when you can."

"I will. Take care." He let go and backed away slowly, still smiling at her. Then he turned and walked toward his car. Halfway down the block he turned and looked back at her. She put her fingertips to her lips and blew him a soft kiss. He put his hand up and closed his fist as if he were catching it, then put it to his heart. He turned back and kept walking.

As she watched him walk away she whispered, "Je t'aime, mon chéri." She wiped her eyes, hoping her mascara hadn't run too much. Then she turned and went back inside, tucking the necklace safely underneath her blouse.

Gladys talked about Tony all the way back to the Plaza. Charles talked about plans and upcoming meetings for his current project. Lily didn't talk at all. She only feigned listening. She missed him already. As soon as they were upstairs, Charles excused himself and went to bed. Lily and Gladys watched the first half of *It's A Wonderful Life* before Gladys finally headed down the hall to her own suite. Lily stayed up to watch the end of the movie and fell asleep on the sofa.

23
MEET ME IN TORONTO

Two weeks after Christmas, the company headed to Toronto. Out of town tryouts were a bit of a luxury that many productions couldn't afford anymore, but then most productions didn't have C.S. George backing them.

When the curtain went down on opening night the show got a good deal of applause and whistles. It was a little long and a few of the numbers needed some tweaking, but over all, it went well. Everyone went out for dinner and drinks afterward to celebrate. When the first reviews came in, most of the news was good. They called the cast talented, the writing bright and funny, and the choreography spectacular. *The Toronto Star*, on the other hand, was less than favorable. While the rest of the cast cheered and toasted to their success, Lily sat alone at a corner table, nursing a Manhattan and pouring over the Star's summary:

The soundtrack to "Love On World Tour" is a hodge-podge of American classics, which when strung together, make for a completely disjointed plot. Writer/director Daniel Josephson proves the old adage that it's who you know in show business. His script, with its contrived story-line, unrealistic dialogue, and inadequate attempts at humor, would never have made it this far if it weren't for his familial connections to Hollywood genius C.S. George and his bank account. Josephson was also fortunate to enlist the help of his sister, Lillian (Josephson) George, whose choreography is a streak of brilliance in an otherwise mediocre show. Mr. Josephson had better not ruffle any feathers at the next family reunion. He's bound to need his brother-in-law's continued support if he ever plans to work on Broadway again.

Lily was so fixated on the last line of the article that she didn't notice Danny coming until he had pulled up a chair and sat down across from her.

"Hey, Sis. What's up?" he said.

Lily quickly folded the newspaper in half and slipped it under her purse. "Oh, hi sweetie. Hey, the news is good, right?"

"The news is wonderful for our first performance. By the time we get back to New York we're gonna be ready to knock their socks off."

"I'm so proud of you! Really I am." She reached across the table and touched his cheek. "You and Steven both. You've done such a wonderful job."

"So have you. They called your work spectacular. You did it. You didn't think you could, but you did."

"*We* did it, didn't we?"

"So what's bothering you?"

"Nothing, sweetie," she said, "I was just thinking about Charles."

"What about him?"

"Ah, well, I was wondering if he and Gladys made it back safely. I haven't heard from them yet."

"And?"

"And... I was thinking about the changes we need to make. I'm still not happy with Natalie's solo routine in act two. It needs more sparkle. There's not enough bang to be seen from the back of the house."

He watched her as she fidgeted with the key-shaped charm on her necklace. "Lil, it's me. Is that really all that's bothering you?"

She paused and exhaled. "No."

"Care to talk about it?" he asked.

"Not really," she said, staring into her drink. "But I'd bet you're going to ask me anyway."

"You do know me, don't you?"

"Yes, my darling brother, I do."

"You're also thinking about *him* again, aren't you?" he asked in a hushed tone.

She nodded. She sat back, and ran her fingers through her hair.

"Am I crazy, Danny? Am I out of my mind to risk ruining my marriage—to risk losing everything—for a man who showed up out of nowhere after twelve years?"

"That depends."

"On what?"

"On whether or not you're still in love with that man."

"If only that were all that mattered," she said, looking away. "I was so angry at Charles, you know? At first. But the past two weeks he's been so much more considerate, so attentive, so—"

"Unlike him?"

"Daniel!"

"Well!"

"So different. Like when we were first married. Do you know, on Christmas morning he actually served me breakfast in bed? And afterward, we went for a carriage ride in central park."

He wondered if she even realized how often she did it—accentuated the tiniest of bright spots, just so that things didn't seem as dark as they really were. She'd done the same thing with their father, making a fuss every time he remembered a birthday or brought home a paycheck, as if it made up for the dozens of times he didn't. "So, he ordered room service and hired someone else to drive you around," he said snidely.

"Stop it! That's big for him. He hates that kind of schmaltzy romantic stuff."

"Right. Do you suppose he was putting on a good show for his sister?"

"I don't think so. He never has before."

"What did he say when you asked him about his involvement with the Tony situation?"

"How was I going to get into it with Gladys there? God, Danny. What the hell am I gonna do?"

"Do you love him? Charles, I mean."

"I can't imagine what my life would be like right now if it weren't for him. For all I know, I might never have recovered from that accident, and look at me now. And what about our home, our work, our life? How can I just ignore all of that?"

"That wasn't a straight answer. Do you love him?"

She thought a moment, then nodded. "Yes. I do. He can be challenging, arrogant, and he's a workaholic. But he's creative and funny. He can bloody charming when he wants to be. And he's attractive."

"In an Ed Harris sort of way," Danny laughed.

Lily just looked at him.

"And Tony?" he said.

She bit her lip and avoided eye contact again.

"Lil?" Danny coaxed.

She looked back up and dabbed at her eyes with her cocktail napkin. "Tony is…" She swallowed. "He's everything I've ever wanted. But he's not my husband, is he?"

"No. But you are in love with him, aren't you?"

She glanced at him. Her eyes glistened and she was still gnawing at her lip. She wanted to deny it, but she couldn't.

"Is it that obvious?"

"Was Liberace gay?"

"Oh God! Really?"

"Yes. The sexual tension alone gives you away."

"What?"

"Come on. You practically climax just standing next to him."

"Danny!"

"Well, don't feel bad. Half the women in the company have the same reaction. For that matter, so does Steven, though I doubt that the feeling is mutual."

"Oh for God's sake!"

"Relax. I'm only joking!"

"Then it's not obvious?"

"To me yes. To the rest of them, no. You're one hell of an actress. You always make things look good on the surface. Lord knows you've had enough years of practice." Danny reached for her hand. "Look, can I offer you some advice?"

She nodded.

"This is a catch twenty-two. You can't go on forever like this and you can't make everyone happy, no matter how much you may want to. Someone is bound to get hurt in the end. Just see to it that it's not you this time. For once in your life, try doing what you *need* to do instead of what you think you *should* do."

"That's easier said than done."

"For you it is. I know." He nodded, squeezing her hand. They sat in silence for a few minutes. Then Danny spoke again. "Well, come on, then." He stood and gestured for her to stand.

"Where are we going?"

"Steven," he hollered across the room. "I'll be right back. I'm just going to walk Lily back."

Steven gave him the thumbs up and waved them off. Danny helped Lily on with her coat. She quickly scooped up her other belongings and followed him out.

"Where are we going?" She asked again.

"Back to the hotel," he said.

"I don't want to be a spoilsport sitting, in my hotel room whilst everyone else is out celebrating."

"Lil, judging by the level of celebration I just saw, you will be much better off going back to your room. You can watch TV, have a cup of tea, get some rest. Whatever you want. It'll give you time to think about what I said. Trust me. It will be just what the doctor ordered. Now let me have your phone for a minute."

"Why?"

"Just give me your phone, please." He held out his hand.

She gave it to him. He played with it while they walked.

Lily was still protesting returning to the hotel when they reached her room. "Trust me," Danny said again, giving her a look.

"Fine!" She dug out her keycard and opened the door, rolling her eyes and sticking her tongue out at him.

"Very mature of you. Would you just go inside already?"

Lily walked in and threw her purse down on the small coffee table. She took her coat off and, as she turned back around to hang it in the closet, Tony came walking out of the bedroom.

"Hello, gorgeous," he said.

"Tony!" she screamed. She dropped her coat on the floor, ran to him, and jumped into his arms, wrapping her legs around his waist and kissing him. "What on earth are you doing here?"

"I sent for him," Danny said.

"You did?"

Tony put her down.

"Well, you've been moping around since Christmas, looking like a lost puppy, for God's sake. I've seen enough broken hearts in my day to know one when I see one, so I sent for him."

"Oh, Danny! You are a gem." She hugged him. "Thank you!"

"Yeah, yeah. Now, just go do whatever it is that you… never mind," he said, waving his hands about. "Here." He handed the phone back to her. "Now, I've taken the liberty of downloading some new music for you."

"How did you get my password?"

"Lil, you use the same password for everything. I could rob you blind if I wanted to."

"What the hell is this?" she asked, looking at the album that he'd added to her playlists.

"It's Hootie and the Blowfish—*Cracked Rear View*."

"I can see that, but what would you like me to do with it?"

"Well, you're going to need something. These walls are pretty thin."

"Daniel!"

"Just try it, okay? It's time to retire AC/DC, for God's sake! Neither one of you is twenty anymore. Trust me. You'll thank me later." He winked at Tony.

"Danny, how in the world did you know that—?"

"Please. I lived with the two of you the summer before I went off to college, remember?" He cleared his throat. "Tony, she's all yours. Just try to keep a low profile, please. I don't need the rest of the group knowing that I've been playing Celestina, setting up your little clandestine meetings." He opened the door to leave. "Oh, and Lil, don't worry about the *Star*, okay?"

"What?"

"The newspaper you have stashed in your handbag. Don't worry about that review. Their theater critic used to date Steven. It ended badly. I could be Gower Fucking Champion and he'd still hate me. I'll see you in the morning." He smiled at her and walked out. "Don't be late, okay?"

She closed the door behind him and slipped her phone into her pocket, shaking her head, then turned her attention back to Tony. He'd taken off his jacket and unbuttoned the first few buttons on his shirt.

"Come here, you." He slid his arms around her waist and kissed her.

"Tony, wait." She pulled away.

"What's the matter?" he asked.

"Nothing. It's just that there's something that I've been wanting to say and if I don't say it right now I think I may burst. Either that, or lose my nerve."

"What is it, darling?"

"Tony, I love you!"

He didn't respond. He only stared at her with a very curious expression.

Puzzled by his reaction, she kept talking in an attempt to fill the uncomfortable silence. "I... I wanted to tell you before. I thought about it even on Christmas, but it just didn't seem like the right time. I haven't been able to stop thinking about you. I wanted to call you so many times while you were away, but I was afraid your family would be too quick to figure things out. Especially Gerald, since he speaks French too. Besides, it's not really the kind of thing you say on the phone or in a text the first time, is it? Well, not exactly the first time, but you know what I mean. Anyway, here you are in front of me and I can finally say it out loud. I love you."

A smile slowly crept across his face, but Lily was sure she could see tears in his eyes. "Is something wrong?" she asked him.

"Do you have any idea how long I've waited to hear you say that?"

"Yes, I think I do actually," she smiled back. "About twelve years. Do you want me to say it once more just for good measure?"

"Yes, please."

"I love you!"

He was too overwhelmed with emotion to even get the words out. "I love you too," he mouthed, going in for a kiss. They hugged each other tightly, savoring the moment. After a few moments she stepped back and raised her eyebrows, smiling flirtatiously. He smiled back and gave her a wink. She took his hand and led him into the bedroom.

"Do you remember the first time you ever said you loved me?" she asked. She sat down on the bed and began to remove her boots.

"Of course I do. April in Paris."

"We were snoggin' on that terrible couch in your little studio apartment."

"You were seventeen." He sat next to her.

"And you were all of nineteen. Such a handsome older man." She paused, smiling at him. "The things we did that summer. We were so young and it was all so romantic." She fell back onto the bed with a desirous look in her eyes. He lay next to her. His hand slipped under her sweater and skimmed across the silken skin on her abdomen.

"You were so young that most of the things we did wouldn't have even been legal in some states," he laughed. He turned onto his side and leaned over her, kissing her behind the opposite ear and making his way down her neck.

"Je t'aime, Tony," she whispered into his ear.

"Je t'aime aussi, Lily. Je t'aime de tout mon coeur."

"Je t'adore, mon chéri." She giggled, feeling a bit like love-struck teenager all over again.

Hearing her effervescent laughter made him smile all the more. "I missed you so much," he said, still slathering her neck with kisses.

"Not as much as I missed you."

"Prove it," he dared her.

She did. Twice. Complete with musical accompaniment, as suggested.

A while later she got a text from Steven.

\- **Omg... Can't sleep. Wish the people next door would quiet down. The woman is a real screamer. Lol.**

\- Jealous?

\- **A little. Did u enjoy Hootie?**

\- Thank my brother for me.

\- **:-)**

24
TWIST OF FATE

Tony stayed in Toronto for the rest of the week. Each day he entertained himself by exploring the city or working on his computer in the hotel room while Lily rehearsed with the cast. In the evenings, Lily would watch the show and then meet him at some out of the way restaurant for a late-night dinner. With Charles off in L.A., it was easy for them to ignore the fact that she was a married woman. But Friday morning came all too soon and with it the end of their romantic fantasy. Lily was awake before the sun. She lay sprawled across Tony's chest, listening to his heartbeat, moving in sync with the rise and fall of his chest. She closed her eyes and tried to make her breaths match his. She thought maybe if she concentrated hard enough on it, she could relax and rid herself of the uneasy feeling in the pit of her stomach. Tony lay awake too. He could feel the tension radiating from her body. He ran his fingertips up and down her back.

"Morning," she mumbled into his chest.

"Good morning, beautiful."

"I can't believe it's Friday already."

"Is that what's bothering you? That it's our last day together?"

"Do you really have to go back tomorrow?"

"I'm afraid so. I have a dinner meeting that I can't reschedule."

"I don't want this week to end."

"Mmm. I know," Tony sighed. "But as much as I hate to leave you and all of this behind, it will be nice to get back to New York and back to work again. I don't know if I would be very good at playing the theater widower long-term." Lily pulled away and moved back over to her own side of the bed. He couldn't see her face in the dark, but he heard her take a deep breath and blow it out forcefully.

"What's wrong," he asked.

"Nothing."

"It's not nothing. What?" he asked, turning on the lamp. She was turned away from him. "Come on now, what is it?" He moved in closer to put his arm around her, nuzzling her ear. With a groan, she turned back to face him.

"I know you'll be happy to get back to work. I don't blame you. It's just that... Once we go back, what's going to happen to us?"

"I don't know. It was nice while it lasted, but it is what it is. We do have to face reality sometime, don't we?"

"What does that mean?"

"Lily, what we've had going on here is wonderful, but it's not real."

"Isn't it? It felt real last night. And the night before that. And—"

"Our feelings are real. Yes. But this isn't real life. In real life, you're the wife of the great C.S. George. With him making a new film, there will certainly be expectations and publicity. We can't just keep carrying on, thinking that we're not going to get caught."

"So what are we going to do?"

"That's really not my call, is it? That's up to you."

"What if it were up to you?"

"It's not."

"Yes, but if it were? What *do* you want?"

"It doesn't really matter what I want. What I want—what I've always wanted—and what I can have might be two very different things."

"But if you could have whatever you wanted, what would it be?"

"Lily, this can't be my decision. It has to be yours."

"Just tell me. Please. I need to hear you say it. What do you want?"

He looked longingly into her eyes, silent for a few moments. When he finally spoke, his voice was soft and tender. "You, darling," he said, caressing her cheek. "I love you. You must know that by now. I would give anything to be able to tell that to the world. I'd love to hold your hand in public, to kiss you on a street corner without having to worry about who might see, or to walk into a room with you on my arm and smile proudly as everyone in the place realized that the most beautiful woman in the world was with me. But we don't always get what we want, do we? Sometimes we just have to make the best of it."

"I'm sorry, Tony."

"For what?"

"I haven't been fair to you. I've been so selfish through this whole thing, and it's been a lot harder on you than I anticipated. On top of that, I've tarnished your reputation by forcing you to become the *other* man."

"Oh, come on, now. I was hardly forced. I'm a big boy. I did know what I was getting into. I'd make the same choice all over again for the chance to be with you. Mind you, I do wish things could end differently. I shall miss you terribly when you leave."

"What if I don't leave?"

"Lily…"

"I'm serious. What if I don't go back with him?"

"There isn't an excuse big enough for you to stay in New York and send your husband back without you. What reason could you possibly give him?"

"You. Us."

"Are you really ready to do that?" he asked. His voice was hopeful.

"I don't know. But I know that I'm not ready to lose you. I'm not ready to risk walking away and never feeling again... the way I feel when I'm with you."

"I don't want to lose you either. Not ever again," he whispered. He wrapped her in his arms and held her close as she buried her face in his neck, unable to stop the tears. She eventually drifted off to sleep again in the security of his arms.

She woke up several hours later to the obnoxious sound of her marimba ringtone.

"Hello. What? Cora? Calm down dear. I can hardly understand you. What on earth is—dear God! No. Of course. No. Absolutely not. I'll be on the next plane. Just stay with him, okay? Please. Yes. Bye." She hung up and immediately ran to the closet. She pulled out a pair of slacks, a blouse, and her suitcase. She ran into the bathroom to dress. She came out a few minutes later fully made up with her toiletries in hand.

"Lily, what are you doing?" Tony asked. She didn't answer. "What is it? You look positively ashen. What's going on?"

"That was Cora."

"I gathered that much. What did she say?"

Lily was already zooming around the room throwing things into her suitcase. "She was calling from the hospital. Charles has been..." She stopped for a moment. She took a deep breath in and exhaled slowly, closing her eyes and pinching the corners of her eyes with her middle fingers as if trying to halt the tears in their tracks.

"What?"

"He's been shot!" Off she went again, emptying several of the drawers and stuffing their contents into her bag.

"What the hell? Is he okay?"

"I don't know yet. Cora didn't know. He's in surgery right now."

"What happened?"

"I don't know exactly. They were attacked. Mugged. I'm not sure. I didn't really stop to ask."

"Can I help you with anything?" he asked as she tore open the nightstand drawer to retrieve her phone charger and a few personal items.

"Yes. Call my brother and tell him. Please. And will you check round here when you leave to see if I've left anything? I'm sorry to run out on you, darling, but..."

"No. Of course. You have to go. Don't worry. I'll take care of things here."

"Thank you." She threw on her coat, blew him a kiss, and ran out the door pulling her rolling suitcase behind her.

* * *

Cora sent the car to pick Lily up at LAX. On the drive to the hospital, news of the shooting was already being broadcast on the radio. According to the reporters, the movie-maker turned hero had defended himself and a lady friend against a mugger and been shot in the process. There was still no news as to his condition. James, their driver, dropped Lily off in front of Cedars-Sinai Medical Center and promised to get her bags back to the house. She climbed out of the car and hurried past a group of reporters that were gathered outside.

"Hey there she is!" one of them shouted.

"Lillian! Mrs. George! Can you give us any update on your husband's condition?"

"Not at this time." She pushed his microphone out of the way with her hand. "Excuse me."

"Can you tell us who the woman is that arrived here with him today?"

"His assistant," she answered, shortly.

"She was pretty hysterical. Are you sure she isn't more than just an assistant?"

"No comment!" She pushed her way past the last one and went inside. "Ugh, the nerve of some people," she thought. Unfortunately, being married to C.S. George meant no subject was off limits and nothing was ever off the record.

She stopped at the information desk for directions to his room. She took the elevator up and hurried down the hallway, her heart pounding in her chest and her heels clacking on the polished white linoleum. When she rounded the corner and looked through the doorway, she saw Charles lying motionless the bed. His eyes were closed. He had bandages wrapped around his head and all about his right shoulder. His arm appeared to be immobilized. Cora was at his bedside holding his hand and crying. Lily cleared her throat and entered the room.

Cora dropped his hand and jumped up when she heard Lily.

"Oh, Lily. I'm sorry, I didn't realize... Thank goodness you made it," Cora said, grabbing a couple of tissues from the box on the bedside table and patting her eyes dry.

"How is he?" Lily asked, going to his bedside and taking his hand.

"The doctor said he came through surgery just fine. They were able to remove the bullet without any trouble."

"Where was he shot?"

"We had just arrived at the studio. We were walking in and..."

"No, I mean where on his body?"

"Oh, gosh. Sorry. I'm not thinking. In the upper right quadrant of his chest, closer to his shoulder."

"Thank God. When you called I thought..." Lily stopped. Cora handed her the box of tissues. Lily took one and dried her eyes too. "Thank God it wasn't any worse. Has he been conscious?"

"Not yet. I think it's just the anesthesia. He did hit his head when he fell. He has some stitches, but they said there was no severe damage. At least they don't anticipate any, but they're keeping an eye on him and will be able to give a better prognosis when he wakes up."

"How long will that be?"

"I'm not sure. I'm sorry I frightened you," Cora said. "I couldn't tell under all the blood what actually happened and he fell down several steps and he wasn't moving and…" She started to cry again.

"It's understandable that you were shaken up," Lily said, without taking her eyes off of Charles. Seeing him lying there was difficult. "I should have been here," she said.

"Don't be silly. You were at out-of-town tryouts with a Broadway show. That's big stuff. Anyway, there wouldn't have been anything you could have done."

"I should have been here," Lily repeated, her voice trembling. "I should have been the one holding his hand. Not…." She swallowed the word "*you*". "God, what if he doesn't wake up?"

"Lillian, don't say that."

"Do we know for sure that there isn't some kind of serious head trauma?"

"Why don't I go get a doctor for you?"

"Thank you," Lily said.

Cora nodded. Lily caught a glimpse of her as she turned to leave the room. She looked tired. Small, compared to her usual quiet, but poised self. She walked without ever lifting her eyes off of the floor. Seeing her that way, Lily actually felt sorry for her.

"Cora," Lily called after her, "what about you? Are you okay?"

"I'll be fine."

Cora left the room and Lily sat next to Charles. She put his hand to her cheek.

What she had really wanted to say to Cora was, "I understand how frightened you must have been. Not only were you attacked, but you saw the man that you are obviously in love with shot. I know how worried you must be, because I would be too, if the tables were turned." She felt no need to explain that, however. Nor did she wish to explain that the real reason for her guilt had nothing to do with the show and everything to do with the fact that she'd been carrying on in a hotel room with her childhood sweetheart. To think that, in what could have been her husband's last moments, she'd been in bed with another man thinking about leaving him. She'd often told Charles that God sent signs if you listened hard enough. One didn't even have to listen that closely to hear this one. This was his way of saying that now was not the time to leave Charles, if ever. Not only that, she couldn't help but feel like the whole thing was a payback and Charles was paying the price for her indiscretions.

Cora came back with one of the doctors, a Dr. Lansing, who looked like he'd just finished his residency last week. He explained that they had done a head CT scan and there didn't seem to be any real damage to the brain from the fall. Although, he had broken his right hip. They had already repaired that damage as well, putting in a plate and screw. He had only lost consciousness for a brief period of time. He was actually awake when he went into surgery and right now it was more likely that he was out from the anesthesia rather than due to head trauma, just as Cora had suggested.

Dr. Lansing said that Charles would probably be hospitalized for at least two weeks, and after that he would need rehab and time to heal. He said that for a healthy male of twenty-five it could take as little as three months for the arm to heal completely, but for a man Charles's age, it would be upwards of six months. In addition, the rehab for a hip injury like his could go on for as much as a year. He said he would check back a little later. Lily thanked him and asked him if he wouldn't mind coming outside with her to make a statement to the press. She hated to do it, but she found it was usually better to give journalists a straight answer and get them out of your hair than to leave them alone to invent their own versions of the truth.

She coached the young doctor on the way out to be sure that he didn't say any more than necessary or get stuck answering excessive questions. "Be brief and vague. Tell them that the bullet was removed successfully and tell them he'll be fine in six months."

"But what if takes more than six months?" he asked.

Lily couldn't help but chuckle at him. "Are you new to the area, doctor?"

"I just moved here from Wisconsin. My girlfriend got a job out here."

"I see. Well, you get used to it," Lily smiled. "If you're worried about it, tell them that, by this time next year, he'll be as good as new. That way you're covered. But, that's it. Nothing more. If they ask anything else, just respond with 'no further comment,' okay?"

The doctor gave a weak nod.

They exited the hospital and were spotted within about ten seconds. The doctor did as he was instructed, but looked stunned when they continued to bombard him with questions. Lily stepped in. "All right, that'll be all. Thank you. No further comments." She put her hand on Dr. Lansing's back and directed him back inside while the reporters clamored behind them.

"How does this affect production of his upcoming film?" they went on.

"That will be all, thank you," she restated firmly. She followed the doctor inside.

On her way back to the room she stopped for two cups of coffee and took one up to Cora, who was still keeping vigil. They sat together and drank the coffee.

Neither of them spoke until Lily finally suggested that Cora go home. Cora was reluctant, but Lily insisted that a shower and a rest would do her good. She promised to update her if there was any change in Charles's condition and sent her on her way.

Once Cora was gone and Lily was alone with her thoughts again, she spent hours reflecting on her life with Charles. Surprisingly, she was no longer as concerned as she had been about whether or not he was Mr. Romance, or the fact that most days he was more married to his career than he was to her. She didn't care if he remembered what kind of shampoo she used or what her favorite flower was. At that moment, she didn't even care to know the truth about Cora or what happened with Tony. The only thing she wanted was for him to wake up so that she would know he was really okay.

She focused on the wonderful memories they'd made over the years, the work that they'd done together, and the occasions they'd celebrated, in public and in private. She thought about the trips they'd taken, like their weekend getaways to the cabin in Montana, where they tuned out the rest of the world and drank wine while gazing up at the stars; they were the brightest stars she'd ever seen. She remembered the countless hours that he'd spent with her in hospitals and rehab and the days he'd spent researching experimental treatments following her accident. *His* arms lifted her out of the chair the first time she tried to stand. *His* arm held her up during her first public appearance after learning to walk again. Now he needed her to be there for him. She couldn't possibly think about leaving him, of turning her back on him when he needed her most. She sat next to his bed and prayed. She prayed harder than she had in years, for his recovery, for forgiveness, and for strength. Strength for both of them to get through whatever challenges lie ahead. After a while, she folded her arms on the edge of the bed and put her head down on top of them to rest her eyes. Worn out from the emotional events of the day, she fell asleep.

She woke up when she felt something very gently touch her face. She looked up, blinking her eyes to focus. He smiled at her.

"Oh, thank God!" she said. She stood up and leaned over him, plastering his cheeks with kisses and ending with one on the lips.

"Hey now, take it easy on me, will ya?" He chuckled weakly.

"Sorry. I'm just so relieved."

"You and me both."

"Are you okay?"

"You tell me."

"The doctors say you're going to be just fine."

"I can't seem to move my arm."

"I know. They've immobilized it to give it a little time to heal."

"How long will that take?"

"Six months or so. For it to heal completely, anyway."

"Six months?"

"For the arm, yes. The hip is another story."

"What?" He was still groggy.

"You managed to break your hip when you fell."

"Oh, God. A broken hip? Lillian, you're married to an old man," he grumbled.

"Oh, stop. You could do with some calcium and a few more vegetables though."

"Yes, Mom!" he teased her. She knew it drove him crazy when she criticized his dietary choices.

Charles continued to fret. "So how long until the hip is working again?"

"They'll probably have you up on it tomorrow, but for a full recovery, a year."

"What about the film?"

"No worries. We'll sort it out and you'll be good as new."

"I can't wait six months to a year!"

"Don't worry, darling. We've only got to get you back into the director's chair for goodness sake. There'll be a slight delay, but we'll manage. You'll see. I'm just so glad you're okay."

"It's dark out. How long have I been out?"

She looked at the clock. "Only about twelve hours."

"But you're here."

"Of course I'm here. I came home as soon as Cora called."

"I'm glad you're here."

"Where else would I be? You scared us half to death, you know?"

"Who?"

"Cora and me."

"Cora? Is she okay?"

"She's fine."

"Are you sure?"

"Yes, darling. She's shaken up, but she's fine. According to the reporters, you saved her. They're not calling you old. They're calling you a hero. How about that?"

"The reporters?"

"Yes, darling. You are still high-profile enough for crews to follow you to the hospital."

"Damn. Did they bother you?"

"Don't you worry about me. I can take care of myself. Dr. Lansing and I already gave them a statement. I'm fairly certain we got rid of them, at least for now."

"Good girl."

"Listen, I'm going to go get the doctors to check you out now that you're awake."

"Okay, but don't go too far."

"I won't." She smiled. "Be right back." She went to the nurse's station to tell them that he was awake, and the team went rushing in. There was barely space for her in the room, so she took the opportunity to go downstairs and check her messages. She clicked the power button on her phone and waited.

By the time the elevator reached the first floor her phone was dinging with messages. The first thing she did was send a message to Cora to let her know that Charles was awake and doing fine. Then she checked her voicemail. She had a message from Nina, one from Danny, and one from Tony. Leaning on the empty reception desk, she listened to the first two.

She was hesitant to listen to Tony's message. She didn't even know if she could handle hearing his voice at the moment. She played it anyway. His tone was calm and tender. His attempt to sound up-beat was fairly convincing, but Lily could hear the touch of sadness.

"Hello, love. I hope you are holding up okay and that Charles is doing okay. I'm leaving now. On my way to the airport. I have your nightgown. You left it hanging in the bathroom. Seems like you have a habit of losing your pajamas on foreign soil." He let out a small chuckle. "Otherwise I think you got everything. I'm sure you're going to need some time to sort everything out. So... Call me when you're ready. I can drop the nightgown off or you can pick it up. Whichever. I'll talk to you later. I... I love you. Bye."

Hearing his voice brought a dull ache to her chest. She remembered that feeling. It was heartbreak, plain and simple, the worst feeling in the world. She put her hand to her chest, expecting the find Tony's key, but felt nothing. She clutched at her blouse, still searching, then let her hand drop. The necklace was gone. She suddenly felt weak, almost physically ill. She had to sit down in one of the chairs near the elevator to keep from falling over. She sat there for a few minutes staring blankly, feeling empty and despondent, but she knew she couldn't afford to let grief get the better of her. She would have to push it out of the way and move on. No matter how much she loved Tony, no matter how much she wanted to be with him, it was Charles who needed her now. She had to focus her energy on him. She deleted the message, turned the phone off again, and went into the ladies room. Fortunately, due to the late hour, no one else was in there. She had a good cry, pulled herself together, and headed back upstairs.

The doctors had just about finished with Charles by the time she returned. They gave him a very good report. There was no evidence of head injury other than a whopper of a headache. They would keep an eye on the bullet wound and incisions from the surgery to be sure he didn't develop any infection. Otherwise, with time and therapy, he was expected to make a full recovery.

After dismissing the doctors, Charles informed Lily that it was time for her to go home and get some sleep. She urged him to let her stay, but he claimed he was tired too, so she kissed him goodbye and promised to be back early in the morning. By the time she climbed into bed, it was almost midnight. She thought she might have trouble sleeping, but she had no trouble at all.

25
SECOND CHANCES

Lily and Cora visited Charles in the hospital every day for the next week. Sometimes they went together, and sometimes they took turns. Cora handled as many of Charles's business affairs as she could. After a day or two he was back to making phone calls and sending messages, but since he couldn't write or type very quickly on his own Cora was forced to take a lot of dictations. In between texting, talking, and emailing with Danny and Nina and watching bits of the show on Skype, Lily helped too, just to give the poor girl a break. Charles was chomping at the bit to get out of there. He hated being cooped up, and he'd already had to delay taping final scenes of his movie, which made him increasingly cross with every passing day. Lily was getting nervous just thinking about him in therapy. He was very busy, very stubborn, and not very likely to be a good patient. She was already preparing herself for the challenge.

On Thursday morning, Lily broke the news to Charles that she would be gone for the next two days. She planned to fly to New York to tie up loose ends and see the opening night performance of the show.

"You're going to New York?" he asked.

"Yes, but just for a couple of days. They're going to run the show one more time for me tomorrow night to see that everything is ready for opening night on Saturday. Then I'll collect my things from the Plaza and be back on Sunday."

"But then you're staying?"

"No," she laughed. "I just told you I'll be back on Sunday. Did you double up on your pain medication again?"

"No. I mean are you staying here."

"Of course."

"How long?"

"How long what?"

"How long will you stay with me? Before you go back to him?"

"To whom?" she asked, catching her bottom lip in her teeth.

"Lillian, don't play dumb. You know who I mean. I've seen the way you look at him when you don't think I'm watching."

"How long have you known?" she asked quietly.

"Hell, I've known it for years."

She frowned and shook her head quizzically. He went on.

"You don't think I've forgotten, do you? That the first name you spoke when you came out of the coma was his, not mine?"

"I ah… I don't know what to say."

"Okay. Well, then let me talk, huh?"

She nodded, still biting her lip.

"Come here. Sit down."

She went to his bed and sat on the edge, afraid to make eye contact.

He put his hand on her hand. "You still have a thing for him, don't you?"

She took a deep breath, blew it out slowly, and nodded.

"Did you sleep with him?"

She nodded again.

"I thought so," he nodded, his lips forming a tight line. "Well, on the bright side, at least you didn't get caught. By the paparazzi, I mean." After a minute he spoke again. "Were you ever going to tell me?"

"I could ask you the same thing, couldn't I?" She stood up and began pacing.

"Tell you what? That I cheated on you?"

"No. That everything we are… everything we had… was based on a lie… a trick. You led him to believe that I didn't want him anymore. You let me think for twelve years that he'd just stopped loving me. I don't blame you entirely. He and I should have talked about it. We should have reasoned things out. But you knew. You knew! You swept in on your white horse and picked me up as if you were the hero, and all while… How could you do that to me?"

"Do you really want the truth?"

"I think I'm entitled, don't you?"

"I wanted you." He shook his head and stared at her.

"Would you care to elaborate?"

"I was used to throwing my money and influence around and getting any woman I wanted. But you—you were different. I threw my money and influence around and you didn't even bat an eye. I was intrigued by the fact that I couldn't get your attention and I was jealous of him because he had you. You became a challenge. I didn't set out to break you up. Not really anyway. I just wanted to create enough of a rift between the two of you to make an opening for me. I wasn't looking to get married. Just…"

"Oh God! Just sleep with me? Was that it? Have an affair with me? Just another notch on your bedpost?"

He shrugged and looked at her apologetically, avoiding the question. "Well, it didn't turn out quite like I planned, did it? Somewhere along the line I fell for you harder than I'd ever fallen for anyone in my life. I cared for you. I loved you. In a way that I'd never loved anyone else. And he gave up way too easily. Then, there you were, alone, depressed, broken. And I had caused it. I decided it was time for me to step up and try to become the man that you needed me to be. So I did. At least I tried. What we became grew out of that."

Lily sat in the chair across the room, staring at him, shocked by his candor.

He adjusted his position in bed and started in again. "Look, Lillian, what I did was wrong. I know that. And it certainly wasn't the only thing I've done wrong over the years. But I'd like to try to get it right from this point on."

Lily shook her head, still trying to digest everything that he was saying. "I've never seen you like this."

"Like what?"

"So calm. About something so huge. Aren't you... angry?"

"I was. Hell, I was pissed."

"But you're not now?"

"Well, that's the funny thing about almost dying, or at least thinking you might die. It changes your perspective. See, I don't know what happened exactly. I don't know if I was unconscious or... semi-conscious. I don't know. Doesn't matter. Whatever state I was in, there was blood everywhere. A searing pain was ripping through my shoulder. My head was throbbing. Cora was screaming. Then there were sirens and doctors or EMTs talking. Who knows? Everything was crazy. I didn't know if I was going to make it. You know how they say that your entire life flashes before your eyes?"

She nodded, her eyes getting moist.

"Well, mine didn't. In that moment, however long it was—felt like time was standing still—in that moment, nothing in my life mattered. Not my friends, not my career. Nothing. Except you. The only thing I could think of was that I wanted to see your face one more time."

"Charles…" she interrupted, tears sitting on her cheeks.

"Lil," he ignored her interruption, "you are the best thing that ever happened to me. You have given me so much over the years, most of which I probably didn't deserve. You brought joy into my life that I'd never known before and you put up with my damned old Iowa stubbornness. I couldn't have asked for a more perfect wife. You were always my greatest asset in terms of public relations, a great networker, the perfect hostess, and the cameras absolutely love you. Of course, what's not to love? You're sweet, funny, incredibly charming, and smart, with a gorgeous smile and a kick-ass body. Marrying you was the best decision I ever made, and I'm damn lucky that you've put up with me for as long as you have. I swore to myself that if you were still with me when it was over that I would put him and all of the other bullshit in the past and try to move on, try to have a future with you. We've had our share of problems, Lil, but I want to start over. I want to make this work. I want to make us work. I don't want to lose you. I know that's not the most romantic declaration. I'm not a hearts and flowers kind of guy, but—"

"No. That was pretty good," she said, wiping her eyes.

"So? What do you say? Can we try to start fresh?"

"Can you live with the fact that I had an affair?" she said.

"Let's not pretend that I'm innocent in that department. I think we both know I'm not."

"If I didn't know it before I figured it out when every visitor you've had since you've been in here was a woman. And Cora. Good Lord. She was practically in hysterics."

"Listen, about Cora—I want to make one thing very clear. I know you've joked about us before, but I swear there has never been anything between us and there never will be. It's just not an option. Even if it were, she cares far too much for you to do that. She's not that kind of woman."

"But there were others?"

"I can't deny that. I can't change it. Not the past, anyway. I can't take it back any more than you can. But I don't want to be that guy anymore—the self-centered Hollywood playboy who's more concerned with his career and his public image than he is with the way he treats the people in his life, especially those he's supposed to love the most."

He watched her, searching for a sign that she believed him—a sign that she believed his declarations. She said nothing, but stood and began to pace again, arms folded around herself, brow wrinkled in a contemplative expression.

He spoke again. "What about you? Can you live with what I've done? You must have been angry too, weren't you?

"I was!" she said, whipping around to face him. "I was angry. I was hurt. I was confused. I thought about leaving you, but…"

"You did?"

"Yes."

"What changed your mind?"

"The moment Cora called and said that you'd been shot, everything changed. Somehow, none of it mattered anymore. All I could think about was the last twelve years of history, and memories, and living, and loving. You needed me. I couldn't just walk away."

"Is that the only reason?"

"No."

"Can I ask you something?"

She nodded.

"Do you still love me?"

"Of course I do."

"Good. 'Cause I love you. I know I never said it enough. It's not really in my nature, but I can learn."

"I'm so sorry, Charles."

"Don't, Lil. Not after all the shit I've put you through."

"I never meant to hurt you."

"We hurt each other. But that doesn't have to matter now. It's in the past. I want to look at the future. I want to make things better. If you'll have me. I want to start over. I want you to come home. And not just because you feel obligated to take care of me, but because you think our marriage deserves another chance. What do you say, Lil? Are you with me?"

26
NOT IN THE CARDS

"Hi," Tony said, smiling when he saw her. "Come in."

"Thanks." Lily walked in and stood anxiously in the entryway.

He leaned in to kiss her. She turned her head so he ended up kissing her cheek. It was not the reaction he'd been hoping for. It gave him a very bad feeling about the impending conversation. Trying to remain positive, he asked, "Can I take your coat?" She took it off and handed it to him. "Your hair looks nice."

"Thank you. I had it done this morning. Opening night, you know."

"Do you want a drink? I have a nice Chardonnay that I picked up at—"

"No," she cut him off. "I can't stay long. Can we sit?"

"Sure," he said. They sat down on opposite ends of the sofa, facing one another. Lily shifted nervously and avoided eye contact. "What's wrong, love?"

She didn't answer.

"Is everything okay with Charles?" he asked.

"Yes, thank you for asking. He's doing quite well, all things considered. They're going to release him next week."

"That's good."

"Yes. He'll be thrilled. So will the nurses," she laughed. "He's not a very good patient I'm afraid."

"So, the news is good. Why so glum?" he asked, even though he was afraid he already knew the answer.

She looked up at him and tears filled her eyes. She hadn't meant to cry, but she couldn't help it. "I'm flying home tomorrow."

"Back to California?" he asked.

She nodded.

"I see." He got up and poured himself a double of scotch. "You didn't tell him then?" He took a drink.

"I didn't have to," she said through her tears. "He already knew."

"So what now?"

"I'm so sorry, Tony. I just can't. After everything he did for me, everything we've been through, I just can't leave him. Especially not now."

"I see."

Tony didn't look at her. He held his position at the bar, downing the glass of scotch and pouring another. She walked up behind him and spoke softly. "Say something, please."

"What do you want me to say? What else is there to say?"

"What are you thinking?"

"Honestly?"

"Of course."

"What about us? What about all that we've been through? What about everything he put us through?"

"We've talked about everything. He's explained everything and apologized for it. We both have," she said.

"Can I ask you one question?"

"Anything."

"When you said you loved me, did you mean it? Or was it just something you thought you should say in the heat of the moment?"

"Darling, please don't think that. Of course I meant it. I do love you. My God. I love you so much. But... I love him too. And he needs me."

"I need you."

"Tony—"

"Tell me, Lily, if I begged you not to go—if I pleaded with you—would it do any good?

She pressed her lips together and shook her head.

"No. I thought not," he said, shaking his head too.

"Tony, please. This isn't an easy decision for me. Finding you again, only to have it end like this…" She choked back tears. "It makes me sick. But I can't just turn my back on my marriage."

"Especially not for some flash-in-the-pan that didn't mean anything."

"Stop it! You know better than that. I would never have been with you if it didn't mean anything. What do think? That I just wanted to sleep with you?"

"Maybe."

"You're angry. You have a right to be. But you know better. I'm sorry Tony. But no matter how much you mean to me, he's my husband. I stood before God and made a promise to him. For better or for worse. I broke that promise, but he's forgiven me for it and he wants to start over. I owe it to him and to myself to try and make our marriage work. I don't expect you to understand."

"I do understand it."

"You do?"

"Of course I do. I know you. You're honoring your commitment to him. You're doing exactly what you think a *good* wife is supposed to do, aren't you? It's what you've always done. Your duty. First to your father, then to your brother, now to him. Never mind your own needs. No matter what happens. Keep calm and carry on."

"That's not fair! It's not the same thing."

"Isn't it?" He caught a glimpse of the tortured look on her face and hated himself for causing it. He took another healthy swig of the scotch and set the glass down. After taking a moment to gather his composure, he spoke again. "I'm sorry, darling." He pulled her to him. "I just want you to be happy. That's all. And after our week in Toronto I thought…" He couldn't let himself finish the thought. Saying it out loud only made it more painful. He let go of her and stepped back. Then he took her hands in his and looked in to her eyes. "It makes no difference now. I promised I would help you figure things out. And now you have. So, if this is what you really want—if he's the one you choose—then, I have to respect that. I don't have to like it." He let a tiny hint of laughter escape, trying to make light. "I have to let you go." He paused, swallowing the rest of his emotions. "No matter how much I'm going to miss you."

"I'll miss you too," she said as she pulled away. "But you know, with Danny and Steven starting a family, I'm sure I'll be coming to New York more often. Perhaps we could see each other once in a while. We could have dinner or drinks."

"Do you really think your husband would tolerate that? Besides, every time we have drinks you either end up in my bed or in my clothes or some damn thing." He forced a laugh. He walked over to the window, looking away to hide his tears from her."

"Can I call you at least?" she asked. "Maybe we could just talk. You know? Like we used to?"

"No. I don't think that would be such a good idea."

"Why not?"

"Because I'll never move on, Lil. Just the sound of your voice stirs things in me that I can't explain. I don't think I can put myself through that. Thinking of you and how much I want to be with you, knowing that I can't have you, it's too much. It'll only make it more difficult. For both of us." He turned to face her again.

She nodded. She didn't like his answer, but she knew he was right. She swallowed hard before speaking again. "Well, I guess I should go, then." She stopped near the door and picked up her coat. "I never wanted to hurt you, Tony. Not then. Not ever."

He took her coat and helped her on with it. "At least this time we finally have the chance to say goodbye," he said, as much to console himself as to comfort her.

"I don't want to say goodbye," Lily said, shaking her head, her eyes still filled with tears.

"I don't think we have much choice at this point. But it was nice while it lasted, wasn't it?"

"Yes it was." She smiled ruefully.

"Just a minute." He walked into the bedroom and came back with the bag of things that she'd left there during their romantic weekend. "Your nightgown is in here as well," he said. He set the bag down. "You also forgot this." He held up the small silver key necklace.

"Oh!" She smiled. "I thought I'd lost it." She stared at it for a moment and then looked at him. "Maybe you should keep it," she said sadly.

"I can't."

"Why not?"

"Because my heart still belongs to you. It always has."

She took the necklace and slipped it into her pocket. "Oh, Tony," she said, falling into his embrace. "I hate leaving you like this."

He said nothing, but hugged her tightly. His eyes closed, he breathed in her perfume, savoring the moment, knowing it might be the last time he would ever hold her. He would have held her forever, but after a minute or so she pulled away.

"So this is it, then?" she asked.

"I guess so."

She looked at him and tried to muster a small smile. She reached out and touched his cheek.

"I am so sorry," she said.

He took her hand from his cheek and kissed it. "We both knew it might end like this," he said softly. "But as much as it hurts, being with you again—even for a little while—it was worth it."

"No regrets?" she asked.

"None."

She looked down. He could see her fighting tears again. He traced her jawline with the backs of his fingers and stopped at her chin, tilting her face back up toward him. They stood in silence for a moment, looking into each other's eyes intently.

"I want you to make me a promise," he finally said.

"What kind of promise?"

"Be happy, Lily. Never forget that you are a bright, talented, strong woman. Believe in yourself. Be proud of who you are. And never settle for less than you deserve."

She nodded and gave him one last brave smile.

"I do have one more request before you go, " he added.

"What's that?" Lily asked.

"Can I kiss you goodbye?"

"Of course," she whispered.

He leaned in and gave her one last slow, gentle kiss. Then he smiled and quietly said, "Goodbye, my love." "Goodbye," she mouthed back, unable to say it aloud. She picked up her bag and walked out.

The cab was waiting for her outside. She held it together until she got back to the hotel. Once she made it to her suite, she tossed her things on the floor inside the door and ran to the bedroom, collapsing on the bed. She cried for hours until she could cry no more.

Finally, devoid of any more emotion, she dragged herself off of the bed and staggered to the butler's pantry. She cracked open the bottle of Bowmore she'd bought for Tony and poured. She swirled it around in the glass and inhaled. The strong smell of it made her wrinkle her nose, but she took a deep breath and threw back the shot of liquid courage. She shot a second pour, hoping it would numb the pain. Then she went in to shower and put on her game face for Danny's and Steven's opening night.

27
SETTLED

In the weeks following the opening, the positive reviews came pouring in. They were getting great publicity and playing to a packed house night after night. Danny and Steven were thrilled. Lily was thrilled for them. Charles was pleasantly surprised that his investment was beginning to pay off after all. He was also pleased to be editing the movie that he was beginning to think he would never finish. It had been a bear of a project, what with his time off for therapy and other interruptions. He was thankful for Cora's help, and Lily, despite his worries, had been right there by his side the entire time. She was a wife, a second assistant, a nurse, and a friend. She even planned a dinner party to celebrate the day the film was picture-locked and invited several of the stars as well as the producers, Jones and Gibson. Diane, Charles's agent and spokesperson, was also there, dressed to the nines and coated in a thick layer of expensive perfume.

During dinner the conversation turned to upcoming projects. Each of the guests took turns trumpeting their sure-to-be summer successes. Finally, one of the more matronly actresses turned to Lily and put a freshly manicured hand on hers. "So, Lillian," she asked in a rather lofty voice, "what about you? Any new charity events on the horizon?"

"No. Not at the moment. I've had a few other things to deal with," she smiled.

"Well, if you don't come up with anything else, I for one would support a career in party planning," a younger cast mate added.

"Or as a personal chef," Jones said. "This leg of lamb is incredible."

"Thank you, Greg."

"And if that doesn't work out she could be your spokesperson, Gibson," Diane added. "She was a great help during the whole shooting incident. Charles, I told you the best thing you could do was to marry her. And you were skeptical."

Lily just smiled, absorbing all of their comments. "Well, it's good to know I have other options if the whole choreographer thing doesn't work out," she added when they'd finished. "Would you all excuse me please? I think I'll go and see about dessert." She stood and picked up her plate. "Are you finished, darling?" she asked Charles, motioning toward his plate.

"Leave it, hon. Rosa can get them."

"It's no trouble."

He glanced around the table and gave her a look that reminded her, "*My* wife doesn't need to be seen clearing dishes."

"Right. I'll just go see if Rosa is ready to serve the cake," she said, lowering her eyes. She smiled politely and left the plates.

"I'll come with you," Cora said, pushing out her chair. "Are you okay?" she asked as she followed Lily into the kitchen.

"Fine."

"Lil?"

"Why wouldn't I be? Rosa, Mr. George would like for you to clear the dinner dishes now, please."

"Sí, claro señora Lillian."

"Gracias, Rosa."

"Lil, don't let that bunch get to you," Cora said.

"Why would they get to me? They were so complimentary of my talents. You know, you'd think that one of them, mainly my husband, might have acknowledged that I do have an actual career."

"I'm sure they didn't mean it that way. None of them has ever worked with you in a professional capacity. They're just commenting on what they've seen. And you know how he is. He's just playing nice with them. He can't piss off the producers before the final cut is finished."

Lily was quiet for a moment. "You're probably right."

Rosa brought in a pile of dishes and picked up the coffee service tray, then left as quietly as she'd entered.

"Why don't you go on back in for coffee," Lily suggested. "I'll be there in a minute."

"Are you sure?"

"Yes. Thanks, sweetie." Cora turned to leave. "Ah, Cora… One question before you go. That perfume Diane is wearing—it's nice. I recognize the scent, but I don't know what it is. Do you know?"

"It's The One by Dolce and Gabbana," Cora said hesitantly.

"I thought you'd know. When I complimented her on it earlier she said that Charles had given it to her for her birthday."

"Yes. He did."

"When is her birthday?"

"October twenty-eighth."

"That's the same day as yours."

"Yes," Cora nodded. She watched Lily's face. She could see the wheels turning as Lily put the pieces together.

"I thought it smelled too rich to be a stripper's."

"What?"

"Nevermind. Do you think he's still involved with her?" Lily asked.

"No." Cora smiled slightly. "I think he's figured out that there is only one Lillian George and she's worth sacrificing the rest."

Lily smiled too, wanting to believe that Cora was right. "Well, we'd better get back in there before the coffee gets cold, hadn't we?"

Cake gave way to celebratory drinks and then talks of marketing and publicity. They finally said their good-byes two hours later.

Lily and Charles sat down on the sofa in the den and sighed, both worn out and happy to be alone. After a few minutes he turned to her and said, "It was a nice dinner."

"I'm glad you enjoyed it."

"You and Cora did a great job putting things together. The lamb was good. A little too much garlic maybe, but good."

"I thought you liked that recipe."

"I do. It was just more garlic than usual."

"Oh."

"It was still good."

"Thank you."

"And... you ah... you look... really pretty tonight."

"Thank you," she said again. She appreciated the compliment, even though it did sound a bit forced.

He smiled at her, gave her knee a gentle squeeze, and leaned in to kiss her. She nearly laughed.

"What?" he asked.

"It's nothing. It just feels..." she didn't know how to finish that statement. Odd? Awkward? It felt almost like kissing a stranger.

"I know. It's been a long time, right?"

"Yes. I guess it has."

"Maybe I should try it again." He chuckled.

"Okay." She smiled.

He did. "How was that?"

She laughed. "Better."

"Good. Maybe we just need to keep working at it. What do you say? Do you want to go upstairs?"

"Oh. Really? Aren't you tired?"

"A little, but nothing I can't handle."

"Are you sure you're strong enough?"

"I had my checkup today. I have a ways to go for a full recovery, but the doctor said I could resume regular… activity. As long as I don't overdo it."

"You don't want to rush it. I mean with a hip…"

"Lil, I've been in therapy for eight weeks."

She looked skeptical.

"Come on. We'll never know until we try, right? So?"

"Ah… okay," she said with a half-smile. "Can you give me a minute?"

"Sure. Go ahead. I'll see you up there."

* * *

When she came out of the master bath in her silk nightgown, he was sitting on the edge of the bed waiting for her. She sat down next to him. He kissed her on the neck as he fussed with the shoulder strap on her gown. She shivered.

"Are you cold?"

"No. I… I'm fine."

He continued. She fumbled with the buttons on his shirt, working to remove it as he slowly eased his hand up her thigh. He felt her tense.

"What's wrong?"

"Nothing."

He kissed her again. She broke free and stood up.

"Charles, we can't do this."

"Sure we can. I'll be fine. As long as you're gentle with me," he joked.

"No. We need to talk."

28
DÉJÀ VU

Lily looked at her watch. Only ten minutes until take-off. She checked her messages one more time. Nothing new. She hit the flower icon on her phone and thumbed through her pictures. Stopping on one of them, she gently caressed the image with her index finger and smiled.

"Ladies and gentlemen, please turn off all electronics in preparation for take-off," the voice came over the intercom.

Lily sighed. Before turning the phone off, she sent one quick text.

- **Be home soon. Love you.**

She put the phone away and buckled her seatbelt. She leaned back on the headrest, ignoring the flight attendant, who was squawking instructions.

"Welcome back to the world of commercial flights," she thought. She closed her eyes and lost herself in thoughts of the craziness to come. To think that six months earlier she'd made the same journey practically against her will. Now she was headed back to New York by choice, and she was looking forward to it.

* * *

Danny was waiting for her at the gate.

"How was your flight?"

"As good as might be expected."

"Good. Here, I'll take that," he said, grabbing her carry-on suitcase. "Is this all you brought?" he asked.

"Well, I was in a bit of a hurry, wasn't I? I spoke with Cora. She's promised to send the rest in a day or two."

"I cannot begin to thank you. You have no idea!"

"Do me a favor, hmm? Don't thank me just yet. Wait until after the performance."

"You're not worried are you?" he asked. She just looked at him. "Are you worried? Shit, Lil."

"Relax. I'm not worried. Are you?"

"I wasn't, but are you sure you can do this? I mean you have less than five hours to learn the steps. And the dialog. Shit!"

"Danny, I don't have to learn the steps. I wrote the steps. As for the lines, she doesn't have that many and I've heard it run a thousand times. Did you find me a clean copy of the script?"

"Yes."

"Have you talked to Brian?"

"Yes. He's meeting us at the theater in an hour."

"Okay. So he and I can go through the solos and run lines. Thank God she doesn't sing outside of the chorus. And what about Nina?"

"Still not well. She said she'd try to come, but I wouldn't hold my breath. She sounded terrible."

"Poor dear. Tell her to stay in bed. I'd love to have her input, but I can do without. I don't think it's wise to try and pull a full rehearsal right now. We don't want the entire cast worn out. They already had a double yesterday. I think I can fake it well enough to please a Thursday night crowd," she joked. "After that we should be ready for the weekend no problem."

"How long can you stay?"

"As long as you need me."

"I'm hoping this flu epidemic doesn't last much longer. Then we can get some of our regulars back in here, and someone can relieve you after a few days."

"Well, Gretchen's bound to be out for a while with her broken leg. How did she do it anyway?"

"She slipped on the ice after the second show. Broke it in two places."

"Jesus! Well, if you need me to stay longer—or forever."

"Ha! Right. I'll keep that in mind."

"No. Seriously."

"What are you saying?"

"Let's just say we have a lot to talk about. But right now I have too much work to do, so let's save it, okay?"

"Are you okay?"

"Actually yes. I really am."

"What happened?"

"Danny, later. Please."

"Okay. Sorry. Anyway, I think I'm going to be quite busy too."

"Doing what?"

"Selling out this weekend's performances. Haven't you heard? Tonight Lily Josephson takes the stage for the first time over seven years. It's going to be quite the comeback!"

29
HOME AGAIN

Lily stood, dressed once again in her street clothes, admiring the quiet set. She'd done it. She'd performed in a live show and survived. One might even say she'd done very well. It felt wonderful. The sights and sounds were more exhilarating than she'd remembered: the music filling the house, the rumble of the live orchestra beneath her feet, the applause and the thrill of the final curtain call. She smiled, pleased with herself, and strolled across the empty stage. She paused once more near the stairs that led off stage, running her hand down the red velvet curtain. It was almost too good to be true.

"You looked beautiful up there," a voice said from out in the dimmed house. She turned and looked out.

"Tony?" She walked down the steps and slowly out to meet him, not wanting to seem overly anxious. "You saw it?"

"I did."

"All of it?"

"Every minute."

"I'm so glad. I was so busy today that I didn't even have a chance to call you. Danny said he had, but I didn't know if you'd come after the way we left things."

"Well, it's not every day that Lily Josephson returns to Broadway. That I had to see."

"I couldn't have done it without you."

"Of course you could have."

"But I wouldn't have. You gave me back a part of myself I thought I'd lost." She paused and smiled sweetly. "Thank you."

He smiled, but looked uncomfortable as if he didn't know how to respond or had too much to say, one or the other.

"Hey Lil," Steven called from the edge of the stage. She turned and shielded her eyes with her hand to see him against the stage lights.

"Steven, darling—we won't be long, okay?" she said, hoping he could take a hint.

"Okay. See you there?"

"Yes. Thanks."

"I should probably get going. You obviously have people to meet. Things to do."

"Actually we are meeting Danny for a bite if you'd like to join us. Unless you have… plans?"

"Plans? No. But I don't imagine Charles would appreciate my presence."

"Well, he's not here. I meant Steven and me. We."

"You mean he wasn't here to see you?"

"No. I think he probably had more important things to deal with."

"What could possibly be more important than seeing you perform for the first time in what—seven years?"

"Well, I imagine right about now he's meeting with his spokesperson and legal team to be sure that his side is the one that is printed and that they're able to fully enforce our prenuptial agreement."

"Your prenup?"

"Mmm hmm."

"Why?"

"Because it states that if I ask for the divorce or give him just cause, I don't get a single cent of his fortune. In which, I might add, I'm not interested."

"You mean…"

"Yes. Last night we... Well, I'll spare you details, but we had a long talk. Or something like that. This morning, I got on a plane and came home."

"Home?"

"Yes. Didn't you get my message?"

"I did, but I wasn't sure it was meant for me."

"It was."

"So by home, you meant here? New York?"

"Yes."

"And he's there? In L.A.?"

"Yes, darling!"

Tony stared at her for a moment in disbelief. "I'm sorry. I'm just... gobsmacked. I'm not sure what's happening exactly."

"Well, you see, there I was with him, in our house, in our room, in our... room."

"In bed. You mean you were in bed."

"Yes. But we didn't... I couldn't... I... " She closed her eyes and sighed. After taking a moment to regroup she continued. "You know, I used to think that I was happy. I used to think that it was enough, the house, the jet, the pool. But it wasn't. Not after I remembered what it was like to be truly happy. I mean, there I was in the place I'd thought of as home for years, and I looked around, and it just hit me. It wasn't anymore. Maybe it never was."

"And this is?"

"Well, it can be, yes. Actually, Wimbledon, New York, Toronto. Pick one. The physical location doesn't really matter."

"It doesn't?"

"No. See, what I've come to realize is that home doesn't have to be any one place. I felt at home in all of those cities because home is not just a place. It's a feeling of comfort and familiarity. A feeling of safety. Of refuge. It's the feeling I have when I'm with you. Home—is where you are."

"And what if it's just nostalgia and the excitement of Paris and all of that? Like you said before?"

"It's not."

"How can you be sure?"

"I went back to California fully intending to make a go of it with Charles. He was trying too. I know he was. But being with him only made me miss you more. As I watched him drink his coffee and eat his pastries every morning, or listened to stories about his day, I wondered what you'd had for breakfast. I wondered how your day was. When I cooked him a meal, I wished I was cooking it for you. I knew you would pick out just the right wine to go with it. That is, if I managed to finish cooking without you distracting me."

They both smiled, thinking about the escapade in the kitchen at his apartment.

"And as I lay in bed at night on my side of the great divide, I yearned to feel your body next to mine."

"Okay. Now you're just talking about sex. If great sex is all we have…"

"It isn't."

"No?"

"No. Ah, well—it is great, but that's not why I want to be with you. Tony, I don't care about sex. I've lived mostly without that for years. I miss your voice, your smile, your touch. I miss *you*."

"I don't know, Lily. So much has happened."

"Oh." She suddenly looked deflated. "I guess I should have thought that… How silly of me to expect that you've been sitting around pining for me for the past six weeks. Have you been… I mean are you… seeing someone?"

"No. But…"

"What?"

"Christ, Lil, I feel like a bloody yo-yo right now. You want me. You don't want me. Then you want me again. What's to stop you from changing your mind again? I don't know if it's worth the stress."

"I hurt you. I know that. I'm so sorry. I was a fool to walk away from you. I know that. But I know now that it's you I want. It's always been you. I can't deny it anymore. I want to wake up next to you every morning and go to sleep in your arms every night. I want to make you breakfast, take care of you when you're sick, buy Christmas presents for your nephews, and I want to spend every moment of every day making up for the time that we've lost, if you'll let me."

He didn't speak. He just looked at her and shook his head.

"What? What does that mean?"

"For God sake, Lily! I can't do this. I just can't." He turned away from her to hide the look on his face.

"Tony! Please! We don't have to rush into anything, but please, don't give up on us. Please give us just one more chance."

Hearing her desperate tone, he turned back around. "Lily," he said through his laughter. "I'm just pissing around!"

"Oh!" She swung her fist at him and he caught it, pulling her toward him.

"Tell me once and for all, Lily Josephson, do you love me?" he asked as he pulled her close.

"I love you!"

"Are you in love with me?"

She felt him tightening his grip around her. "I am. Completely. In love. With you," she said in between short, shallow breaths. "Are you. With me?" His hands had slipped inside her coat and were now caressing her back as his lips closed in on hers.

He leaned in so close that his lips were nearly touching hers and whispered, "Once in love with Lily, always in love with Lily." Then he kissed her long and hard, making up for a little lost time himself. By the time he let go, she could barely breathe, but she managed to pull herself together.

"Does that mean you're willing to give it one more go?"

"Does this answer your question?" He kissed her again. It took everything she had to keep from going completely weak in the knees.

She pulled away after a moment. "I like that answer, very much."

"I like you very much," he said, trying for a third time. But she put a finger to his lips to block his attempt.

"We should get going. Danny and Steven will be wondering where I am."

"Do we have to meet them?" he asked, nipping at her ear.

"Yes."

"For the record, I do care about the sex. I care a lot." He kissed at her lips as she laughed, her teeth catching his bottom lip once or twice. "Couldn't we just go home. Fifth Avenue home, that is, and…"

"We shall darling. Later." She wiggled her way free and started up the aisle.

"You know I don't wait well."

"I'll do my best to make it worth the wait, darling. I promise."

"Hoo yeah!" he called after her.

She reached back and took his hand, leading him the rest of the way up the aisle and out the front door just to avoid any crowds that might still be gathered by the stage door. As she stepped out onto the street in front of him, he watched her face light up. The flakes of a late snow fell around her. She looked back at him, smiling with a girlish joy that only he could bring about. His smile widened and his heart felt full.

"Come on, then," she said, tugging at this hand.

"What now?" he asked as they walked up the Great White Way.

"Food. I'm starving!"

"No, angel. I was thinking more long term. What are you going to do now?"

"Oh!" She giggled. "I don't know. Broadway, West End, choreography, coaching. I haven't decided yet. But I know I can go anywhere. I can do anything I want. As long as it's with you."

ABOUT THE AUTHOR

A native Ohioan, Cathryn K. Thompson has always had a passion for drama and the arts. She is a lover of languages, a Toastmaster, and a former dance instructor with a brown belt in Kenpo karate.

www.catkthompson.com

www.ingramcontent.com/pod-product-compliance
Lightning Source LLC
Chambersburg PA
CBHW022146170626
46807CB00005B/2098